Intersections

W. S. Fuller

CCB Publishing
British Columbia, Canada

Intersections

Copyright ©2024 by W. S. Fuller
ISBN-13   978-1-77143-581-9
First Edition

Library and Archives Canada Cataloguing in Publication
Title: Intersections / by W. S. Fuller.
Names: Fuller, W. S., author.
Identifiers: Canadiana (print) 20230534805 | Canadiana (ebook) 20230534813
 | ISBN 9781771435819 (softcover) | ISBN 9781771435826 (PDF)
Subjects: LCGFT: Novels.
Classification: LCC PS3606.U55 I58 2023 | DDC 813/.6—dc23

Front cover artwork: Antique compass with clipping pass.
Picture © Sitade | iStockPhoto.com

Publisher: CCB Publishing
              British Columbia, Canada
              www.ccbpublishing.com

This tale is dedicated to those among us who face the angst, joy, mysteries, contradictions, human frailties, tragedies, and triumphs of life with an open and inquisitive mind...while maintaining a fierce dedication to stand for what's true rather than false, the conquest of good over evil, and the inherent dignity of all humanity.

Intersections

Book 1

Chapter 1

Inside the mile-long pipe, just large enough for a man to squeeze through and lying on the bottom under twenty feet of dark, murky seawater, Petty Officer 3rd Class Andre Rivers glances at the illuminated dial on his watch. The explosion of panic and fear confirm it was a mistake. *Halfway... God... only halfway. The dreams... always here, the worst place... fifteen minutes to either end. Goddamn why'd I look. Calm down... steady kick... smooth breaths.*

Continuing to move forward, he kicks his fins and pushes with his hands against the rough surface of the pipe, so close to his body it offers little leverage. He knows the quickest way out is strong, rhythmic kicks, with his arms at his side, but his fight with fear causes a wasted struggle for speed. Slamming through him again, he makes the mistake of dwelling on it for that sliver of a second it needs to find the corner in his mind to wedge, lodge...to become immovable.

Sucking air rapidly, almost violently, the urge strikes to spit out the mouthpiece, but he bites down tighter, again tries to calm himself. He takes deep, measured breaths, presses his eyes together, tries to shut out everything interrupting the steady motion. Trying to make his mind go blank...he focuses on only moving, breathing to a beat. It works. But not for long, and when the panic slams back through him he knows he might die. Giving up flashes through his thoughts...the gentle comfort of the oxygen deprivation as he begins to succumb, stops fighting. *No way out, no one to help. Let go, do it. Jesus, all you have to do is keep kicking and breathing.... it's all your mind, goddamn it. Think about sex, Janet's ass, concentrate, like when you were young and tense.*

Reaching down, he rubs his crotch, remembers it could make it worse, then realizes he's not moving at all. *Dear God, help me.* Sucking on the mouthpiece harder than ever, frantic, he can't seem to breathe. He tries to kick, but his body has twisted and he scrapes his shoulder hard against the wall of the pipe. His vision clouds. *Spit it out, get it over.... give up you bastard, you lowly, cowardly bastard.* Eyes wide in panic, he watches the pipe narrow, the sleek, silver-white death head, hounds with bared fangs…feels his silent scream to the heavens…and thrusts his mouth wide open to let out the cry. Water rushes through his throat to fill his lungs. Gagging...

"Andre! Andre!"

Coming awake, bolting upright, gasping for air in hoarse, raspy grunts, body shaking, mouth open trying to scream… Andre Rivers, Navy Seal, collapses back onto the bed as he realizes where he is.

"Andre, you all right man," his nine-year old brother Kevin asks, his eyes huge with fear as he stares down at him.

"Yeah, man. I'm O.K. Just a bad dream."

"Yeah, but you been havin another one of those real bad dreams the other night. I get all scared when I hear you makin those noises and shakin the bed like that."

"Don't worry, little man. I'm fine. Everybody has bad dreams sometimes." Andre puts his arm around Kevin and draws him close until the boy's head tucks in against his chest. He glances over to the mattress in the corner where his other brothers are still asleep. *Third time since I've been here. Time to get back.*

Chapter 2

"So tell me how you're doing in school, Kevin," Andre asks as they stand in line at the Dairy Queen.

"Not too great. You know, I mean, I don't like it too much. It's dumb, you know."

"How's Floyd doing?"

"Real bad, man. He's always talkin about quittin but Mama says she'll kick him out if he does it."

"What does Mama say about you guys not doing so good?"

"She gets all mad when she has to go to the school and she finds out we're doin bad, but she don't say much other times. She's always workin so much."

"O.K. Geno, what do you want? An ice cream cone or a chocolate sundae with nuts, whipped cream and a cherry like Kevin and me?"

The four-year-old has to look almost straight up to see the face of his six-foot two-inch brother. "A sundae with a cherry."

This child, the youngest of his eight brothers and sisters, is irresistible to him, with the large, round, inquisitive eyes and soft voice. Andre reaches, and in one effortless motion sweeps him up into his arms, as he has done at least a dozen times today. "I better get you up here so you can watch em make your sundae and see how good it's gonna be," he says, his face only inches from Geno's. "Would you put an extra cherry on that one for this little man here?"

"Sure," comes the reply from the large woman with the broad smile as she fills the cup with ice cream. An even larger smile breaks across the little boy's face as he watches, and Andre resists the urge to squeeze him too hard.

Walking back to the apartment, they pass the men and boys in front of Marvin's grocery; some talking, some drinking from paper bags, or shuffling back and forth, or just sitting. All their activity aimless. Then the open, heavily barred doors of the Uptown Bar and the sharp click of pool balls from the table just inside. Pearl's Styling Salon is on the next corner and across the street there's the playground, with runs going on at all but the most skewed of the four netless baskets.

"Can we play, Andre?" Kevin asks. "Or you play and we'll watch. Man, you can put it in those dude's face."

"We'll go back and get the ball and maybe by then there'll be a good court empty."

They walk on in silence for a few moments before Andre speaks. "Kevin, you know you and your brothers got to start doing better in school. You got to make something of yourself. You don't want to be like all these dudes around here that don't have nothing to do but hang out and get in trouble, do you? Don't want to end up like Bo and Anthony, do you?"

"I want to be like you, Andre. Be in the Navy and go all the places you been. Go to some islands."

"Yeah, me too. And swim like a fish like Mama says you do," Geno says, looking up and stumbling off the curb, his big brother grabbing him just before he tumbles to the pavement."

"Yeah, well I did pretty well in school, and I graduated. I

should have gone to college and I may still go. Then I could do a lot more than I've done. But if you don't study and finish school you ain't gonna be nothin, man. Nothin but a bum. I'm gonna start writing and checking on how you're doing. Don't let me down. You got what it takes to be somebody, both of you, all of us do, and I'm not gonna ever forgive you if you don't start trying harder. We're gonna be talkin about this some more, man. You better get used to it."

Chapter 3

Scores of yachts, mostly sailboats, of all sizes, from all directions, are heading toward the small anchorage in Great Harbor. Close to fifty appear to Alan Hardy to already be on a hook, as he stares through the binoculars.

"Ease the sheets," Alan shouts, "we'll go over and have a look."

The big ketch, hard on the wind for the final miles of the six-hour passage from Charlotte Amalie to Sopers Hole, falls off, her deck comes almost level, and her bowsprit joins in the chase for the island of Jost Van Dyke, British Virgin Islands. The binoculars are eagerly passed around as they close quickly at ten knots on the floating armada in the twenty-knot breeze.

"Forget Cane Garden, mates, now this looks like one serious damn party," Alan shouts from the helm, eyes again glued to the glasses as they are now close enough to see what's going on. "Let's get everything down, and quickly. It's going to be tight enough finding a spot for this beast under power. She'd grab half the anchor rodes in there if we come in hot and under canvass like we usually do."

It becomes a challenge to lower, flake the sails, and prepare the anchor considering the distractions of the scene they are now, slowly, under power, moving into. Boats of all descriptions and sizes, from a few that dwarf their seventy-two-foot bulk to a variety of small craft and day sailors with perfunctory cabins fit only for small animals. People are everywhere, of all descriptions, more than a few stark or semi-naked, shouting from boat to boat, waving drinks, diving off booms, spinnaker flying over neighboring vessels, streaking in and out of this deliriously mad maritime maze on brightly colored sailboards, buzzing and scurrying about in dinghies.

"Incoming," screams the crew of the sloop they are passing astern of, and suddenly there's the splat of a large water balloon as it bursts on their doghouse, just long of its intended target.

"Heavy artillery, mates, someone get ours. All right, drop the hook, this'll do." Alan barks orders, begins to back the diesel down, then pops open a beer as the heavy running clang of the anchor chain signals Zulu Warrior has found a spot of water and empty bottom she will fit into for the night.

Sam comes up from below with the heavy strips of inner tube, twelve feet long and a foot wide, they will secure to the shrouds and use to launch their own fusillade and begins heading down the rail to start the rigging process. The tanned back, ass, and legs of what appears to be an incredibly beautiful, naked girl suddenly flash by, enormous shock of white-blond hair streaming straight out in the wind, as she passes within a few feet of them, pulling back and down on the boom of her sailboard. Sam stops dead still to stare. Within seconds another body, dark and muscular, also darts past. Her companion...or pursuer... following closely in her wake.

"I'm in love," Alan bellows from the stern.

"Which one?" comes the reply from the foredeck, "The bloke's ass is just your type."

"Fuck you, I'll stay here forever if I can find her, or another one like her."

Foxy's Beach Bar is hosting the opening night blow-out for the annual Wooden Boat Regatta. Foxy, a.k.a. Philicianno Callwood - club owner, entertainer, raconteur, purveyor of all manner of available items, substances, and services - is the legendary island king of cool and guile.

But can a mere shore party possibly top the debauchery, spectacle, and hellacious good time had by all in the harbor this afternoon? Sam had contemplated that on the dinghy ride to shore…is still not certain of the answer… but now reckons if this party doesn't, it will at the least be a photo finish.

Two electric guitars, numerous gasoline drums, tambourines, and an ever-growing choir of backup singers and screechers belt out a blend of reggae and island bebop. In front of the band and local swayers, the cement floor is crowded with sweaty, writhing bodies, many dressed to the minimum… hopping, jumping, sliding, stepping, shaking and humping to the driving, lilting, never-ending, sensuous beat. Beer bottles drop, shatter, and no one seems to notice. A large, fiftyish white man, with white hair, matching, bushy beard, huge, protruding belly, dressed in a sarong, sports a bone through his nose…while a tall, stunning native with long, yellow-crusted dreadlocks moves sensually while caressing a woman that could pass for a Newport dowager. Accents and languages are as varied as the revelers and toast after toast is hoisted, to everything possible, and no one in particular.

Sam is chatting with a Canadian on a bareboat charter who is incredulous at the whole scene when the white-blond head comes into view. Turning, compelled to stare, her impact on Sam is immediate, intense. She also turns, their eyes meet. She is exquisite. Perfect, razor-sharp features, high cheekbones, large, oval, azure eyes. And the hair…wild, frizzled, halfway to her waist. Leather sandals tied with thongs around her calves, white shorts with wide legs that come barely to the tops of the gorgeous thighs, a thin white tank top that reveals small, perfect breasts shaped like grapefruit halves topped with erect nipples…force Sam's eyes downward before quickly returning to the mesmerizing eyes.

There's no sign of her afternoon companion…she seems to be alone…as she abruptly turns and walks into the crowd. Sam follows, and after squeezing through a mass of quivering dancers, ends up at the bar. The stunning white hair is nowhere to be seen. Out back native women roast pigs in pits in the ground, the strong aroma brings hunger to Sam's mind, but the girl is not there either and the thought of food vanishes quickly.

Back at the bar, Sam orders another beer and accepts a conversation with a Brit skipper of a private charter. Suddenly she again appears, standing beside the band, her flat, intense gaze seeming to burn through the path between their interlocking eyes.

"You know her?" the skipper asks.

"No, do you?"

"Not really. She's German, crew on that hundred-foot Swedish ketch with the French name and Italian port o'call. They've been down here for a couple of weeks before heading to South America to pick up a charter. She seems strange, a real odd bird. Only bloody reason I can figure she'd be doing this with her looks… maybe a guy. But I haven't seen one."

The girl turns, walks in front of the band and out toward the beach. Sam turns quickly back to the bar and changes the subject, mind racing for a way to escape from the talkative Brit without seeming obvious, but unable to think clearly through his constant monologue. *To hell with it.*

"Enjoyed talking to you."

Stepping quickly away from the bar, following in her direction, Sam walks out from under the palm thatched roof and onto the sand. Moving away, the noise and chaos begin to subside. The beach is a crescent, perhaps a half mile around, and the full moon illuminates a scene of beached dinghies and motionless bodies reminiscent of a failed amphibious assault. A few are entwined couples, but most are solitary figures to be stepped over as they lie still in the sand, in varying positions, as if dead. Yet likely having raised the white flag against the onslaught of abject drunkenness. Or been overwhelmed by it. Halfway around the arc the bodies become less frequent, there is no sign of her, and Sam stops, thinks about going back. But decides to continue because the quiet is soothing and the night so beautiful. Suddenly, ahead, the faint sound of a female voice, humming.

Lying on her stomach in the moist sand, stunning head of white hair resting on her crossed arms, only a few feet beyond the gently lapping sea, she is naked. Sam's eyes follow the perfect taper of her long, slender legs, to the gorgeous curves of her bottom, the slender waist, and again, the hair. The huge, rising moon's reflection off the shimmering sea casts a silvery white, satin glow on her bronze body. Tiny goosebumps are illuminated on her buttocks, raised by the zephyr of a breeze…or her own stirrings.

Now beside her, knees in the sand, Sam brushes the hair aside.

The German feels the warm, moist tongue against the nape of her neck, circling, then starting to move slowly down the small of her back. Tracing lower, across her ass, to her thigh, there is also the faint brushing of fingertips on the inside of her other thigh. The warm wetness and touch caress her in concert, sending a delicious shiver through the length of her body. Reaching her calves, they linger, then start back up the inside of her thighs, gently but steadily moving higher. Her legs slide apart in accommodation.

Catching a whiff of the scent of sex, Sam begins to brush and twirl the thatch between her legs. The white mane raises, there is a soft moan as the hand settles, fingers part and brush across the moist folds, and the hot tongue moves faster and harder up and down her buttocks next to the cleft.

Sam feels the girl twist to turn over and suddenly they are wrapped tightly around each other, squeezing every possible inch of their steaming flesh together. Their mouths lock with an explosion of heat and current.

Three bags of trash drop onto the floor of the dinghy. Sam climbs down the boarding ladder, steps into the rubber boat, cranks the motor, and starts through the harbor for shore. Instead of scattered along the beach, as they were last night, bodies now lie or curl on most every available flat spot of most every boat. Stretched out on decks, hanging in mainsails, slumped in cockpits. There are few signs of life except for an occasional bleary-eyed face that lifts and glances her way, then buries itself again, as if trying to reject the day.

Sam's mind seizes on last night and she tries to clear it, knowing she needs focus to weave the dinghy through the maze of boats, anchor lines, and coral heads. No use. Giving in, she cuts the throttle back to idle, slips the gear into neutral, and drifts. *Well, it happened. Guess I thought it might. If there was ever a doubt I don't fit the mold of women who aren't into physical attraction and visual stimulation without a good dose of romance, affection, or love...there's damn sure none anymore. First time I've had sex with another woman, and we*

13

didn't say one goddamn word to each other until it was over.
Pure physical lust, nothing but, at its zenith. But then...the
sexual energy and heat generated in the harbor and that
party...huh...if they had dropped in on that scene, cloistered
nuns might have been looking at each other.

She loves romance, affection, knows it's better with that.
But also knows, for as long as she can remember, she's been
attracted to bodies, velvety skin, gentle curves, muscles,
asses, the soft steel of erect cocks, breasts, faces, voices,
actions, circumstances. She doesn't respond as easily or often
as most men, but enough to make her different than many
women. Why? When did it begin? Nature or nurture? She's
always thought peoples' diverse sexual stimulants,
idiosyncrasies, are learned. Surely the basic drive is inborn,
the biological urge to mate, but the variations on the theme,
the specific turn-ons and turn-offs, foreplay, fetishes outside
intercourse, she attributes more to nurture than nature. There
are so many differences from culture to culture that
substantiate her view.

Many women don't seem to develop and master these
sexual possibilities easily...their ideas about arousal and
fulfillment are often so different from those of men. Even those
who lived through the sixties' sexual revolution, who were
right there in the middle of the philosophy of free love and
sexual equality for everyone. And the animal kingdom...
there's often only one aggressor there, and we're not so far up
the evolutionary ladder for that to all be out of us. It's a good
thing, anyway, this "love to a man is a thing apart, tis a
woman's whole existence", or however the saying goes. If all
women heated up as quickly as men, or as I did last night,
many of the great milestones of human achievement would
still be waiting to happen.

Will I do it again? Maybe. Does it mean I'm bisexual?

Will I prefer women? Don't think so... seriously doubt it. Can't see it taking the place of being with a man, of that kind of relationship. But it was white hot. Wanton comes to mind. But different. One more experience. Maybe it was the whole scene, maybe not. Maybe it will take someone else who looks like that, acts like that. Pure, unadulterated, physical lu.. Jolted... almost sliding off the seat as the boat bumps something solid and stops, Sam feels heavy metal rub across her shoulder.

"Hi sweetheart, come aboard and have a Bloody Mary."

Looking up to find the voice, she sees a large man, sun-flambeaued, big belly hanging over knee length, flowered bathing trunks, smiling down at her from the motor yacht whose hull and anchor chain her dinghy is now wedged between.

After taking the trash ashore Sam is back at Zulu Warrior, ties the dinghy off, strips off her T-shirt and shorts, and dives over the side. The cool shock turns quickly to luxurious immersion, and she hangs suspended, slowing her rise to the top, enjoying the exquisite, sublime feeling. After swimming out fifty yards or so, then back, she pulls herself up and flops over into the dinghy, reaches for the bottle of Joy, and soaps and washes her body and hair. She dives in once more to rinse off, then climbs up the ladder to the cockpit. After spraying the salt water off with the shower on the transom, she faces the bow of the boat and the trade winds that will dry her while she begins to comb out her hair. After a few moments she notices Alan peering up from the companionway. Winking at him, she continues combing, her inhibitions having long since vanished with the frequent nudity on board and among the yachting community in these latitudes.

Alan gazes longingly at her. *Short, petite, tan everywhere, but not as brown as the rest of us. Maybe as dark as a real redhead can get. Neat, muscular legs, perfect triangle of untrimmed reddish-brown hair, round, full, but firm ass, narrow waist, medium- sized tits that hang ever so slightly, small nipples...just on the slender side of voluptuous. Wide, gorgeous, friendly face, expressive green eyes, perfect nose, long, luxurious, wavy red hair...and small, wonderful freckles.*

"Samantha, love, if I had a body like yours to curl up with I would never, so help me God, ever again, pursue and bring home another cow like the one that's still asleep in my berth, snoring loudly."

She continues to pull the comb through her hair, eyes closed now against the glare of the morning sun off the water. "Why is it, Alan, that the many wonderful traits of Aussies....cheerfulness, courage, spirit of adventure, are so often completely overshadowed by the blatant sense of chauvinistic sexism that your country's men always seem to wear around like a sandwich board?"

"It's in the genes, you know. My forefathers were convicts, not women's liberationists. Yeah, it all goes back to the penal colonies and the bloody Brits that came up with that. I can't be blamed, love, only pitied and consoled." He raises his eyebrows and smiles. "Don't imagine it's possible for us to ever change."

Chapter 4

Caroline Brockton comes awake just in time to see the hard eyes peering from the slit in the ski mask before the tape slams across her mouth. The bed covers are stripped away, she is jerked over onto her stomach, a hand presses the side of her face roughly into the pillow, her arms are pulled behind her back and her wrists are taped. As she feels a sharp pain in her buttock, she sees the barrel against the head on the pillow next to her, then a flash, hears the muffled 'pffft', and tries frantically to twist and turn away as a warm stream of blood splashes on her face and she tastes vomit rise through her throat and fill her mouth. Quickly rolled and pushed into a large bag, she knows she is being carried over someone's shoulder, down flights of stairs, as she bounces and sways, then outside where the subzero temperature and howling wind attack her nakedness through the canvas. She begins to shiver uncontrollably before everything goes black.

Chapter 5

The eggs he ordered over medium are served barely cooked, with watery whites, the way he used to hate them. But the way he's learned to appreciate after endless mornings of the European breakfast staple of hard bread, hard bread, cold cuts, and more hard bread. It's very good bread, it's usually free, and that's usually important. But Christopher likes an occasional change of pace, particularly on a morning that he's fighting a mild hangover and is about to spend three or four frigid hours standing on a mountain in blowing snow.

Finished with breakfast, he is on his third cup of coffee and reading yesterday's edition of the Times of London when he hears the familiar, heavily accented voice. "Christopher, how are you this morning? I hope you had a large breakfast, for you will need it today."

He looks up to see the stocky body and broad, smiling face of Karl Mueller, blue eyes twinkling under the thick blond brows and crew cut.

"Good morning, Karl, sit down and have a cup of coffee or tea with me, or breakfast if you haven't already eaten."

"Only a quick cup of tea. I have eaten, many hours ago. One of the technicians is ill and I have been waxing and sharpening skis since the middle of the night. It's going to be cold today, Christopher. The wind has come up quite strong. If it continues to snow the visibility could be bad. They could possibly cancel the training runs."

"I know that would screw up the schedule and the days off between races for your guys who also ski the slaloms. But from my perspective, looking out this window and feeling a bit rough from drinking too much of that wonderful Austrian beer you've hooked me on, I'm not going to be that disappointed if they cancel it."

"Yes, but the decision is never made until we have been up there long enough to become stiff with cold. So, Christopher, I think either way you are going to freeze, at least for a while.

"How is Nygren going to approach this last training run. Is he going to go all out? He was pretty slow yesterday."

"I think you will see him much faster today. He needs one good run before the race. He has been, how do you say, distracted," Karl lifts an eyebrow, his expression reflecting mild disgust.

"And you don't approve of any distractions, eh, Karl?"

"The World Championships are a very important event, particularly in my country. And the rewards of winning for the racer are great. I believe all the hard training, the...tough, being tough it takes to get to this championship, should not be wasted. Chances should not be taken because of distractions. I must go now. When will you come up to the course?"

"I'm waiting for the weather to clear. I have this feeling." Christopher saw the brilliant brightness of the sun illuminate the magnificent image of the Matterhorn through the window an instant before Karl finished his question. "I'll be damned, maybe the FIS should hire me as a weather forecaster," he says, gesturing for Karl to turn and look. "I couldn't be worse than whoever they use, and they could probably easily top my salary."

The window suddenly goes gray with swirling snow in the foreground as Karl is looking out. "Maybe the salary should be lower. Your first performance is not good," he says with a broad grin. "At these altitudes there are often small breaks, but only small ones today, Christopher. Don't wait too long. You might miss something interesting trying to stay warm. I will see you on the mountain." Karl pats his friend on the back and walks out the door of the hotel cafe.

A promising young racer twenty-five years ago when it was common to participate in all the World Cup alpine events, Karl took a hideous fall in his first year on the Austrian national team at the famed Hahnekamm downhill and miraculously escaped with what was thought to be a strained knee. Determined to race a few days later in the giant slalom, the knee collapsed and practically disintegrated when he jumped hard on his edge to round a gate. Not only did it end his career… he still walks with a slight limp.

Typical of the breed of youths who grow up in the Tyrol region of the Alps, spend much of their early years on skis, and get to the elite level of the sport, Karl never wants to leave it. His warm, friendly, but reserved persona belies a steel-hard, no-nonsense approach to competition.

Christopher heads back up to his room in the hotel Zermatterhoff, enjoying, as always, the ride in the elegant, glassed, creaky lift, operated by the formal, but genuinely friendly, Jurgen. *This is what excellent service should really be about. Not the latest in technology, or lightning speed, but courteous, warm efficiency, the result of studied tradition, and a sense of elegance in the surroundings and staff.*

Entering the tiny room, he slips into the navy blue and white gore tex ski suit, wrestles his boots on, grabs his gloves, hat, goggles, small, portable recorder, and walks back to the lift for the trip to the basement and the ski lockers.

Reluctantly, he pushes the heavy door open and enters the

gray, white world of snow, wind, and frigid cold…in no way less cruel than he imagined from the scene out the window and Karl's warnings. As he moves toward the train and queue he will have to stand in he tries not to dwell on the certainty it will be much worse on the mountain.

The downhill course has been set on Gornergrat, one of three ski mountains rising from the lovely, quaint Swiss village of Zermatt. Each has its own primary lift system out of the high alpine valley where the town is nestled, and Gornergrat's is certainly the most unusual. And to Christopher, the most pleasant. Klein Matterhorn has its huge cable-cars that span spectacular gorges and glaciers, and the route to the slopes of Sunnegga is a ride through a dark tunnel up the inside of a mountain on a cog railway moving at an angle approaching vertical.

Set against those marvels of engineering, the lift he is about to board is antiquated, but elegant. It's a train; the exact type of train that carried him from Zurich on a steady climb into this region of magnificent peaks, valleys, picturesque villages, farms, and finally to this renowned mecca of skiing, mountaineering and everything winter chic. Red cars leave from the station behind a traditional engine and make the gradual climb to the upper lifts. There is a great deal of above timberline terrain on these mountains, and Gornergrat resembles a gigantic mound of vanilla ice cream, melted enough to create uneven indentations, and blur the definition of its original shape.

At times, on the ride up, the clouds lift enough for Christopher to marvel at the landscape that so fascinates him. The fact he's seated on a train, slow and warm enough to affect a pleasant delay to his entrance into the brutal environment that awaits him at the top...causes him to relish every minute of the ascent. Just before reaching the end of the climb, they emerge from a cloud layer into brilliant sunshine, the surrounding peaks close enough to jolt the senses, jutting abruptly and magnificently out of the white-gray blanket below. And the most magnificent, as always, is the stunning monolith of the Matterhorn. He doubts the training runs will be canceled now, unless the visibility is too dangerous on the lower sections of the course, and he zips his jacket and lowers his goggles as they slow to a stop.

Once outside he clicks quickly into his skis and pushes off for the downhill traverse and short surface lift ride to the start house, the force of the wind blowing up the slope to slow his forward motion. Cringing, he imagines what it would be like without the sun, as even with its radiance and reflection off the snow at this altitude...it's cold as hell.

Sliding off the lift, Christopher scans the clumps of brightly clothed racers, coaches, trainers, ski techs and course workers, busily engaged in stretching, massaging, ski tuning and speaking into walkie talkies, and locates the red and blue clad figures of the American team.

"Billy, how does the schedule stand?"

"Hey Christopher, it's just been clear up here for the last fifteen minutes or so and they've announced a ten thirty start. Pretty damned foolish, you still can't see shit on the lower half, and the wind is too strong," Billy McCormick, the coach of the men's team replies, shaking his head as he continues his work on a ski binding with a battery powered screwdriver.

"Is the schedule pretty much the same as yesterday?"

"Yeah, Baxter will go at the end of the first seed and the rest sometime before the days over."

"I'm going to see if I can find a place to watch and hide from the wind. I'd like to talk to you later if we could."

"Sure, I'll be up here or at the bottom, or look me up back at the hotel."

Christopher pushes off and starts down the outside of the course. After dropping no more than a few hundred vertical feet a cloud laced with small ice pellets slams into him, everything in front of his eyes goes white, and he slows himself with an awkward snowplow while turning his head and raising his gloves to shield the bare skin of his face against the frigid, burning fusillade. As he often does when conditions are like this, he thinks of the irony of something he loves so much, that he's done every chance he's had for so long, that he's spent so much time and money on, that has given him so many moments and hours of pure joy and excitement...and yet at times can be so excruciatingly miserable. Waiting, his back against the gusts until they ease, he continues down, slowly, straining to see in the flat light, in no way resembling the expert skier he is.

Finding a spot below the first headwall, where the course makes a sweeping turn back to the left and is partially protected from the howling wind by a large snowbank, he stops, pulls off his gloves, and presses the palms of his hands against his cheeks and nose to ward off any early stages of frostbite. He then removes the tape recorder from the inside pocket of his suit. The sky is still overcast, but the visibility has improved, and he can now see the spot at the precipice of the headwall where the racers will first come into view, as well as the spot they will disappear below him.

Christopher has seen many downhill runs over the past three months, but the first racer still elicits a "Jesus Christ" from him as the body in the skin-hugging, red and white suit of the Swiss team pre-jumps the headwall at sixty-five miles per hour, hurtles through the air, low, in a tuck, arms and poles forward and rotating, and lands on the icy course, gasping for air, the wind audibly slapping against his body as he straightens slightly. Next comes the raw, grating, scraping screech of the edges desperately biting into the snow to make the precision, seventy-mile-an-hour, sweeping turn that takes him a few feet from a catastrophic collision with a fence and a twenty-five-foot drop onto the catwalk below it. As suddenly as the racer appeared, he disappears.

To Christopher, skiing fast is a thrill, but it's hard for him to comprehend the lack of fear and caution that allows downhillers the concentration necessary to make their damn-the-torpedoes, always-on-the-edge-of-disaster charges down the mountain. And this level of speed, energy and effort, it's so different...graceful at a distance...but up close, violent and stunning in its intensity. He understands if you begin when you're very young, and gradually become accustomed...again and again...to the speed. But still....

The last of the skiers who will be in the first seed for the race tomorrow and have the advantage of skiing their training runs before the snow becomes rutted, have passed him. Hans Nygren, the great Austrian downhiller and current World Cup leader, was not among them, and Christopher decides to ski to the bottom to find out why. If he's injured or ill just one day before the race and Karl can arrange an interview with him, it's a story that will be played up by the wire services.

The two miles to the bottom are so frigid that he stops a few times to warm his face and hide briefly in places that provide protection from the wind. When finally down, he clicks out of his skis, lifts them onto his shoulder, and is hurrying to the warmth of the lodge and a cup of hot chocolate when he see Baxter Harding.

"How was your time?"

"Chris, hey man, not too bad. I'm sixth so far. Jesus was it bad up there. Half the time I couldn't see a damn thing. Maybe I'm faster when I'm blind."

"Do you know what happened to Nygren? He hasn't come down yet."

"Yeah, we were just talking about that. You know the Austrian primas, though. Probably decided he'd wait till it clears or maybe not run at all today."

After some thirty minutes of relief in the lodge, Christopher heads back outside and looks for someone he knows from the Austrian team, or Billy McCormick. Seeing neither he decides to take the chair and poma lifts that will take him back to the top to look for Karl. The ride up is not as bad as he had expected. The sun is now out on the lower part of the mountain and with the wind mostly at his back, it's bearable.

When he slides off the lift above the start house he sees only a fraction of the crowd that should be there in the middle of a training run. He doesn't see any Americans and only a few of the Austrians, standing in groups of twos, heads lowered. And then he sees the short, stocky figure sitting on a bale of hay, with his face buried in his hands.

Christopher moves over to him. "Karl?"

"Please do not bother him, you must leave him now," comes a sharp, heavily accented voice from one of the two men standing to Karl Mueller's side.

His friend looks up and Christopher sees his eyes are red, there are tears frozen on his cheeks. "It is all right," Karl says in a soft, but steady voice, to the other man.

"What's happened?"

"He is dead. Hans is dead. His body was found in a room at the Mont Cervin. Someone has killed him."

Chapter 6

The package is placed on the desk in front of the receptionist in the top-floor, elegant suite of offices by a tall, sinewy black man wearing ankle length black cycling pants, a black leather jacket, and a blue bandana tied pirate style around his head. Before Shirley Donaldson can speak, he is back through the door, steps into the elevator he had put on hold, and begins the descent to Fifth Avenue and his bicycle.

Ten minutes later, after a circuitous, daring dash in and out of moving traffic down West 49th, south on Seventh to 42nd, west to 8th, around the block and then north and into Central Park, the bicyclist approaches a man seated on a bench next to a frozen pond. The man hands the cyclist a hundred-dollar bill and he is quickly back on the bike and gone.

Amy Hawes, Joseph Brockton's executive assistant, receives the package with the second batch of inter-office mail for the day. She slices open the neatly taped, small, corrugated box, as she does with all of Mr. Brockton's mail, and begins to open the yellow, padded envelope inside when she sees the 'PERSONAL AND CONFIDENTIAL' on the lower left-hand corner and 'Caroline Brockton' on the upper left. *Probably a birthday present. Better let him open it.*

After sorting his other mail, she opens the ornate double doors behind her, enters the enormous, lavish office, walks across the Persian rug, lays three letters on the leather inlay in the antique, hand carved desk, then places the package beside them.

It is 2:40 p.m. before Joseph Brockton returns from lunch with Robert Wembley, Chairman of Morgan Stanley. He doesn't usually take so much time away from his office for long lunches, but the two are old, close friends, and it has become a ritual, though seldom more than a monthly one.

Seating himself behind his desk he quickly glances through the five messages, then notices his daughter's name on the yellow envelope. He cuts the single layer of clear tape and removes a video cassette. Pushing away from the desk, he moves to the bookcases and cabinets built into the wall behind and to his left, opens two heavily molded wooden panels and pulls a television and deck out on a sliding platform. Swiveling it toward his desk, he inserts the cassette, leans back in his seat, picks up the remote control, and engages the PLAY button.

Nothing but snow appears for what seems an inordinate amount of time, so he pushes the fast forward button until he detects a change in images, releases his finger, and instantaneously feels his breath catch as a wall of fear slams into him.

His daughter, kneeling, in a brown robe, a wide strip of silver tape across her mouth, hands behind her back, her hair mussed and her eyes wide with fear, fills the screen. She is motionless for perhaps a minute and then a black clad arm with a black glove enters the picture and rips the tape from her mouth, jerking her head violently to the side as she utters a terse, taut cry. Turning her face back to face the camera, she speaks...slowly, trembling.

"Daddy, please do whatever they say. They'll kill me if you don't. Please help me."

The screen goes blank with a dark background and then a typed message appears in white.

```
Do not tell anyone anything about what
you have just seen or the existence of
this tape. We are monitoring your
actions. If you do not follow our
instructions we will kill your daughter.
```

Joseph is conscience of his heart pounding against his chest when the intercom comes on.

"Mr. Brockton."

"Yes."

"There are two men here to see you. Federal agents. They say it's urgent."

A sense of alarm…of danger…causes Joseph Brockton to feel panic. But his iron will fights back, he steadies himself, and answers Amy Hawes with a calm "I'll be with them in just a minute," as he quickly removes the cassette, pushes the TV and VCR back into the cabinet, closes the doors, and places the tape in his briefcase. Sitting squarely behind his desk again, he takes a couple of deep breaths and tries to focus his racing mind on the reactions he knows he must now make. He pushes the button and hears Amy Hawes answer.

"Show them in, please."

The door opens and two well-dressed men enter. Joseph, careful not to give anything away, sizes them up as well as he can in the few seconds it takes to walk around the desk to shake their hands as they introduce themselves.

"I'm David McCrary and this is Richard Waite. We're with the F.B.I."

"Please have a seat." He goes back to his chair behind the massive desk. "What can I do for you?"

"Mr. Brockton, have you heard from your daughter in the

last few days?"

"What's wrong?" he says in a flat voice, his eyes darting from one man to the next to convey alarm.

"We need to talk with your daughter if you could tell us how to get in touch with her," Waite, the younger of the two men, says."

"Gentlemen, please be honest with me. I want to know what has happened to cause you to come here."

"Hans Nygren, a member of the Austrian ski team, was found shot to death this morning in Zermatt, Switzerland, where the World Championships are now taking place. He was found in a hotel room registered in your daughter's name. She hasn't been located." Richard McCrary keeps his eyes locked on Joseph's after he speaks.

Returning the steady stare for a few moments, Joseph swivels his chair to the side, drops his head, takes an audible, deep breath, and sits very still. He knows he is doing well. He turns back to face the agents. "I last heard from her four or five days ago. She was in Vienna."

"Have you heard from anyone concerning her whereabouts?" McCrary is clearly in charge of the interview.

"No." The answer is quick, and again flat.

"Have you ever heard her mention Nygren's name?"

"No."

"Mr. Brockton," McCrary continues, leaning forward in his chair, his words slower, measured, "It is critically important that you let us know immediately if anyone contacts you about your daughter or you hear from her. I don't think I need to tell you why. In your position, you know what something like this could be about. Don't even think about trying to handle it on your own. Remember, there's already one body. We'd like to put a tap on your phones, here and at your home."

Joseph senses danger in his answer but doesn't hesitate. "Don't you think that's a little premature. There could be an explanation for this, and I'd rather not have to alarm my wife until we know a little more. Has she been seen in Zermatt?"

"We don't have information on that yet. Interpol just contacted us a couple of hours ago and they didn't have any information other than what we've told you. No one will know we have a tap on the phones. I'd really like to go ahead."

"All right."

"Could you give us all your business and residential numbers, including any private lines you might have."

He quickly jots down the numbers on a sheet of legal paper and hands it to McCrary. He again fixes the agent with his eyes, a stare, trying to penetrate him and show emotion at the same time. "You must also let me know immediately if you hear anything at all." He looks over at Waite with the same intensity for a moment and then back at McCrary.

"Of course," comes the reply.

The two men rise to leave, and Joseph shows them to the door, shaking hands before they walk out of the office.

After the doors are closed behind them, he takes the few steps to the couch and collapses into a seated position, leans his head back until it rests on the soft leather. Off guard now, the full force of the terror crushes down on him. Mind racing, in chaos and confusion, the thoughts and emotions meld, and he feels flashes of panic. Again, he tries to calm himself...and fights a sudden urge to draw his body up and weep.

For a number of minutes Joseph Brockton doesn't move. When he does rise his thinking has cleared...he knows there are numerous decisions he must make, no matter how provisional at this point...and realizes he must begin going over the possibilities and choices. Now...in detail.

Amy Hawes sees the light flash, picks up the phone and hears the familiar voice. "I'm going out for a while. I'm not sure if I'll be back or not."

Moving to the closet, he grabs and wraps a white cashmere scarf around his neck, pulls on the dark grey, double breasted wool overcoat, black leather, fleece-lined gloves, picks up the briefcase, walks through the door to the back entrance of his office, down a short hall, through another door, and into the elevator. Exiting the building, he heads north on Fifth Avenue, bending into the teeth of a stiff, cold wind cutting through the afternoon gloom of another of New York's seemingly endless gray, raw, winter days. He has not considered calling for his limousine, as he wants desperately to walk. Alone.

Joseph's concentration and frenzied thoughts on what lies ahead are broken only momentarily by the recognition of the need to stop for traffic lights and blocked intersections. The blocks run by in a stream, and he is unaware of exactly where he is until alongside the park and opposite the elegant building where he keeps a twelve-room apartment for the nights he does not make the trip back to Long Island. As he approaches his destination, he hesitates...decides to keep moving...and again is immersed in thought until reaching Ninety-Second Street, where he makes the decision to go into the park at the next entrance.

Telling her...Jesus God is going to be horrible, but I need to go ahead and do it. Nygren's well known, the World Cup is a big deal...it could be on the evening news or the front page.

At least the front page of the sports. I wonder if the media knows. Damn. Should have asked if the media over there knows about Caroline, the room. Maybe I didn't do as well as I thought. She's been everything to us. Both of us equally, but Jane never stops to consider this kind of stuff can happen, what she would do, how she would handle it. I've thought about it hundreds of times. Is it making it easier? Goddamn it no, doesn't feel like it, but maybe the decisions, what I'm going to do, maybe they're coming quicker. If I tell her now she'll want to know what we're going to do. If only they would contact me, so I would know more before I tell her. But she needs to be in on it from the beginning, what we're going to do. Or maybe I shouldn't tell her anything more than what the F.B.I. told me. They'll question her for sure. Christ, they could be doing it now. Don't think I asked them not to. Goddamn it. I think I said something about not wanting to upset her before we know for sure.

The thought continually recurring to him, that makes him feel he might surrender to his fear, is the image of her in the robe, the tape being ripped off. It makes him shiver to his spine, want to shake his head and drive the image from his mind. He has never been able to bear the thought of her being hurt, much less actually seeing it...and imagining how frightened she must be. Forcing his mind to think of the money, he considers how he might handle it. Looking up, Joseph sees the museum just ahead, completely unaware of how far, or for how long, he walked into and back out of the park.

Climbing the steps from the massive lobby to the second floor and entering the section that houses the collections of European paintings, he moves steadily until he passes into the first of the rooms filled with works of the old masters. He slows his pace, stops to gaze at a few of his favorites, those so familiar to him, then sits on one of the upholstered benches.

Joseph comes here often, as he does the Museum of Modern Art and the Guggenheim. But this is his favorite spot, a place where he seems able to think clearly. The tranquility and dignity of the museum, the magnificent depictions of the scenes of chaos, serenity, of noble purpose...have always been comforting, uplifting in difficult times; times when crucial decisions have been demanded of him.

It occurs to him his acceptance of what has happened is on two distinct levels. There's the recurring tendency to want to question if it's all real....an unreal, almost surreal sense of amazement at how suddenly this horrid intrusion has appeared in his life, how everything will change now, will have to be considered differently. And all because a video tape showed him what has happened so far away, caused by God knows what circumstances. On another level he knows he accepted the reality of it from the first moment he understood what he was watching. From that instant his ability to ascertain and accept facts, the truth, allowed him to accept Caroline's kidnapping and the possible outcomes. And at this moment it seems a very long time since he hasn't been burdened with this life-altering crisis.

Losing track of time, he sits with his thoughts and is surprised to see only a few minutes have passed each time he glances at his watch. He's now able to think clearly, at least in the short stretches when his mind stills before resuming its hectic race from one scenario, or horror, to another. Suddenly restless, anxious, and convinced he has formulated his actions as well as possible for now, he stands, pulls the phone from his coat pocket, and calls for the limousine that will take him home. There will be more time to think on the ride. Far too much time. *God I wish she were here in the apartment, wish I could get it over with...now.*

The headlights of the black Mercedes limo illuminate the four-foot-high natural stone wall that runs along the full half mile of the Brocton's property that fronts the road. The wall abruptly ends in massive stone posts, the iron gate between them swings open, and the car starts up the gravel drive. A huge, rambling, gray clapboard mansion sits some two hundred yards back on a low hill overlooking a perfectly manicured lawn that falls off into a thick stand of trees. In the back a larger lawn slopes more gently towards huge rocks that rise from the shore of Long Island Sound. After the car takes the fork that leads to the side of the house and the garage, Joseph is quickly out of the back seat and into the house. He walks purposefully down the hall that leads into the huge foyer, up the circular stairs and toward the bedroom suite.

Jane suddenly appears in the hall and catches him off guard. She opens her arms, and he wonders for a moment if she knows, but sees the smile. Embracing her, he speaks before she can. "Darling, something's happened. You must listen to me very carefully."

"Caroline?" Oh God. What..?" Sheer terror fills her eyes.

"She's been kidnapped."

"Oh God, no."

All her weight falls on him as she goes limp in his arms. Squeezing her head and chest tightly against him, he is silent for a few moments, then speaks softly, as softly and strongly as he can. "She's all right, but we've got to be as calm as we can. If we're going to help her we've got to think and act clearly."

Jane Brocton speaks in short gasps, between sniffling and trying to hold back her tears. "How do you know she's all right? Where is she? How did you find out? How long have you known?"

"Let's sit down and we'll talk about it."

"But…"

Wrapping his arm around her, she leans her head on his shoulder as they walk into the sitting room that adjourns their bedroom. Bright yellow flames lick toward the top of the mahogany and Delph-tile encased fireplace, and they sit facing each other on the loveseat in front of it.

"I got a tape this afternoon. Caroline was on it. She looked like she hasn't been hurt, she spoke clearly. The F.B.I. came to my office just after I'd seen it, but I didn't tell them about it. I acted like I didn't know anything."

"Where is she."

"She was in Zermatt when it happened. Or at least that's what they think. It didn't say on the tape."

"What do they want?"

"I don't know. Well, hell, I'm sure money, but the tape didn't say anything other than not to tell anyone anything about what was on it, what I knew. I'm sure they'll be in touch with us."

"Why didn't you tell them? God, Joe, we've got to tell them."

"We've got to wait until we know as much as we can about this, and then decide what to do. I'm sure it's going to be about money and I can somehow arrange that. If the best chance of keeping her safe and getting her back is to not tell them, that's what we've got to do. If it's to tell them, then we'll do that. But right now, I don't see how waiting until we hear from them can hurt. The kidnappers made it very clear I shouldn't tell anyone."

"I want to see the tape."

"I'd rather you not."

"There's something on it you're not telling me, isn't there? Goddammit, you've got to tell me the truth." Her voice and eyes are desperate, pleading, as tears roll down her cheeks.

"I've told you the truth. She's all right, and if you insist on seeing it you can. It's just that you're not going to learn anything other than what I've told you and there's no reason to get even more upset than you are now. We've got to think clearly."

Joseph stares at the now expressionless face of his wife as she gazes, transfixed, at him. Her aristocratic beauty with the sharp, perfect features, lofty cheekbones, large, doe-like brown eyes and dark, stylishly short hair - he can't recall her ever looking finer to him, ever causing him to feel more in love with her, even through her tears and pain.

Jane Brockton's head slowly sinks until it lays against his chest, and she begins to sob, softly, her whole body shaking. Nuzzling his cheek against her hair, he strokes through it with his fingers. And then his tears come, in a flood.

Chapter 7

The small pub is crowded and filled with a tobacco-scented haze; Europeans not yet health conscience or trendy enough to cause any perceptible percentage of the patrons to resist the urge to puff away. But then Christopher thinks it would be blasphemous for a decent bar not to be permeated by the pale of heavy smoke. He is occupying a spot at the bar, which has become a habit for him during his stay in Zermatt; at least on the days he arrives in time to keep from standing. Elsie's is one of the villages favorite hangouts for locals, racers, beautiful women, good conversation and raucous times, any one of which is enough to lure him inside and develop a real affection for a place.

"Do you think they'll delay it more than one day?"

"I don't think so. I mean…in light of what's happened it's certainly going to take the edge off, but there's too many commitments, too much pressure from too many places to go ahead, to get back on the schedule. Another one, Christopher?"

"Sure."

"Two beer," Billy McCormick says to the bartender, holding up 2 fingers.

"What about the Austrians?"

"There's some talk they'll pull out, but I can't see it. It's too important to them. I think they'll use the 'we thought about it but it's what Hans would have wanted for the team, and the country, and so we'll continue on' bit. And then they'll probably go out and kick everyone's ass even worse without him. Actually, that's not fair and maybe not true. They seem to be really shook. It'll probably distract some of them. What do you hear from Karl?"

"I haven't seen him since this morning on the mountain. He's usually in here, but I don't think so today. He looked pretty rough up there. Jesus, just when you start thinking these places and this life really is like Disneyland, so removed from the real world, this comes along and slaps a big dose of reality back into you."

"Have you heard anything at all about what happened?" Billy asks.

"Naw, I went to the press conference, if you want to call it that. It's pretty obvious the local constables aren't real seasoned in answering questions about murders in their little kingdom, and that they're not getting too much advice on spin control from whoever else might be involved. We were told he was found dead of a gunshot in a room at the Mont Cervin. We were told that over and over. And that's about all we were told."

"What the hell was he doing in a room at the Cervin? Was it his room? He gets a lot of special attention, but they usually stay together and they're at the Zermatterhof."

"They wouldn't say."

"Christopher, who else would be involved? Interpol must be around here by now, wouldn't you think, and probably whatever national agencies the Swiss have?"

"Yeah, I'm sure, and of course the Austrians too," Christopher replies, "and then there's the security for the tour, and the event. This place is crawling with people who ought to know more than they're putting out right now."

"Well, I've got to go. We've got a team dinner tonight.

Being a sleuth is part of your business, so I'm counting on you to find out what happened and let me in on it."

"Billy, I'll be glad to tell you whatever I know, but I've just begun to get the hang of deciphering injury reports and the psychological warfare of training runs. And when I'm not doing that, I'm delving into the complex questions of how hard the beds are and how warm the beer is at the great and not-so-great hotels on this continent. Murder is a little out of my line."

"Have a good evening."

"So long."

Christopher decides to walk to the Mont Cervin on the chance he might run into someone he knows, to see what might be going on. The early winter darkness of the Alps has descended and bitter cold attacks him as he leaves Elsie's. It seems the instant it gets dark, the temperature in all high mountain towns immediately drops through the floor. Moving quickly down the narrow street, past the quaint, gaily lit shops, restaurants, and pubs, weaving in and out of the browsers and strollers, his shoulders raised and hunched forward in a futile effort to create warmth, he thinks of the pity he has for the crews that must work on the mountain at night...in the dark, frigid, hostile world of the peaks above him that were sunlit and inviting just hours before. *But there was that midnight run in the moonlight, the bright, milky white glow that illuminated zillions of diamond-like sparkles in the fresh, uncut snow...the stillness...and the descent through the surreal patina of shades of only white and shadows. One of the great experiences of my life.*

Entering the hotel, Christopher sees no familiar faces in the lobby. He heads for the bar, wondering for an instant if it might be closed, but then realizes the management would want to play this down as much as possible...business as usual.

The Matterhorn Stube is crowded, but a few spots are open at the bar, he ambles over, hangs his coat on an ancient, elegant, freestanding rack, and orders a beer. After again glancing around for someone he knows, again unsuccessfully, he turns his back to the crowd and finds his gaze stopped cold as he looks directly at a stunning woman, across from him, leaning forward and talking to the bartender. Tall, with short black hair, a beautiful round face filled with exquisitely chiseled features, huge dark eyes, and pouting, pink lips. She's wearing a black leather jacket with enormous shoulders and all sorts of vents and zippers...sort of a hybrid flight and motorcycle number...and a collar generously trimmed in what appears to be mink. There is a cigarette jutting from between the splayed fingers of her drooping wrist, held as perfectly as only the right personality and amount of practice will allow.

Suddenly looking up, her eyes lock on Christopher's. There is nothing but a flat expression, but the eyes linger, then her face turns back to the conversation, she takes a long drag, and Christopher looks away.

After a few moments in the leaning-on-his-forearm while-pretending-to-be-engrossed-in-the-surrounding-activity-he-is-scanning pose, he decides to change images and take on the pensive, preoccupied look. Waiting what he judges a safe amount of time, he again faces the bar and orders another beer. She is also looking out at the crowd, fingering her glass, and appears totally oblivious to him when he risks a glance. Then she quickly turns and again their eyes meet. This time she smiles, he smiles weakly back, and then he turns his head, feeling sure his stupid little grin is welded to his face. *Don't turn away, you fuckin' idiot. Go talk to her. What more do you need? God, why are you so bad at this?. Jesus, it should be simple. At least look back up.* He does and she is gone. *You stupid son of a bitch.* And then he notices the cigarette pack, which looks from his vantage point to be half full. *If she comes back, swear to God, if she comes back and I get one more chance, I'm over there.*

He finishes his second beer and orders another. She's still not back and he thinks about asking the bartender who she is, where he can find her. Possible reasons, scenarios that would explain his interest, run through his mind, and then it occurs to him he'd better check out the guy's English before he spends too much time on his story. Signaling by slightly raising his hand and smiling toward the bartender, there is suddenly a voice from behind him and a gentle hand on his shoulder.

"Excuse me, do you know anything about what happened here today? I've heard something about a murder."

The voice is rich, enchanting, melodic, the accent and inflection unmistakably British...crisp, educated, blue- blood British. A siren song to him. Christopher turns, and the face is even more striking at only two feet.

"Yes, Hans Nygren was found shot to death here in the hotel."

"He's a skier, isn't he.?"

"A member of the Austrian ski team. Their best downhiller. Probably the best in the world. Are you here for the World Cup?"

"No. I would be here now even if there were no races."

"Are you on holiday?" Christopher, emboldened, is not about to let the conversation lag.

"Yes, I just arrived. There is an enormous amount of

security around. It's rather disconcerting in a place like this. I must get my cigarettes."

"May I join you?"

"Yes, please do."

Below the jacket she is wearing baggy black wool pants tucked into short, black leather boots with pointed toes, and walking ahead of him she appears slim and regal in the smooth grace of her gait.

"Would you care for a cigarette?" she asks, as they reach the pack of Marlboros.

"Actually, I would, but so far I've been successful at quitting, and it might be a bit too much of a reminder."

"You would probably choke. How long has it been since you've had one?"

"Over two years and I definitely do not think I would choke. I'm sure the first one would taste every bit as wonderful as the last one did. Do you like really fine, Godiva quality chocolate?"

"Yes, of course."

"Have you ever given it up for any length of time?"

"No."

"Well, try giving it up for a while and then, after a few months, have a piece. The taste is incredible. It'll be the best piece of chocolate you'll ever have in your life. And I think that's exactly what one of those damned cigarettes of yours would taste like to me."

A sly grin crosses her face and her eyes sparkle as she looks intently at him. "Why would you possibly resist something you know will give you so much pleasure?"

"If you keep putting it like that, and I keep thinking about it, I'm sure I'm going to forget why."

"At least you are not one of those dreadful people who act as if they are close to death if they are within ten meters of someone who is smoking. You know, there seems to be quite a number of Americans like that."

"No I'm not, and yes I know. We have a phenomenon in the U.S. called the bandwagon."

"Bandwagon?"

"The explanation is really dull. I don't think you'd find it that interesting."

"You might be surprised. I am a very curious person."

"Well then ask me something else, about anything other than smoking and bandwagons."

"Tell me about the murder. What happened?"

"Sorry, let me add murder to smoking and bandwagons. I really don't know, and neither does anyone else I've talked with. The authorities are saying only that he was found shot to death. They're keeping a very tight lid on everything so far. It's puzzling."

"Would you like to know more about it?"

"Yes, I would."

"I should be able to find out. The manager of the hotel, Peter Molterer, is an old and dear friend of mine. My name is Juliette. What's yours?"

"Christopher."

"I'm starving, Christopher. I've not had one bite since this morning and two glasses of gin on an empty stomach is telling me it is time to have dinner. Would you join me?"

"I'd love to." He motions for the bartender's attention as he is pulling francs out of his pocket to pay the bill.

"It is taken care of sir," comes the man's quiet voice.

"Well..." He turns to her. "Thank you."

He retrieves his coat, and they walk out into the lobby.

"What would you like to eat?" she asks.

"Have you been to Zermatt before?" he replies.

"Many times."

"Good. That means the decision is yours. I like all types of food, I've only been here for a couple of days and know very little about the restaurants."

They walk through the cold streets close to each other as she presses her arm and shoulder against his. A gloved hand suddenly encircles his elbow and the other closes on top of it. He feels his heart beating, the excitement course through him. *Be charming, be cool. God this is fun.*

They arrive at a small, intimate downstairs restaurant, and after ordering drinks, peruse the menu. He gushes about his love for fondue, and she prefaces her suggestion they order with a condescending but amusing reference to American tourists in Switzerland.

"Exactly where is your home, Christopher?"

"Raleigh, North Carolina. Do you know where that is?"

"I have been in Cape Hatteras in North Carolina and Hilton Head in South Carolina. Is it close to either?"

"Not too far."

"I thought I recognized your accent as southern. It's charming."

"Thank you, yours is more than charming. I love the way people from your country speak the language...the dialects and impeccable usage. I can listen all day."

"Oh really?" Again, there is the warm, wry smile.

"Where do you live?"

"In London."

"And what do you do there?"

"I own an art gallery. I'm the daughter of the landed gentry you sometimes read about...who has been given the means to pursue my fantasies and keep myself occupied. And what about you, Christopher, what do you do?"

"I'm a writer."

"What kind of writer?"

"Right now I'm covering the World Cup ski circuit for a magazine and doing some other articles on the European travel scene."

"You look like a novelist, not a travel writer."

"Well, I didn't want to mention it. The southern male's sense of modesty, you know. Or at least wait until I'm officially awarded the Pulitzer. Next month, at the latest."

"Are all men from the southern United States modest? It seems that some of Faulkner's characters were, and certainly Eudora Welty's."

Jesus. "Well, some of Faulkner's were a little bit of everything; and yes, I would say that's a fairly accurate description of many men who grow up in the south. At least of past generations, and probably including many of mine." He hesitates, smiles. "But the polar opposite of modesty...a trait of that mythical Southern Gentleman...is also on display...and seems to be increasing."

"And how about you? How modest are you really?"

"Well, I discovered early on that everything I enjoy doing I enjoy much more when I'm stark naked and trumpeting my pleasure and proficiency at the top of my lungs to anyone within ear shot."

"Everything, Christopher?"

"Absolutely everything."

She takes a long, slow drink of her gin, and, holding the glass just below her chin with both her hands, looks into his eyes for a moment before speaking. "I know the owner here also. There is a secluded table in the back. I know you would prefer to be here in the open, but I would worry about someone complaining. Let's move back now, before they serve our dinner, and you can take off your clothes and enjoy your meal that much more. Anderl." She motions to the waiter.

"Uh..."

"Yes Christopher?"

"Under any other circumstances I'd be thrilled by your suggestion, but remember, we're having fondue. And I'm looking forward to it so much I couldn't think of changing my order. And sometimes...well, you know, when you eat fondue, you sometimes spill the hot oil or cheese...and if I were naked...well, it could be extremely dangerous."

"Are you going to write a novel that will win a Pulitzer Prize?"

"Why don't we just start with a novel?"

"And what will your novel be about?"

"I've got a lot of different thoughts bouncing around, but something with some real meat, depth, you know, that discusses the truly critical issues of our times."

"And what are the critical issues of our times?"

"Sex, money, violence, a little romance...those are damn sure the critical issues for selling books. It's the old dilemma...the bullshit makes money, gets published, and the good stuff often doesn't. I'd love to be able to combine them, but then it would probably turn off both the trash hounds and the literary snobs, and no one would read it. What do you like to read?"

The sommelier appears with the cabernet Juliette ordered, and after precisely the correct amount of time, the waiter, with two pots of simmering cheese and plates of bread. After the few minutes it takes for the organization of food, dishes, and utensils dining on fondue requires, he notices her diligently devoting all her attention to preparing the first few bites. "Maybe we should have ordered something that doesn't require so much work."

"Yes.... I mean, no, this is wonderful," she says, with a hint of apology. "Please, you must forgive me. It's just I am so hungry...but I do apologize for being rude. What were we talking about? Sometimes I become totally immersed in making a glutton of myself."

"It's understandable if you haven't eaten all day. You were going to tell me who you enjoy reading."

"I've been through my stages, you know. I read many of the great writers and philosophers while I was at university. And I suppose for a bit after I was out. But it seems now I am content with being more of...what was the term you used, a rubbish hound? Never heard that before, but I do like it. Tocqueville, Sartre, Dostoyevsky...Faulkner...Roth, Updike,

47

Hesse...when I was trying to be an intellectual. But Le Carre is more my style now, although his last two efforts have seemed quite slow. And I rather like your Anne Rice. She's written some very interesting fantasy. I recently read Bonfire of the Vanities by Tom Wolfe. Is that what you are referring to? He seems to attempt to illuminate important issues through sensationalism and satire."

"Yes, in a way. He can be very good. And a large step above my definition of trash hounds. Why have you moved away from the classic, more literary writers?"

"I became weary of so many heavy, often pessimistic thoughts, and despair, and contemplating such serious issues and grave consequences. I decided I did not want to...that I am not the type of person who should spend so much of my life immersed in a state of melancholy. Or pretending to be. It was a stage I suspect. The young, concerned intellectual. Very noble...I told myself. I'm quite sure I was never totally comfortable with it. I'm also sure it was part of an act, trying to establish a reputation as a serious thinker...a person with depth. And the change in what I read was symbolic, it paralleled other areas of my life. I decided to not worry as much about what I could not affect and just enjoy myself."

"And do you enjoy yourself most of the time now?"

"Yes, Christopher, I do." This time the grin grows into a broad smile.

He looks at her for a long moment, as the waiter places more pots between them, trays and dishes filled with small slices of raw tenderloin, chicken and shrimp, vegetables, and numerous sauces. After they finish this course another pot arrives with hot, thick, creamy chocolate, and they empty the bottle of wine with the exquisite dessert. The conversation doesn't wane, is warm, stimulating, animated, the subjects serious, silly, and avant-garde.

"Juliette, are you going to ski tomorrow?"

"Yes. I'll likely sleep late, but I will be on the mountain by noon."

"They've rescheduled the race because of Nygren's death so I have the day off. Would you come skiing with me?"

"Yes, that would be lovely."

"Where do you like to ski when you're here?"

"There's something about each area that I love. The access, trails, and sun at Sunnegga; the views at Gornergrat; the trams, restaurants and runs into the village from Schwarzsee; the views at Testa Grigia. And the run down into Cervinia...it's likely my favorite run anywhere."

"So maybe we can go to Italy tomorrow?" Christopher asks, a pleading grin on his face.

"It would be best to start early for that, in order to have time for lunch before coming back. And if the weather is not good, or closes in, the ridge at Testa Grigia and the Theodulgletscher are very uncomfortable places to be in the late afternoon."

"Well, whenever...I'd like you to be my guide. I've never been to Cervinia and my Italian is very weak."

"But how is your French?" She leans closer, her weight on her forearms, and fixes him with the deep, dark eyes and warm smile.

"Weaker still."

"And your German?"

"Nonexistent."

"Your Greek?"

"Greek?" He asks, feigning surprise.

"And your English?"

"Next to yours it sounds like my second language."

"So, Christopher," she laughs heartily now, "you are not fluent in any of the sexual cultures, none of them at all?"

"My, my, aren't we clever? I'll have to back up and remember what you said. German? I might be able to follow the rest, but German?"

"I must go now. We've been here forever, and I am very tired."

His mind is racing as they walk back out into the night, and he suggests they find a bar with a cozy fireplace for a nightcap.

"No, I really must go. Where are you staying?"

"At the Zermatterhof."

"I will call you in the morning. Christopher, what is your last name?"

"Cabot."

"Goodnight." She turns and begins to walk away.

"Juliette, wait," he calls and starts after her. "Let me at least walk you back to your hotel."

She turns but doesn't stop. "Thank you but I am fine. I will talk to you tomorrow."

Her pace and voice tell him not to follow.

His thoughts confused, Christopher decides to go back to Elsie's for another beer or two. *Jesus, she's gorgeous, the voice and accent, and smart, crazy quick...enjoy my dinner more if I'm naked? Goddamn...More than a few references to sex. Why the hell did she leave so suddenly? At least I don't have to worry about what I'd have said when we got to her hotel. God I hope she calls. Probably has a boyfriend waiting for her. Gorgeous Italian hunk with a Ferrari. She'd have to. Maybe not. Real free spirit. Hell of an evening.*

Christopher walks back to his hotel at close to midnight, quite high from the evening of drinking. He wishes he had left out the last stop at Elsie's. Or maybe he's glad he went back. He had a lot to think about and doing it over beers was enjoyable.

"Mr. Cabot, you have a message sir," the man behind the desk says as Christopher walks past him toward the elevator.

Must be Juliette, wants me to come as quickly as I can, won't take no for an answer. Riiight. "Thank you." He takes the small envelope, opens it, and removes the slip of paper.

> Brockton puzzle answer reason
> off day registered Caroline for the
> to room is to your and the your the
> guess who?

Goddamn, what the hell...who the hell...guess who? Jesus. If they only knew how drunk I am. Man, who could it be? Her?

Christopher tries to decipher the message on the elevator, but it doesn't begin to register...nothing but a jumble. Once inside his room he falls on the bed, turns on the reading lamp and stares again. He gets up, grabs a note pad out off the table and begins to write the words out in a vertical column. *Caroline Brockton. Caroline Brocton!* He sees and recognizes the name as soon as he has the first two words down. Scribbling quickly now, it starts to fall into place, and his mind quickly clears.

Holy shit! Caroline Brockton. Thoughts now racing, he makes a conscience effort to slow them and make some sense of what he thinks he knows.

It's got to be her. Very clever indeed. He picks up the receiver, hesitates for a moment, then places it back on the phone. *What if she's with somebody, maybe the guy who told her. Come on, she's not going to interrupt that to take time to send a message. I'll call Joe. Jesus, I'll give Joe a call and the story. He'll love me.*

Again he starts to make the call, this time staying with it and allowing time for the hotel operator to make the connections that will give him an overseas link to the U.S. The wait is not long, he hears three or four rings, and a female voice answers.

"Could I speak with Joe please?"

"Yes, just a moment."

This all seems to warrant another beer and Christopher wishes he had taken one out of the small icebox before he made the call. Pulling the telephone cord as far as it will stretch, he leans over, and with his legs wide apart and arm fully extended, just manages to open the door. He lowers the receiver for the seconds it takes him to reach for the bottle, the opener, and remove the top. Settling back onto the bed, propping himself against the headboard, he is taking his first long draw when he hears the familiar, gravelly, deep "Hello."

"Joe, it's Christopher. How are you?"

"Christopher, I'm fine, how the hell are you? Are you still in Europe?"

"I'm fine, and yes, I'm in Switzerland."

"I was thinking about you today. Saw where that skier was killed. Are you still covering that stuff?"

"Yeah, I am. And that happens to be why I'm calling. What's the latest on it in the states?"

"Just that he was found shot to death in a hotel room. That was it."

"Is it getting much play there."

"I don't think so. I got it off the machine this morning. The sports section had a pretty nice little piece, but it was mostly bio and a few quotes about what effect it might have on the team and the event. Said security is really tight over there."

"Well, they haven't said much more than that over here either. It's strange. No details. But I think I've found out why. Do you know who Caroline Brockton is?"

"Sure. Joseph Brockton's daughter. Shows up in a lot of pictures with the international party set. Looks like she does her best to spend her fair share of the old man's billions, as if any army of extravagant splurgers could even make a dent in it."

"Hans Nygren was in a room registered to her when he was found."

"Whoa....How did you find that out?"

"Doesn't really matter, but the source is good."

"Are you sure?"

"Yeah. I was calling to see if you'd run it with my byline, then I figured you'd want the glory for yourself but would be eternally grateful and indebted to me for life. But now I'm thinking maybe you could snoop around with some of your contacts with the feds and see what else you can dig up. What do you think?"

"If it's true you've got to figure they're thinking kidnapping and they're waiting for something...or maybe they already know. Unless it's something totally different."

"Like what?"

"Hell, I don't know. These days...maybe she's a member of an Austrian separatist group. I've never heard about one but they're all the rage you know, everywhere else. In any case, the first question is how long we have before the authorities are forced to release some information or someone else finds out. How many other people who might let it out do you think know?"

"Man.... I don't have any idea about that, but I'm right here where it happened and so far I haven't come across a soul who admits to knowing anything."

"I'd love to release it and I'll do it with your name but let me go to the office first and see what's there. We've got some time to make the morning papers. I'll check some sources. And if somebody else already has it maybe we can dig up something for a follow-up. Christopher, there's something you'd better think about. If they're holding this for what they think is a good reason, and your name comes up, they're going to be all over you. You're going to have to make some decisions about protecting your source. It could get pretty nasty."

"Jesus, yeah, I guess you're right about that. Fame has its price, right?"

"Let's arrange a time to talk tomorrow. If I decide to do something with it tonight I'll call you back, but let me do some checking first. Call me later, or in the morning, as soon as you've heard the latest, seen the papers. Christ, that's going to be real late...or early here. That's okay."

Christopher gives Joe his phone number, says goodbye, drains the beer and lays flat on the bed. Excited, his adrenalin is flowing, but he's tired. Fighting for the energy to get up and strip, he quickly pulls back the sheet and down comforter, switches off the light, and crawls in. The night seems light outside his window and after staring at it for a few moments he closes his eyes and settles his thoughts on Joe Amato and what his old friend will do in the next few hours.

Chapter 8

Dr. Gerard LeFont has the arms of his seat in a death grip as the plane passes so close to the ridge and road that he's sure he sees the eyes of spectators widen as their upturned faces flash by just below him. The sensation is of falling vertically, not the gradual descent of most landings that cause him acute, suffocating anxiety on each occasion he goes through one. Closing his eyes...he awaits the bump and skid, or cartwheel, or spin. The bump comes, followed by a bouncy, then smooth roll that tells him he has survived. As the plane slows rapidly, he is pushed against his seatbelt, and only when it is just short of a dead stop does he release the armrest, place his sweat- soaked hands on his trousers and alter his rigor mortis-like, straight-ahead pose to turn his head and look out the window. He's startled to see a large expanse of incredibly hued turquoise water just a few feet from the plane. *Miss the fucking hill by inches only to end up in the goddamn sea.*

After clearing customs, LeFont is met by two men who introduce themselves as Gary and Michael. They take his one carry-on bag, walk past the collection of locals who always seem to be in the business of hanging out in tiny island airports, and usher him into a jeep parked just outside.

Palm trees, one story cottages, and restaurants occasionally hide the view, but within seconds they are alongside the beautiful bay that the runway dives into. LeFont doesn't look, keeps his eyes glued to the back of the front seat, even as the jeep climbs the tight, twisting, steep road to some five hundred feet above the water, where a spectacular view unfolds down on what is surely one of the most perfect crescents of beach imaginable. Passing a house suspended over a steep cliff, they crest the hill, then drop suddenly down and to the right as the road plunges toward the next sparkling cove and advancing columns of white surf. LeFont's hands have found the side of the seat and the low-cut door for their sweaty clutch during this harrowing journey, and he fights the urge to scream out loud—*You ignorant bastard, slow down.*

The road flattens as it squeezes between the roaring surf of the windward shore and the dramatic rise of the green hills on the other side. After only a few miles they are at the eastern tip of the island, bend around to the south, and begin to climb again. Rising a few hundred feet through switchbacks, they drop back down beside the sea, then the jeep suddenly veers onto a small driveway pitched at an angle so severe it reminds LeFont of the cog railway he once let himself be intimidated into riding. After a short, torturous climb that has them staring at the midday's powder blue sky, the jeep levels in a gravel courtyard and comes to a stop. A small, gray, stone villa with a red tile roof is in front of them. Once the men lead LeFont inside, it's immediately clear the house is anything but small. Tiered and cut into the steep hill, what they entered was just the upper level. Two lower floors spread out like fans with large, open, tile-floored areas that look out across a magnificent scene of frangipanni, wisteria and orealander, to vast stretches of sparkling sea and distant islands. There are overstuffed rattan chairs, sofas and lounges throughout, and large fans, their blurred blades whirring almost imperceptibly. LeFont sees it all, but his eyes linger on nothing, his mind attaching no value.

"Would you care for a drink, or perhaps something to eat, Dr?" Gary, the younger of the two men, asks in a voice that sounds just off from British. LeFont thinks possibly Australian. "Everything you might want is here and all you have to do is ask."

"I am very tired. Could you show me to my room? I would also like to shower." His English is clearly understandable, but heavily accented.

"Of course."

He is led to the lower level and down a hallway to the left. They pass a striking, young, dark-skinned girl watering plants. An island native, LeFont reasons, as his eyes linger on her long, slender legs. Shown into a room midway down the hall, he nods his head impatiently at Gary's instructions on the indoor and outdoor shower options and other amenities of the house, before finally uttering a terse "Yes, I can assure you I will be fine, I am very tired now." LeFont moves to the door to try and hasten the man's departure.

After a considerable stay under the hot shower, his small, naked, reed-thin body lies spread eagled on the bed beneath the cooling breeze of the fan. Listening to the almost constant wind gusts rattle the trees and bushes outside the open, wooden blinds, he wonders how long it will be before he can leave the island, where the girl is, and again how long it will be. He feels himself begin to drift off. Within seconds he is fast asleep.

Chapter 9

The knock on the door is violent, startling. He comes awake, groggy, and gropes for his pants in what seems like the same instant in time, failing to find them before the door bursts open and two men step quickly inside.

"Are you Christopher Cabot?"

Forgetting for the moment about the pants, and relieved at their well-dressed, non-menacing appearance, he answers without hesitation. "No. I'm Fidel Castro. What the hell do you want?" How did you get in.?"

"Please answer the question? Are you Christopher Cabot?"

"Yes I am."

"We would like to ask you some questions."

"Who are you?"

"My name is Thatcher and this is Wilson. We're from Interpol," the taller, older of the two men answers as they both hold up what Christopher assumes to be some sort of identification. "How did you determine that Hans Nygren's body was found in a room registered in the name of Caroline Brocton?"

"Jesus Christ. That son-of-a-bitch, didn't call."

"Would you please answer the question?"

"Was it in the paper?" Christopher asks.

"Yes, in this morning's Washington Post."

"Goddamn it. Look, this is all a real comedy of errors," he

says as he spots the trousers, slides off the bed, turns his back, and pulls them on. "I overheard it in a bar and called an acquaintance of mine in the states, in the newspaper business, to see if there was anything about it over there. I was just checking it out. I mean it seemed pretty strange that nobody was saying anything yesterday."

"Who did you overhear it from?"

"How the hell should I know. A couple of guys sitting next to me."

"Where were you?" Thatcher, the only one of the two who has spoken, asks him.

"At Elsie's."

"What time?"

"Jesus, it was a long night. Ten, eleven o'clock, something like that."

"How long were you there?"

"Maybe a couple of hours, or a little more, or a little less. Look, I'm a ski and travel writer who occasionally gets into some heavy investigative stuff like the quality of the Wienerschnitzel at the hotel restaurant. I was just curious. I didn't know anything was going to get into print, much less with my name on it. You can't trust the goddamned American press, you know. They're like vultures." *Did I say that?*

"Yes, and you're one of them." After a pause, Wilson finally says something.

"Yeah, but I don't deal in that kind of thing. People don't break your door down because of what you write about the death-defying fall Yugoslavia's favorite son took in the second training run."

"What did the men look like that you overheard?"

"I don't know. I mean I just don't pay that much attention to guys next to me at a bar. One of them was real tanned. Middle aged. You know, maybe he's one of these Swiss ski gurus, legends, guides you see around this place. Skin looks like a fine saddle."

"What exactly did they say?" Thatcher is doing the talking again.

"I don't remember that either, not exactly. Just something like Nygren was in Caroline Brockton's room. She's an American socialite."

"And that's all?"

"All I heard."

"Did you ask them anything about it?"

"No."

"Why?"

"I think an incredibly beautiful woman happened to walk by at that precise moment. Look, I don't know. I just didn't ask them."

"Who did you call in the states?"

"Didn't you get his name out of the paper too?"

"Yours was the only one mentioned."

"Wonderful. I ought to tell you just so he could go through this, but I know I don't have to do that. I'm sure you can find out if you need to. Look, it was a stupid move on my part to make the call, or to not insist that he keep it to himself. I screwed up, O.K.? But that's all there is to it. I don't know anything that's going to help you, and neither does anyone else I know. Now I would like to be able to go to the bathroom if you would please excuse me."

"This is very serious business, Mr. Cabot," Thatcher says, "We will likely be in touch with you again. And you might prepare yourself for a long day. We had the advantage of learning about the article almost as soon as it was on the street. The blokes from the Swiss and Austrian offices should be here any minute. Good day."

Christopher is into the numerous layers of ski clothing as fast as he can, doesn't shave, and considers not brushing his teeth until he remembers Juliette. He makes the trip down to the basement, boots lightly buckled, grabs his skis and poles, and steps out into the bright, clear, frigid morning. Walking quickly, he makes a couple of turns down side streets, then enters a small cafe.

After ordering coffee he begins to consider his options. He'd like to call Joe, but decides against it, at least for now. It's ten-thirty and he should be getting a call from Juliette soon, but he's sure if he goes back to the hotel for her message he'll be seen. They'll stake out the lobby and his room as soon as they find out. If he calls...he could try that...but they might not give him the message, or maybe they'll read it when it comes in. He chuckles to himself. *Jesus, real cloak and dagger stuff.* Deciding to call Juliette and heading for the phone he suddenly realizes he doesn't know her last name. *Did I ever know it? Ever ask her? They won't give me just Juliette's room. Dammit.*

Over four rolls and three cups of coffee he continues to mull over his next move. A few times he starts to call the hotel but doesn't. Finishing his breakfast, he pays, grabs his skis from outside in the rack, and walks in a brisk pace, heel to toe in the rigid boots, toward the Mont Cervin.

Arriving at the front desk, he asks if there is a message for a C. Cabot. The answer is no, and he asks the man to check Christopher. Same answer. Then Chris C. The note is handed to him. He walks back outside before unfolding it. *Very, very clever. Damn is she quick.*

of worker Chapel at Sol beginning at route of ceiling homeland to vertical

He unzips his pocket and reaches for a pen, but his face breaks into a broad grin while still fumbling for it, and he starts walking quickly back toward the cafe. *Worker of the chapel ceiling...Jesus...the route to Michelangelo's homeland at noon. I'd bet a zillion she'll be there.* Christopher feels a rush he hasn't felt in a long time.

At ten minutes past twelve he first catches sight of her walking toward him. Unmistakable...the strikingly tall, slender, white-clad figure, long strides and graceful gait, even in ski boots. She has on a white fur hat to match the perfectly fitted, one piece nylon suit, and gold sunglasses attached to a gold and black braided cord that hangs around the back of her neck.

"You should be a writer of riddles...or a riddle-writer, you know," he says as she comes alongside of him and lifts her skis from her shoulder.

"I would have made the message far more difficult last night if I had known you were going to use it to try to become famous."

"I apologize. I had no idea this would happen. Are you mad at me?"

"You should have known. It's not that difficult to put together. You did know who she is didn't you?"

"Of course."

"Yes, I am mad at you Christopher, but if you'll find a

tissue, I'll consider forgiving you. I left without any and my nose is dripping dreadfully."

"I thought you didn't want to go into Italy starting this late."

"We don't have to stay long. But I thought it would be a good idea to get you as far out of Zermatt as possible. It can be a quick trip."

They jam into the crowded cable car that will take them to Furi, then Schwarzee, struggle to the outside for a view, and end up pressed tightly against one another, barely able to move.

"Forced intimacy. These things are nirvana for dirty old men," he says quietly, his face just inches from hers.

"And what about dirty young men?"

"I'm not complaining."

As they rise above the tree line the unfolding vistas are spectacular in the noonday sun. Glistening, vast stretches of white, broken only by huge rock faces and sheer cliffs, all starkly contrasted against the cobalt blue of the sky. Each time they cross a tower and the car dips...then sways gently back...then forward...Christopher feels the familiar uneasiness in his stomach, tries to look across rather than down at the enormous drop. But all and all it's a wonderful ride, due in no small measure, he realizes, to their bodies being pressed so close together. Occasionally stealing a look when they are silent and gazing out, he finds her even more beautiful today than he did last night...her face, in his eyes, close to perfection.

"So does your friend, the hotel manager, know you told me?"

"No, but I found out about the article through him. He was

called in early this morning by the authorities. They were furious about the leak and were trying desperately to find out who it came from. I thought I might put Peter in a compromising position if he knew, and he's such a dear friend. It will all settle down soon enough. That kind of information is difficult to keep hidden for any length of time."

"Well, it was really stupid of me. I was curious about what the story was in the states. The beer and wine no doubt impaired my judgement...seriously impaired it."

Looking at her again, becoming slightly intoxicated by the scent she wears, he feels the car slow, signaling their arrival at Schwarzse. Shuffling out like an obedient herd, they walk along the mesh grate, then enter the searing brightness of a high alpine snowfield on a cloudless day. The glare is debilitating, his eyes shutting reflexively until his sunglasses are on. Stepping into their skis, they head for the first of two long poma lifts that will take them up and across the glacier, to the top of the ridge that runs between Klein Matterhorn and the Matterhorn itself. Not a fan of the numerous, lengthy, frigid surface lifts found here and at most resorts in Europe, he thinks that if he's going to ride these two, this is the day. As he leans back and allows the lift to pull him, he shudders at the thought of what it would be like up here in snow, wind, and cold. *But today...there's nothing that could make today any better.*

They slide off at the top and he is compelled to look back at the Matterhorn, as he always is, wherever he is. He has never seen it from this angle, this close, though it seems to be visible and dominate the view from any place one might be in Zermatt or the surrounding area. They are at the highest point accessible by lifts on the surrounding mountains, and it feels to him like the roof of the world.

"Juliette, is that mountain as awe inspiring to you as it is to me?"

"Yes."

"Well, what do you think? Do we have time?"

"I think we should make time. We will get back," she says, turning and pushing off, skating across the flat trail along the ridge. He follows closely behind, alternately poling and skating as the flat continues for some distance, with occasional stretches that are slightly uphill. Finally rounding a corner to enough of a drop for their skis to slide unaided, panting in the thin air from the climb, he lowers his arms and allows the force of gravity to move him along slowly. She stops and he comes alongside her.

"It's ten kilometers down into Cervinia. Follow me."

He sees quickly she is a strong skier. The form isn't perfect, but it isn't bad...and she likes to go fast. The four inches of fresh snow from yesterday's storm is silky, the trail just steep enough to allow plenty of speed with a relaxed technique, and they dart and swoop across the rises, drops, and twists in the terrain as they fly down the mountain toward the border. When their legs begin to burn and their breath is short, they stop, laugh, and swear it might be the best run ever. After sharing their mutual awe at the jaw-dropping scenery, they are off again. Halfway down the seven-mile-long run there is a small restaurant, and as they sit on the deck in the warm sun, the sound of opera in the background, drinking large glasses of beer…their talk is animated, there is much laughter, and questions are asked. Then they are flying again, racing toward Italy in an exuberant descent.

After walking through the streets of the quaint village of Cervinia and window shopping, her hand encircling his arm, they enter a small pub and order glasses of wine.

"Tell me about your family," she says.

"I'd rather talk about yours."

"I have already told you about mine, at least part of the story. It is your turn."

"I have two brothers, and a father. My mother died a few years ago."

"I am sorry."

"She was a wonderful person."

"What was she like?"

"Kind, considerate, gracious, gentle. Very gentle. But with an inner strength of steel. And bright. Interested in everything. A real fascination with the world."

"You sound as if you were very close to her."

"I guess. I'm not really sure. But I admired her very much. She was a great Southern lady."

"What is different about a great southern lady and a great northern lady, or great western lady, or…God, you would be a writer. What is this great southern mystique that so many people have made so much money writing about?"

"She would have been a great lady anywhere. I'm not sure about the mystique. Maybe…maybe it's only what you just said, that it has been written about, dissected, romanticized so often, and for so long. Maybe a similar mystique could be created about any region and its' people. But then maybe not. The people…there are so many paradoxes. Collectively…a real schizophrenic personality. There's an enormous depth of genuine warmth, kindness, concern, generosity, a true gentility, and graciousness, elegance, diligence, ingenuity, creativity, humor, spirituality, courage, honor. And then there's bigotry, oppression, smoldering hate and rage, xenophobia, homophobia, among other phobias, ignorance - all equally genuine. And, and hair-trigger violence, arrogance, parochialism, and self- righteousness. Maybe it's the traditions. They seem so hard to break, to defy all reason. It's a relatively short period, you know, compared to your country, that the southern part of my country has been settled. And the history and culture are so rich. But I don't know if our history should bear the brunt of responsibility for molding the people. Or if they're too weak…ignorant…too proud…to break free."

"I suspect many of those contradictions are inherent in many cultures…maybe they are more on display with the abundance of accomplished southern writers and cataclysmic events such as your civil war." She pauses, then continues. "What do your brothers do?"

"One's a lawyer. The other's a surgeon."

"And your father?"

"He's also a lawyer."

She studies the unshaven face…olive complexion, even features, framed by longish, luxurious, brown wavy hair. And the eyes - deep set, mysteriously dark. Handsome, and at the moment, melancholy. "You look as if something is bothering you. Is it your father, or your mother? Or am I being too inquisitive? Asking questions I shouldn't?"

"No, you're not. My father's a very successful and prominent person. The quintessential, driven man. And he expects all his sons to be like him. I'm not and it causes problems."

"Are your other brothers like him in that respect?"

"More so than I am. Or maybe they just go easier with the program. If you look at it on the surface...I mean, they're well on their way to emerging from the mold, following in the hallowed footsteps, and I'm writing stories about skiing and trying not to grow up."

"Is that what you are doing, avoiding growing up."

"I don't know. That's a recurring problem with me. I sometimes have a hard time figuring out just what the hell I am doing."

"Why do you think you are not more like your father, like your brothers?"

"Sorry, but I don't know the answer to that either. And I've sure thought about it enough. It seems like I've always been in a state of rebellion, against a lot of things, but particularly him. Or maybe it's my mother. She was so different. Maybe it's caused by my relationship with her, or what I perceived her going through, consciously, or unconsciously. You know about mothers and sons."

"Yes, and mothers and daughters. The woman is always the problem, you know."

"I know, but I disagree. Men are totally fucked up, much more so than women. Women are fucked up too, but not like men. Everybody has an act, the roles they use to hide who they really are. Men though...God, it's like, theirs are so entrenched, all pervasive, hopelessly twisted. It's not all their fault, of course. Or maybe it is. In any case...it's a real goddamn mess."

"Interesting thought coming from a man."

"True thought." He glances at his watch and looks outside, where a cloud cover has brought a gray cast to the afternoon. "We'd better start back. If it stays overcast it might be a real bitch by the time we get to the top. We've got a long way to go."

"I'd love another glass of wine."

"So would I," he says, slumping down in his chair, "but as relaxed as I am now, one more and I might not make it back."

"Good. I'll order another and we'll stay. Nodding to the waiter, who is standing patiently against the wall, then moves toward them, she says, "altri due bicchieri per favore" Her Italian sounds perfect.

"We can't stay long. We're going to have to drink fast, and you may have to drag me back to the lift."

"I don't mean stay for the glass of wine. I mean stay for the night."

Christopher laughs. "Right." Then, with a serious, questioning look, "You can't be serious?"

"Oh yes, Christopher, I am quite serious." Her sparkling eyes and wry smile delay his reply.

"I've got to be back for the women's downhill in the morning, and I don't have anything with me."

"We'll buy a toothbrush, and a razor if you insist, though I rather like the stubble look on you. And you had best not tell me you had rather watch women in helmets with huge thighs ski than stay here with me."

"It's not what I'd rather do. It's my job."

"You are acting much too responsible and conscientious for someone who refuses to grow up and is as fucked up as you say you are."

They both laugh and then he looks at her very intently. "Jesus."

They finish the wine, find a restaurant, dine on pasta in honor of being on Italian ground, stop and buy two more bottles of Italian wine, then check into a small, quaint hotel on a side street. Entering their room Christopher is concerned about how much he's had to drink, unsure as always about the opening move, but deep in heat.

Removing his boots, he starts to take off the outer layer of clothing, but stops to open one of the bottles, then pours the glasses, turns and hands one to her.

"To a wonderful idea, and the crazed person who suggested it," he says. Their glasses touch. After one sip they are suddenly embracing and a long, scintillating, luxurious kiss has broken the ice. He thinks to remove her layers of clothing slowly, to heighten and savor the mysteries of her body. But within minutes, and no protest on his part, they are entwined on the starched down comforter on the four-poster bed, still reveling in the hot, sweet taste of each other, and now the free, electric sensation of one naked body against another. When the writhing becomes frantic, he lets it go for a minute, then slows the pace by quieting his body and starting at her neck with his fingertips and tongue. Caressing, slowly, every inch of her, he explores each wonder of the silky skin, slender curves, smooth, firm muscles, and fine, black hair. A feathery touch, a hot tongue...he misses nothing. Her sounds are soft, stirrings of tranquil pleasure as he moves over her, gently turns her, and starts again. When he again finds her mouth with his and lowers his weight onto her, the delicious simmer comes immediately to a boil, she pulls him strongly and quickly into her, and they thrust and move together with an exquisite, tight precision...for a long time. When it comes, the shudder and rush is as intense as he can remember and makes him want to gasp and cry out as she does.

They lay still and silent for some time, hard breaths loud

in their ears, then begin to laugh and talk as she smokes. She gets up and pours them another glass of wine. Later, when he does the same, she watches the trim, muscular body. Not heavily muscled, as if he works at it, but rather like a soccer player, without the huge legs. And when he turns to the side she stares at the shrunken, shriveled, sagging clumps of flesh that, at times like this, resemble nothing to her so much as the vestige of a crude, ancient evolutionary appendage, or some ridiculous prehistoric body decoration. But when brought to life, to her gaze or touch, can cause an explosion of longing and lust in her.

A few minutes after he has settled back onto the bed he feels a delicious charge as her fingers barely touch and slide up his thigh, and then ever so delicately trace his genitals before gradually encircling and beginning to caress them.

Juliette slowly plays her tongue down his chest, paying special attention to his nipples, and across the smooth, flat stomach. She sees the object of her previous amusement becoming sleek, thick, and beautiful...exciting her as she watches the dramatic change.

Everything he did to her she does to him... and more... and better. A true maestro. All delicate bliss, then surging desire, then delicate bliss, and a few times he pushes her away to avoid it coming to an end. After making love again...this time slowly, tenderly... there is no cigarette or wine, just exhaustion, contented minds and bodies. Embracing, they quickly fall asleep.

Chapter 10

"Mr. Brockton, John Slade has been here for almost thirty minutes now, and he's beginning to shift around and look at his watch. He looks very impatient," Amy Hawes says as soon as she closes the door behind her.

Jesus. "Show him in," Joseph says as he realizes how long he has been lost in thought.

"I'm sorry, John, I was tied up and didn't realize how long I've been keeping you. My apologies."

"None needed. Everything's in order for the offer for Rappaport. We just need to know when to move. I think we should go ahead as quickly as possible. That is, unless you have anything to cause us to delay. It'll be hard as hell to keep it from getting out if we sit on it for much longer, and if you remember there were rumors not so long ago in a couple of their papers. Someone could have a contact somewhere." Slade studies Brockton's face, waiting for an answer, but there are no clues and no reply. "Joe...."

"Yes, uh, well...I agree with you. I think we need to move quickly. There is one other minor thing though. But it shouldn't take long. I'll let you know something by tomorrow at the latest. Thanks for finishing everything up so quickly and coming by." Brockton rises, signaling it is time for the attorney to leave, and then walks him to the door. "Give my regards to Liz."

John Slade stops, turns, and fixes Joseph's eyes with a warm, sympathetic stare. "We're thinking about you and praying for you."

Returning to his desk, he sits and buries his head in his hands, cursing the fact he can't concentrate on anything for more than a few minutes, that he must carry on business, and now possibly be faced with dealing with the media on something else while consumed with Caroline's situation.

It has been almost forty-eight hours since he received the tape, thirty since the article, and he has heard nothing else. Jane is frantic, and it seems more frequent that he finds himself fighting the urge to lose control. He thought staying busy would help. It hasn't. But the office is a refuge from the media. Tempted to level with the F.B.I. more than a few times, he has resisted, convinced waiting offers the best chance. He can always go to them if he thinks the odds have changed. *But don't these damned people know I can't put them off much longer. Not talking to your daughter for a couple of days is one thing, anything longer under the circumstances and they'll wonder why I'm not a total wreck. Hell, I am. Or be convinced I know more than I've told them.*

"Has the second mail delivery come yet?" he asks Amy through the speaker.

"Yes. But there's nothing for you that you need to see."

"I'll be out for a while. Probably a couple of hours." Joseph has decided to go to the athletic club. A game of squash and a workout suddenly sounds good, will relax him, he hopes.

He walks out the front entrance, handing his assistant two documents to be faxed. At the end of the long, elegantly paneled and wallpapered hall he passes the reception desk and pushes open the double doors.

"Mr. Brockton, excuse me sir," Shirley Donaldson calls to him. He stops and turns towards her

"A courier just delivered this package, said you were expecting it and to get it to you as soon as possible. I thought you would want it before you leave."

"When did he leave it?"

"He just got on the elevator."

Joseph turns and starts for the elevator, then turns back for the package, then hurries back toward the doors, telling himself to slow down. Once hidden from the desk he glances quickly, sees no one in the hall, sprints for the elevators, and slams his finger against the down button. It opens immediately and he lurches in, simultaneously pressing the lobby level and the button to close the door. Starting to open the small Federal Express package, he thinks better of it, then stuffs it into the large inside pocket of his overcoat.

As the door opens, he strides quickly out and breaks into a run across the huge marble-floored lobby and through the revolving doors. Once outside his eyes frantically search up and down the sidewalk, then the intersections. The only couriers he sees are flashing by at speeds generated from leaving other buildings. He starts to reach for the package, but again decides to wait. Looking around once more, this time for McCrary or Waite, or the press, or anyone else that might be eyeing him, he starts walking, in a long, rapid gait.

Sitting on the bench in front of his locker, he rips open the adhesive strip and looks at the label behind the plastic sheath. His name and address are typed in, but the section for the package's origination is blank. He starts for the toilet, then lays the package on the bench and quickly strips to his undershorts. After locking the door to the stall and sitting down, he opens the package and pulls out a folded, overnight envelope. It is addressed to him in Caroline's handwriting, with her Paris address listed as a return and an origination in

Vienna, Austria. He tears it open and removes two envelopes. One is addressed to him, again in Caroline's handwriting. The other is blank. Inside the one bearing his name is a matching, folded sheet of elegant linen stationery, with a distinctive CB embossed in script in the upper left-hand corner. The handwriting is hers. The stationery he doesn't recognize.

Dear Mom and Dad,

Just arrived back in Vienna after a quick trip to Zermatt and the World Cup. Had some friends arriving unexpectedly for an opening and parties so I rushed back. Saw some great skiing while I was there, although just the prelims. Schedule hectic here now, but I will call you in a couple of days. Could you please wire more funds -- It gets more expensive here by the day, and I've bought some really interesting pieces. I can't wait...

Joseph lays the letter in his lap without finishing it and fumbles to open the blank envelope. There is again a single folded sheet, with the message typed.

```
$25,000,000 WIRED TO THE BANK ACCOUNT
ACCOUNT LISTED BELOW -- WITHIN 48 HOURS

        BANK OF THE CAYMANS
        ACCT.#8463299904tcl
        GRAND CAYMAN ISLAND

REMEMBER, WE ARE WATCHING YOU. TELL NO
ONE. FOLLOW THESE DIRECTIONS EXPLICITLY
OR YOU WILL NEVER SEE YOUR DAUGHTER ALIVE
AGAIN, AND SHE WILL SUFFER BEFORE SHE DIES.
```

His gut contracts. Shivers shake his body to the core. Quickly he goes back to her letter and finishes reading it.

Then rereads it. There are no clues. Leaning back against the top of the toilet seat, he tilts his head back, closing his eyes. *They're not going to make any damned mistakes.* Attempting to quiet his mind, he focuses on trying to think clearly. *Should I call McCrary or wait until he contacts me again. Call him now, anything else would look strange. But I've got to talk to Bob first.*

"Robert Wembley, please. This is Joseph Brockton."

"Hello Mr. Brockton. He's at lunch. He should be back within an hour."

"Do you know if he had a luncheon, or where he might be?"

"He went to lunch with Peter Isman. They're at the Yacht Club."

"Thank you."

"Would you like me to leave a message for him?"

"No, thank you." *Perfect*

Robert dresses, leaves the athletic club and heads south on Sixth Avenue. He turns left on 44th and halfway down the block walks below the massive, gray stone window frames sculpted to resemble a galleon's transom, up the steps, and into the imposing structure of the New York Yacht Club. Charles, the doorman, greets him by name and takes his coat.

"Charles, I believe Robert Wembley is downstairs having lunch. Could you find him and give him this, please," Joseph says as he hands the man a small, folded sheet of paper. He then walks up the open flight of stairs and into the model room, to a grouping of burgundy leather, chesterfield couches beneath one of the windows, and sits down. Unlike the hundreds of other times he has been in this iconic, ornately decorated room, he pays no attention to the incredible array of large, intricate ship models, some in glass cases, or the walls lined with half hulls and magnificent nautical art. For as long as he can remember he has had a love affair with boats, the sea, and its lore, and has always thought this room was likely the ultimate landlocked environment for anyone who shares his feelings. Today…he hardly notices.

"Hello Joe."

The voice shakes him from his whirring ruminations, and he stands to greet Robert Wembley. "I've got something very important to discuss with you Bob…I'll need a few minutes."

"Peter and I are just finishing lunch. I'll be right back up."

Robert Wembley was biting into one of the club's famous macaroons when he was handed the note with the word urgent underlined. It's not like Joe to find him here and send that kind of message unless it is indeed something grave, and because of the story in the paper he assumes it is about Caroline. But as he walks back to the dining room he has perceived no clue in his friend's demeanor, except his preoccupation when Robert walked in. Then again, it's hard for him to imagine much what would make Joe Brockton appear rattled, at least on the outside, while knowing full well the kind of internal emotion his friend is capable of enduring.

Arriving back in the dining room on the lower level and quickly excusing himself to "deal with something that requires my immediate attention,", Robert heads back up the stairs to the model room.

"What is it Joe?"

"You could probably guess."

"Yes, I probably can."

"Bob, what I'm about to tell you, and ask you, must be kept just between us. Absolutely no one else must know. It is, literally, life or death."

"Christ, Joe...you know you have my word. You don't have to go through that."

"I know, and I apologize, but in this case..." Joseph pauses for a moment before continuing. "Caroline's been kidnapped. They want twenty-five million deposited to an account in the Cayman Islands. I desperately need your help."

"No one knows?"

"Only Jane, but she doesn't know about the ransom. They just contacted me. Sorry I had to lie to you yesterday when you called, but I'm sure you understand."

"How long have you known they have her?"

"The day before yesterday."

"So before the story."

"Yes."

"Don't you think you should go to the F.B.I? God, they must be all over you."

"They are. But I'm convinced my best chance is to try it on my own first. Whoever these people are, they appear to be real pros. And they made it explicitly clear I wasn't to let anyone know."

"Do you...have you heard from Caroline personally?"

"They sent me a tape. It was the first I knew of it. She looked OK, but scared as hell, begged me to do what they asked." Joseph feels his eyes suddenly fill, but continues to look straight at Robert.

"God I'm sorry Joe. How's Jane taking it?"

"Not quite as well as I am," he says, making a feeble attempt to chuckle as he brushes at the tear sliding down his cheek. "You've got to help me get that money down there, Bob, and before anybody finds out what's going on. The threats are ugly and I think they're dead serious."

"You know there are a number of problems with doing something like this?"

"Yeah, I know, but I also know it can be done."

"Well, let me go get started. Is there any problem getting in touch with you?"

"Yes. I refused at first to let them tap my phones, but then I figured these people are smart enough not to call anyway, and I was right. And I realized it would look funny if I persisted. I'll call you tonight, try to talk in code, but we'll need to meet in person. A place with absolute privacy. Likely here again. What time will you be home?"

"By six thirty."

"Thank you, I'd better get back before someone gets suspicious. I'm glad I didn't choose espionage for a career."

Chapter 11

Almost three hours into her watch the brightly illuminated green lines and numbers of the compass are beginning to work their spell, and Sam is struggling to keep the needle within a few clicks on either side of 92 degrees east as Zulu Warrior charges upwind. She looks up, but within minutes the ghosts appear again in the black intersection of sea and horizon, and her eyes jump blearily back to the dial. Readjusting her hands close to forty-five degrees from the raised band on the leather wheel cover indicating a neutral rudder...with slight, subtle movements... she watches the needle's swing narrow until it hovers dead on their intended course. But again, the green pulses, blurs, and she looks up, shaking her head to clear her senses. Sam thinks of how small her universe is, right now, in this place. Crossing an ocean, miles from the nearest land, one might think there would be a grand sense of space. But there is only the compass, the cockpit, the small portion of the deck ahead that is illuminated. On a moonless night, unless looking up at the breadth of the heavens, everything compresses. Just this small space around you, only what you can see. She imagines what it might look like from above, and a distance, the boat reduced to a speck, moving almost imperceptibly through the vastness. Her focus returns to the business at hand, to steering from her little platform, while listening to the sound of the hull slicing water, plowing through the seas before they rush by and give her the sense of moving much faster through the dark abyss than the large yacht's actual speed.

"Hey beautiful, it's a few minutes til, but I'm here and ready, whenever," come the words from Giles, looking up from the companionway. "Does sleep sound good?"

"I'll stay the ten minutes and a little longer if you'll be kind enough to put some coffee on for me. I'm going up front to gaze at this sky before I call it a night."

A few minutes later Giles steps back up into the cockpit with a steaming mug, hands it to Sam, snaps his harness to the rail and steps behind the wheel to start his three-hour watch at the helm.

Moving forward of the mast, on the high, weather side of the deck, Sam lays back on the smooth, worn teak and revels in the eighteen knots of trade wind rushing over her. The seas are relatively flat for open water in the Caribbean...and the ride is sublime. Looking skyward, she watches the arc of the main and top of the mast cut like a scythe through the infinite billions of sparkles in the black sky.

"Would I be disturbing the pretty thoughts in your pretty head if I joined you? Glorious night, luv. Goddamn glorious night."

"Alan, do you ever try to imagine the tens of millions of stars in the smallest of galaxies, then endless millions of galaxies, all moving apart at incredible speeds, and the quasars and black holes, the endless possibilities for other planets, and other life. And where we fit in, right here on Zulu?"

"Christ, Samantha, on a night like this my mind's on other things. Maybe I'm not capable, or maybe it's choice. I'll go with the latter. Surely, luv, there are other things you were thinking about."

"My old boyfriend, but only for an instant."

"Bad to worse, unless you tell me about your sex life, in detail. Is he the bloke you sailed to Papeete with?"

"Yeah."

"So I'm all ears, the perfect confidant, big brother, with a soft shoulder to absorb tears. Why aren't you two still together?"

"It's not very interesting...dramatic...nothing like that. It just didn't work, and it never could have. You learn about someone real fast when you're in a thirty-five foot space with them, alone, twenty-four hours a day, and neither one of you can leave."

"He was studying to be a doctor like you, wasn't he?"

"A doctorate in philosophy, Alan, that's what I was studying for, and Will was getting his doctorate in psychology. Tell me about Saint Maarten."

"Great bars, casinos, good restaurants, lots of tourists, stewardesses on holiday. And then there's Saint Bart's."

"Well?"

"Beautiful women, incredibly beautiful women, and men, Samantha, beautiful Frenchmen. And the island itself, it's gorgeous, spectacular...might be perfect if it wasn't so damned French."

The heavy, clanging drum roll of the anchor chain awakens her from a deep sleep on the couch in the main salon and causes Sam to get on her knees and peer out the hatch at the harbor at Phillipsburg, Saint Maarten. But her last watch at the helm and long adventure with the night sky, only a few hours in the past, and the gentle, cooling breeze blowing down on her through an open hatch, cause a luxurious, tired contentment that is too much to overcome. Lying back down, she quickly loses consciousness.

When she finally awakens for good it is two o'clock in the afternoon. Lazily fixing herself a cup of coffee, she goes out into the cockpit. Everyone has left, she is alone on board, and Sam smiles as she imagines the whole crew already hard at play in the casinos and bars. Propping her back against the cabin she opens the weather-beaten copy of THE SCARLET PIMPERNEL that she exchanged for her equally worn copy of LORD JIM in a quaint island hotel and begins the classic. The pages turn quickly for the next hour, her concentration unbroken until the end of a chapter allows her mind a moment to seize on the thought of a shore shower.

Back in quick order from below with clean clothes, a towel, and her toiletries, she suddenly contemplates the excellent chance of being marooned on Zulu Warrior without a dinghy. Sure enough. *Damn. All dressed up and nowhere to go.* Scanning the turquoise water in the large, round harbor, she sees a very small boat coming in her general direction from quite a distance down the shore. As it draws closer, she goes to the foredeck and waves her arms. There is no immediate course correction, but then the bow of the craft swings toward her.

A handsome, lanky black man with a neat, full beard, in shorts, sandals, and a grimy chambray work shirt, the buttons open and shirttails tied, pulls the little pram alongside, lifts the oars from the water, and swivels the locks until the blades rest inside the hull. She looks down onto his sparkling eyes and broad grin.

"Hello, welcome to Saint Maarten."

"Thank you. Could you be so kind as to give me a ride to shore?"

"My pleasure. I'll pull down to the ladder."

"Thank you so much," she says, "no telling how long I

would have been stranded if you hadn't come along."

"Must be an Australian crew to leave a beautiful woman aboard without a ride." They both laugh.

"I'm Andre," he says, sticking out his large hand.

"I'm Sam."

On the short trip to the dock she receives directions to the showers and the recommendation of a restaurant in an adjacent building, and is soon luxuriating in the strong pressure and seemingly endless flow of warm water…things foreign to showers on board. Without the return of her land legs, she rocks and rolls in the stall.

Andre sees her sitting at the bar, eating a hamburger, and the thick, tousled red hair and lightly tanned skin against her pale green, blousy, short dress causes him to say quietly and to no one, "Jesus."

"I hope you're not already too full to let me buy you another beer. Or maybe you'd like to have a pina colada for dessert," he says, as he sits on the bar stool next to her.

"I'm not too full, but I won't accept your offer. You must let me buy you a beer for rescuing me."

"If you insist Sam. Would you like another?"

"Yes, please."

"Could we have two Heinekens, Jon," Andre says, "So how long is the magnificent Zulu Warrior going to be in Saint Maarten?"

"I'm not sure. This is a ship without much of a schedule."

"Where are you in from."

"The Virgins. We spent two weeks there. A couple of days

in Saint Thomas and the rest on the British side, mostly in Road Town and Virgin Gorda."

"And what's next?"

"Down island, as everyone around here seems to say. I don't have much to do with making the plans, but it sounds like Antigua's next, then Guadeloupe. How about you, do you live here or are you a transient?"

"I live here, but I guess I'm still a transient. Just a little longer term than you."

"Where are you from?" she asks.

"St. Louis. How about you. I'm guessing it isn't Sydney."

"New Mexico. How long have you been here?"

"About three years," he says.

"You must like it."

"Yeah, it's O.K. It's O.K. I won't complain."

"So what do you do, Andre? Do you work or are you independently wealthy enough to be able to just hang out?"

He looks at her for a long moment, his eyes probing hers. "Sam, there aren't many people that look like me from St. Louis that are independently wealthy. Wealthy, perhaps a few, independently or legally, not much of a chance. I work."

"And what do you do?"

"Did you notice the black catamaran, 'Shadow', as we came in?"

"Yes."

"Well, there's another cat, a sister ship, 'El Tigre', about the same size, sleeker and a little faster, that's usually moored alongside her. I'm the skipper."

"And what does 'El Tigre' do?"

"Makes a trip to Saint Barts and back every day. Cargo's primarily tourists, some locals, occasionally something of value stashed alongside the rum punch and pina coladas. Sometimes she charters out for groups."

"I've heard Saint Barts is wonderful."

"It is. And you now have an official invitation to be the special guest of the captain on tomorrow's trip. I'm a terrific island guide."

"Sounds great. Where is she now.?"

"Down at the yard. Roller furling needed replacing, and I was doing some other minor stuff. That's the reason I was so grubby when I picked you up. Excuse me for a minute."

She watches the tall, slender, lithe figure, white safari shirt hanging from broad shoulders, move gracefully away from the bar.

"Two more beers, please," Sam says.

"He's not about to let you pay for these, you know," Jon says from behind the bar in his clipped, proper English.

"And why not?"

"He's a real gentleman, gallant, Andre is."

"I ordered two more. I hope your limit isn't one," she says as he sits back down.

"Sam, you ever met anyone in this part of the world who has a limit of one?"

"Hardly."

"So did you get aboard at Sydney, or did she start there?"

"She started there, but I got on in Papeete."

"Doesn't sound like a mass migration route, New Mexico to Tahiti. If you're not following the herd, some special reason? Or special person? And where in New Mexico?"

She hesitates for a moment, then says in a flat voice, "Los Alamos."

"Yeah? They work on some pretty hairy stuff out there. Was your father...or mother...a scientist?"

"Yes. My Dad. Anyway, I sailed to Papeete from San Diego with my boyfriend."

"Is he here with you?"

"God no. He's safely back in school."

"You sound relieved. Would it be improper for me to ask why?"

She laughs. "Jon was right about you."

"Wha.."

"Will talked me into taking the trip because it would be a great adventure, romantic. Before the first week was over it became obvious he wasn't much of an adventurer or a romantic. Narcissistic, vain, weak, scared. He had the boat, the sea, the whole incredible environment...me, running around naked much of the time, sex whenever we wanted it, however we wanted it, plenty of great books, time to talk. And after the initial excitement he spent most of his time in deep depression over the pimples he'd developed...probably from his hideous karma...and scared to death every time he saw a dark cloud and the wind got above 15 knots."

"How long had you known him?"

"Not long enough. Actually, that's not true. But until we were in a situation where he couldn't hide, couldn't fool me, he did fool me. He was studying to be a psychologist, and I don't know if it played a major role. I suspect it might have. But he was in desperate need of one himself, and very, very good at hiding it."

"And what were you doing in San Diego?"

"That's just where we left from. I was in school also. With him."

"Were you studying to be a psychologist?"

"No," she says, her expressive face breaking into a wide grin, the bright green eyes sparkling. "Something much more exacting, more precise, incredibly practical. I was working on my doctorate in philosophy."

"Wow...so how much longer do I have before you're going to leave unless we start discussing heavy stuff?"

"Don't worry. I'm not sure the heavy stuff was ever relevant enough...at least for me. Just time consuming. That's one of the reasons I left."

"Where were you in school?"

"Cal-Berkely."

"You definitely know how to intimidate a guy. So the romantic adventurer shrink is back in class. What happened to the girlfriend he dragged out to sea?"

"Became an intrepid seawoman and seeker of romantic adventure. Actually, I'll probably decide to do something serious again after we reach Europe...if we ever do with this floating fraternity party."

"And what will that be?"

"I really don't know. Something I enjoy, but something that's productive, you know...contributes something. Once I backed away from it, what I was doing seemed so esoteric, elitist. I was into it because I didn't want to get involved in all the corruption and greed that seems inherent in most of the great American dream." She laughs. "Now I don't know."

"When you left school did you know you weren't going back, or at least not for a while?"

"The trip was supposed to be just a vacation. We were going to take six months off. But I was already pretty restless...disenchanted. When we reached Tahiti, I was so glad to be rid of Will, so anxious for a little more adventure without him...to see some other places, have more time to think. I knew I was confused about a lot of things. And then I met Alan from Zulu."

"New boyfriend?"

"God no. Women's public enemy number one. No, just kidding. That's much too harsh. He's a terrific guy in a lot of ways. Just tries to uphold the banners of chauvinism and sexism all by himself, and usually succeeds. But if I really needed help, there's no one I've ever known that I'd go to first. Enough about me. What's your reason for ending up in paradise?"

"Too long and involved a story for now. Not really that interesting. And I'm going to have to go. Would you like me to run you back out?"

"Well...if you promise you don't mind, I forgot my laundry and if you could take me out to get it. I'm sure somebody will be back by the time it's done, or I'll go into town."

"I'll be glad to."

When they are back at the dock, she has thanked him and told him how much she has enjoyed the conversation, he asks her again how long they will be in Saint Maarten.

"After hearing Alan describe all this area has to offer, and Saint Barts, it could be quite a while. Then again, maybe just a few days."

"Well, I'll be disappointed and terribly depressed if I don't see you on El Tigre tomorrow. She sails at ten o'clock. Have a nice evening." He turns and steps down into the pram, pushes off, and she watches his powerful, rhythmic oar strokes move the little boat swiftly in the direction of town.

The big, sleek, orange catamaran eases out of the slip promptly at ten. Some twenty people are aboard, all with the look of tourists except for one middle-aged couple.

Andre is smooth, jovial, his presence commanding as he explains the itinerary, safety precautions, and how quickly one's skin will burn at these latitudes if not saturated repeatedly with protective lotion. There is shelter under the large bimini top, but not enough. Sam notes how the passengers react to the tall, jet-black man, long muscles rippling under his open shirt, as his friendly voice and deep, dark eyes address them. She tries to imagine which women are intrigued, which aren't, which men are intimidated. As they approach the entrance to the harbor, the mainsail and genoa go up, and there is a surge in speed. Once clear of the rocks and reefs they turn upwind toward Saint Barts, bear off and trim the sails for a beam reach, Jimmy Cliff's reggae begins to blare, and the bar opens.

It's Sam's first time on a big ocean cat and the speed astounds her. After watching Andre turn the helm over to one of the two crew members and expertly work his charges to assure their trip is off to a great start, her attention shifts back to the group as they grease up and order their first bloody mary, pina colada, rum punch, or beer of the day. Mostly a young crowd. Mid-twenties to late thirties, with a few older exceptions. One very attractive couple stands out; the girl in a tiny, high cut bikini, the guy with the look of a successful attorney, or broker...tortoise shell glasses, athletic build, but pale. A number of bodies are not quite as well kept, some with suits perhaps a style too bold, and plenty of uneven, splotchy red skin from a previous day without Andre's recommended dosage of protection. There is not much mingling yet, everyone staying in their own space.

She is the last to get a drink, and with a seltzer water in her hand moves up front and lays back on the huge trampoline that stretches between the two hulls. The water rushes by just below her with a sound that says everything about power and speed, and the ride on the springy, rubberized, webbed surface is luxurious and wild as they blast along in a full twenty knots of steady, trade wind breeze. Closing her eyes, she lets her body go limp, exhales to fully relax, then finds her hand tapping on the trampoline to "Johnny Too Bad's" steady, reggae beat.

By the time they glide into the inner harbor of Gustavia, Saint Bartholomey, many drinks and two hours of sun later, El Tigre's passengers are far more into socializing than when they left. The scene surrounding them is pure picture-postcard. A narrow, oval harbor full of impressive yachts at anchor or moored stern-to, rimmed by sun-splashed, red tile-roofed white buildings, rising into green hills flecked with bright orange hibiscus and red bougainvillea.

After deftly backing the big cat into a stern-to position along the quay, Andre gives everyone the scoop on what to see, to shop for, options for getting around the island, and instructions to be back by four o'clock at the latest. His tone, though jovial, leaves no doubt he'll sail without any stragglers. After helping the last of them with the step up onto the concrete government pier, he turns to Sam. "Are you hungry?"

"Starved."

"Good. We'll grab a bite and talk about what to do next."

She envisions a quaint Mediterranean seacoast village, in the middle of the Caribbean. This is what it would be like. After a short walk through the narrow streets lined with shops, they enter the shaded courtyard of an ancient looking bar with a sign reading 'Le Select'.

"This is one of the few real sailor's bars you'll still find on these tourist-filled islands," Andre says. "Nothing fancy or put on here. It's a great place to hang out, some real characters if you're around enough, and they have terrific cheeseburgers. God, what happened to my manners. I should ask you first if you even like, or want a cheeseburger?"

"A cheeseburger sounds wonderful," she says.

The place certainly looks authentic as they step inside and toward the bar. Fairly dark, not particularly clean, old, abused wooden tables and chairs...real, faded, seagoing burgees covering the walls and hanging from the ceiling. And the feel...damp, cool, smell of old smoke, with a fan whirring overhead. A real respite from the blistering heat of the noonday, tropical sun.

"Andre, bon jour," comes the deep, gravelly voice from the large man behind the bar.

"Bonjour, Jean-Paul, could we have two cheeseburgers and...what would you like to drink?" he asks, shifting his eyes to her."

"A Heineken."

"Two cheeseburgers and two Heinekens, please."

Sam looks past Andre to a table in the corner where three men and a girl are sitting. The two men with their backs to her, hunched over beers, are large, tan, one with blond, spiked hair, the other with a blue bandana wrapped around a bald head. The girl opposite them is very young, beautiful, exotic looking; maybe Polynesian, with dark, copper-toned skin, a wide face and long, jet black, braided hair. It's the man she is sitting close to her that Sam cannot shift her eyes from. Frightfully pale, thin, he's much older, probably late forties or early fifties, with a narrow, angular face, a large hook nose and stringy, reddish-brown hair. Wearing thick, black-rimmed glasses, he looks terribly out of place so close to her, with them, in this place.

"Excuse me...I need your attention please. We've got a big afternoon ahead of us. Remember, I'm the island's best guide, and as soon as we finish lunch, I'm at your beck and call."

"Oh...uh excuse me. Sorry." Sam quickly wrenches her attention back to Andre. "Yes, I'm looking forward to it. But you've got to tell me what we should do."

Motioning her to a table just opposite the bar, he continues, "I'll give you the possibilities, and you can make the decisions. Of course, there are a few things you must see."

"And what are those?"

"Bay Saint Jean, the road around the island, a few wonderful beaches, the rest of the town, the cemeteries. There's a holiday here tomorrow and you must see how they're decorated."

"That all sounds great. How do I choose?

"I guess just where we go first. Do you want to lay on a beach, or shop?"

"Well, I'd…"

"Excuse my interruption, but I'll suggest a solution. I'll give you the grand tour, but a quick one. Then if there's some place you want to spend more time we can do that. Or maybe we'll just see everything we can and you can come back over with me again and go wherever you'd like." Andre's face breaks into a wide, Cheshire cat grin.

Sounds fine to me."

Two large, juicy-looking cheeseburgers and Heinekens arrive, and Sam wastes no time in taking the first bite. Silence settles over the table as their attention shifts to addressing their hunger and thirst.

"By the way, this is a wonderful cheeseburger."

"Thought you'd like it. Excuse me for a second," Andre says as he gets up and walks over to speak to Jean-Paul at the end of the bar.

Sam steals another long look at the table in the corner. The two younger men are talking in animated conversation to the girl while the older man, still sitting very close to her, is reading a hardback book. Suddenly, he looks up and peers above the pages directly at Sam, squinting boldly through the glasses until she quickly breaks the eye contact and turns toward Andre at the bar.

"Are you ready," he asks, returning to the table. "We've got a lot of ground to cover."

They walk into the small courtyard outside the door and Andre reaches for what looks like an old but well-maintained motor scooter. "Jean-Paul lets me use his bike when he's working. Climb on."

"Is there a bartender anywhere around here you're not good friends with?" Sam says as she throws her leg over the small seat and tucks in against Andre's back.

"I hope not." The motor comes to life, and they bolt off through the streets to the familiar, low-pitched whine of a Vesper scooter.

Leaving the shopping district after just a few short blocks, they accelerate rapidly as the road runs along the harbor before turning sharply uphill and inland. Sam squeezes her arms tight against Andre's rock-hard stomach to hold herself on as the bike tilts for the climb. After three or four tight S-turns the road levels, they stop, and he tells her to look back. The view down on the town and harbor from here is stunning, an even lovelier sight than from below, and after moving another fifty yards across the ridge to where the road crests in another direction, they stop again. Her eyes follow a severely sloped airstrip to its' termination below them in a lift producing rise, just feet from a large, beautiful, turquoise bay.

"That's Bay Saint-Jean, one of the most perfect bays and beaches in the Caribbean," Andre says. "Maybe the most beautiful. And the airport. It's a spectator sport here. The locals come out to watch the controlled crashes it takes to get a plane down between the ridge and the water."

They make the short sprint down to the bay, park the scooter and walk through a small open-air restaurant and onto the beach. A perfect white sand crescent, close to a mile around, with a series of reefs that start well out, break the surf, and leave nothing more than ripples when the sea reaches the shore. But the wind is not broken, blowing steadily, briskly, and brightly colored sailboards carrying brown, muscular men and lithe, topless women shoot across the incredible hues of the crystal-clear water.

"Andre, I saw a sign that says no nudity when we were walking in. They don't seem to enforce it."

His deep, hearty laugh erupts. "This is a French island. And the French are different, a little looser than we are. The sign means no total nudity. The beaches that have no signs...a few of the beaches here, you don't have to wear anything."

Aa they stroll along the slight slope of the sand Andre points out the quaint, elegant looking restaurants, with linen covered tables on decks that jut out onto the sand; which have good lobster and wine for lunch, which are best for dinner, which of the cottages discreetly placed among the palms are the best places to stay overnight.

"Do you windsurf?" he asks.

"Yes, we have two on board. I've just learned since we left and I'm not very good. But I love it."

"We'll come back when we have more time. This is a perfect place for it because the bay is so wide, the wind always blows in, and the reefs make for calm water on the inside. Or would you like to go now? I know the guys that rent them. They'll let us use a couple."

"I'd be shocked if you didn't know them," she says, looking up at him with a smile. "But let's wait, I don't want to miss the rest of the tour. Alan was right. About everything about St. Barts."

The little bike again takes them up a steep hill, on the other end of the bay, and as they reach the top Andre pulls over to the side so they can look back down. Much higher this time, the view of the bay is spectacular. Off again, the road plunges at a dizzying angle, then flattens, then rises, twists, then drops once more. They speed along, circumnavigating this island of lush green hills rising steeply from pounding surf and serene bays, all filled with varying shades of wonderfully translucent, emerald, turquoise water. The stunning vistas seem endless, the tiny villages quaint. They stop at two small cemeteries, shaded by huge, ancient trees, encircled by white picket fences, and walk among the white crosses and stones, each gaily bedecked with all manner of beautiful island flowers for the coming festival. Andre points out small inns and restaurants tucked into the hills and along the shore and some of the more spectacular, precariously perched houses of the rich and famous....or infamous. They stop twice for beers and the owners come over to greet them, speaking to him as if they were old friends.

The road turns inland and after a short rise and drop they are back on level ground and the scooter suddenly heads to the left onto a dirt path. "One of the most beautiful beaches on the island is down here. We have enough time to go for a swim if you'd like or we can just take a look and head back to town to browse around. It's just a couple of miles ahead."

"A swim sounds wonderful," Sam says.

The well-trodden, smooth dirt path is a quarter mile long, empties into a small, perfect cove, carved out between towering hills, lined with sparkling sand tilting up gradually from the water's edge to a row of palms. Again, a reef stops the rollers, the gorgeous sea just lapping at the beach. Perhaps ten people are sunning or in the water, most of them nude. There was no sign.

"This is a question I'm sure I know the answer to Andre, but do you know someone here we can borrow a towel from?"

He laughs heartily...that deep, throaty laugh. "I doubt it, but I know someone in town that will let us shower so we don't have to leave the salt on us the rest of the day. It's so close and the ride back will dry us quickly."

Sam wonders if she should just take off her cover or strip off her bathing suit too. She wonders about Andre, what he'll think, what he'll do, as she pulls the cotton dress over her shoulders. Then, quickly, in an uninhibited moment of decisiveness, she unsnaps and drops her top, pushes down and steps out of the bikini bottoms, and sprints toward the water.

Looking away as she began to strip off her suit, Andre now watches the mop of wind-blown red hair and petite, luscious body, each beautifully rounded buttock bouncing pertly up and down, as she flies across the sand and launches, missile-like, into the sea.

Sam stays under for a long time, luxuriating in the cool, soothing water. When she comes up, she takes a few strokes back toward shallow water, stands, pulls her hair back out or her face, turns toward the beach to see Andre a few feet away, his dark, wet body glistening above the black shorts.

Perfection to his mind, her body and lovely face, with her hair back, render him silent and still for a moment. But he quickly regains his composure, turns his head, shifts his gaze to the natural surroundings, and asks, "Have you ever seen a better spot than this?"

"If I have I can't recall it. It's wonderful. Everything about this island is wonderful."

They stand in the water and talk for a few minutes, Andre trying desperately to keep his eyes on hers, then start to walk out for the trip back, discussing how they would like to spend a whole lazy day here. As she reaches the midway point in the sand and her clothes she notices the bronze, slender legs tapering into the gentle curves and dark crevasse of the girl's ass, and the braided, black hair. Then she sees him. Seated under the shade of a palm tree, in a short beach chair, about five feet beyond the girl. He's also naked, his pasty white, sickly-thin body a stark contrast to hers. The hardback book is in his hands, but he is peering over the top of it at Sam.

Self-conscience now, she turns her side to him and dresses quickly, leaving her top off under the cover. As they continue back to the scooter, they pass closer to the couple and Sam can't resist the urge. She instantly snaps her head back as she sees his eyes turned to follow her and his erect penis.

As the scooter moves slowly along the path she speaks into Andre's ear. "Did you notice that couple on the beach? The beautiful girl with the strange looking man? They were in Le Select too."

"Yes. Why?"

"Just curious. Really strange looking pair."

"Stay here long enough," he replies, "and you'll see lots of curious things...and folks."

After showering in a hotel whose manager is a gigantic, friendly Norwegian, they leisurely tour Gustavia, stopping for ice cream, then meet the rest of the crew and passengers for the trip back to Saint Maarten. 'Shadow' is now also alongside the pier, ready to head back, and what appears to be the usual afternoon race between the two big ocean catamarans is agreed to and wagered upon. Once they clear the harbor and turn onto the heading for the downwind, homeward leg, the crew pops a large orange spinnaker with 'El Tigre' emblazoned across it, and the contest is on. Sam only thought she had learned something about speed under sail on the trip over. The water literally boils in their wake as they scream along at close to twenty knots under the huge chute. With the sun low the sea's surface shimmers. A glorious ride. At first the group on board is again sedate after their day of sun, drinking, shopping and sightseeing, but the exhilaration of the race and the open bar soon transforms them into laughing, shouting revelers, with only a few holdouts snuggled quietly against one another.

With 'El Tigre' comfortably ahead on a straight, easy course to steer, and most of those on board forward or at the bar, Sam moves close to Andre, at the helm. "You're really good at this, you know. And you seem to enjoy it so much. A connection I imagine."

"It has its' moments," he says. "Actually, I do enjoy it, most of the time." He's silent for a few seconds. "But like I said. Most everything down here's transient. I imagine I'll be movin' on before too long."

"Why?"

"Things change. People change. It just doesn't seem like a permanent thing to do. Won't always offer me the things I really want."

"And what are those?"

"I'm not sure."

"You never told me how you got here. To this place and job you like and you're great at but you'll probably leave."

"Where do you want me to start?"

"Wherever you'd like."

"I was in the Navy before coming down here. Before that I was in college for a while, a junior college." He looks down at her, smiling. "I'm sure I had the brain, but I just couldn't quite scrape the money together to go to Berkeley. I played ball on a scholarship, but I screwed up, got in with the wrong crowd, got lazy, into some trouble, nothing serious. I figured the Navy would straighten me out, and that 'see the world' stuff turned me on. There were a couple of plans that would let me go back to school when I got out. So I saw some of the world. Europe, Middle East, down around here, but I also found out I loved the sea. I decided I wanted to get into a special, elite unit. The SEALS. Do you know what they are?"

"I've heard of them. Commandos, right?"

"Yeah, the most prestigious special operations group in the military. They do everything special forces, the green berets do, but they're also underwater specialists, divers. Real heavy duty, clandestine stuff. It sounded like great adventure, and the quickest way to be somebody. Anyway, it took me a while to get accepted, but I made friends with the right people and finally got in. The training, the courses, were brutal…really high washout rate. But I hung in. The mental part, the stress, was the worse. The physical I handled OK. I finished, graduated…was assigned to a unit and spent a couple of months in more training. That's all Seals do – train. Except when a mission comes along." A melancholy smile spreads across Andre's face.

"Go on."

"During one of the training exercises I had an accident. I recovered, but had some…let's say…limitations. SEALs can't have limitations."

"Are you all right now?"

"Yeah…anyway, I was pretty bummed out. Gulf war happened a couple of months later. Worthy cause to liberate the Kuwaiti people. My buddies fought…and I was stuck behind a desk. I decided to leave the military as soon as I could. I came down here to figure out what to do next. Some guys from the French Navy told me about these islands, and there's another ex-SEAL I know in this part of the world that encouraged me." He pats the large wheel he is steering from. "This was a case of just being in the right place at the right time."

"How long have you been here?"

"Just over three years."

"Andre, they are gaining on us, and everyone on board has already counted their money," comes the cry from Lea, the lovely young crew member from Amsterdam, as she pours glasses of rum punch. She darts her eyes quickly at Sam, still smiling.

"Michael," Andre yells, "ease the pole out a bit. We'll head up and see if we can stop everyone from looking so concerned. As they change course thirty degrees from dead down wind the spinnaker shifts outboard and begins to pull the windward pontoon up. El Tigre takes on a noticeable heel, the strong breeze they had been moving with begins to rush over them, a collective cry of exhilaration rings out, and drinks are raised all around. The sleek black enemy off their starboard quarter may be no farther behind, but under the big orange chute the feeling is she soon will be.

Chapter 12

66 J oe, this is Christopher."

"Where the hell have you been?" Joe Amato's voice sounds more than mildly inquisitive.

"Hiding out. Were you able to find out anything about Caroline Brockton?"

"Have you talked to the F.B.I. yet?"

"Hell yes, and every other law enforcement dick head from every group, country and continent except the Arctic, and I'm sure they'll be lurking around here tomorrow. Man, were you ever right. I left for a day and went to Italy. Thought things might calm down by the time I got back. They were waiting for me on the damned mountain. No byline is worth this. But better me than you, right? Anyway, I think I've got them convinced I don't really know anything, but I don't trust the phones, and I'm paranoid about being followed."

"Well, I'm afraid I can't be of much help. Either old man Brockton doesn't know a damn thing or he's going to do it his way. What I'm hearing from inside is he hasn't heard anything unusual or been contacted, and he got a letter from her a couple of days after the body was found postmarked from Vienna. Of course, they don't believe him. You think you're being attacked? You ought to see the media over here after that poor son-of-a-bitch."

"I'll call back sooner next time. Or call me if you hear anything. Just leave a number and time, not a message."

"I know, Christopher. I'll run anything decent you can get to me, so keep your ear to the ground. Does your source know anything else?"

"No. And unless it's something really good I don't want to screw with it again. Definitely not with my name. It's not worth having to deal with all this crap. In any case, I'll talk to you in the next few days, if not sooner. And I'm not about to thank you for giving me my ten minutes of nightmarish fame."

Christopher hangs up the receiver of the public telephone in the Zermatt train station, buys a three-day old copy of *U.S.A. TODAY*, and walks back toward the hotel. Stopping in a small cafe, he orders a cup of coffee and goes straight to the sports section to check the standings, not wanting to read the headlines, anything about Caroline Brockton, or any of the other dismal news of the world. He feels tired, depressed. After spending practically all of two days with Juliette, he hasn't heard from her in the last twenty-four hours...she hasn't returned calls he's left at the hotel. Trying to read, he instead wonders where she could be, stares at the paper without a word registering, wonders why she hasn't at least called or left a note, finally does read. Perhaps a paragraph. *Well, it isn't like it hasn't happened before. But God, we had such a great time, the whole time.* Giving up, he leaves the paper on the table and heads for Elsie's.

The Après Ski crowd arrives early on cold, snowy days and the room is packed and loud with talk and laughter. Pushing his way through the throng, Christopher squeezes out a body width of space against the bar. Still thinking about Juliette into his third beer, his mood has lightened; the ambience and alcohol soothing the familiar fear and gnawing in his gut...of loss...and hurt.

The familiar, tanned face with close cropped blond hair appears in the doorway, quickly scans the room, and then moves to greet friends and acquaintances. After a few minutes his eyes again seem to be searching for someone, and as soon as they fall on Christopher, Karl begins to make his way to the bar. "I am very glad you are here, Christopher. I need to talk to you."

"Would you like to go somewhere there's more privacy?"

"No, this would be better." His voice is soft, almost a whisper, but steady. A strained, intense look covers his face. "But we must not appear to be discussing anything so important, and our conversation must be brief. I believe I can trust you, Christopher, and you must tell me I can."

"You can trust me, Karl, I give you my word on that."

"I have some information on the Brockton girl. You must do something...she is in grave danger." His friend's voice is almost a whisper as he crowds close, pressing his muscular chest against Christopher's shoulder, their faces only inches apart but their eyes focused elsewhere to avoid the appearance of important conversation.

"You should go to the authorities," Christopher replies.

"I cannot do that. This is where you must trust me. If the authorities here find out I believe she has no chance to live."

"What can I do, Karl?"

"You will think of something. Perhaps the authorities in your country. Now order another beer and let's smile and talk about skiing for a moment."

"Okay," Christopher says, then laughs out loud at nothing. "Who will win the women's slalom tomorrow?"

"I believe it will be Eva Russi. Our team is still upset. And Annamarie, well, our women's team is very upset." Karl's attempt at a sly laugh is weak. "She is on a boat called 'Purity'. It should be at a group of islands called the Dutch

West Indies within a few days."

"Has she been kidnapped?"

"I have told you all I know Christopher. You must not ask me more. I must be able to trust you. You must never tell anyone we had this conversation."

"You can trust me, Karl. Is she all right?"

"I believe she is. Now."

Karl's eyes begin to fill, but before Christopher can say anything his friend makes a heroic effort at a large grin, reaches his arm around the American writer, and slaps him on the back. "I must go now and talk with the coaches. I hope to see you on the mountain tomorrow."

"Can I...."

Karl moves quickly away from the bar and joins the others at a table along the wall.

Christopher's mind churns, with blazing speed and considerable confusion. Looking away from Karl's table and down between his forearms, he stares at the ancient, cigarette scarred wood finish on the bar as he leans on it. After a lost amount of time in trancelike thought, with no clarity coming to the chaos inside his head, he realizes he should look around, talk to someone. He decides to leave. Then that he should have another beer. Ordering another, he makes small talk with the bartender, drains the last half of the bottle and heads for the door. On the way out he walks over to Karl and without ever stopping pats him on the back. "See you tomorrow...and save a couple of St. Pauli's for me in case I come back after dinner."

By the time he reaches his room he has decided to call Joe Amato, then changed his mind...at least five times. He thought about the F.B.I., decided to call Juliette again, or go to the Mont Cervin and look for her. And then not to. Opening his door, he takes one small step, then turns immediately left into the bathroom, the five beers having taken their toll.

"Where the hell have you been?"

His face breaks into a grin as he hears the crisp, beautiful accent. "Where the hell have you been?" he shouts, trying to lend irritation to his voice as he impatiently waits to empty his bladder and thinks it takes longer than it should. Walking around the corner he sees her lying on the bed, reading, in one of the skin-tight leotards she favors and a huge, oversized, rose-colored sweater. "I've been trying to get in touch with you for over a day. You could have at least returned my calls." His tone is still sharp, and he senses a mistake, by the hard look in her eyes.

"Calm down, Christopher. I told you I had friends here. I needed to spend some time with them."

Her matter-of-fact reply catches him off guard, makes him unsure how to respond. His voice turns sheepish. "Sorry, it's been a long day."

"Tell me about it. Anything interesting?"

He wants to tell her but hesitates. He needs time to think.

"A ski race is a ski race is a ski race." Sitting on the bed beside her they begin to talk, but within minutes are embracing, kissing, then stripping off each other's clothes. Caressing, slowly, thoroughly, the flowing curves and silken skin of her long, slender body...as he did in Italy...he throbs with excitement. But he notices she doesn't spend as much time on him as before. And maybe she's not as frantic as he uses his tongue or is inside her. Or maybe it's just his imagination. He wonders.

"I'm absolutely ravenous again, Christopher. Are you

hungry?" You've not already had dinner have you?"

"No. And after four or five beers and no cigarette after a cataclysmic orgasm...hell yes I'm hungry."

The wiener schnitzel is the best he's ever had, and more beer and the intimacy of the intense, animated conversation has lessened his concerns He decides to tell her. When he has a chance.

Decision made, Christopher launches enthusiastically back into the current conversation. "I used to think it was practically all nurture. But I've changed my opinion significantly over the last couple of years. There's just so much difference...far more and far more ingrained than can be explained away by what we're exposed to when we're young, or later."

"But the hideous attitudes and actions that large groups of people have been taught, or acquired, and even often seem to enjoy, numerous times throughout history. Christ, Christopher, that should be proof of the role nurture must play. If that energy and dedication were put to work changing sexual attitudes and practices...it may be where you live, you know. We may not be the same over here. I mean, of course there are differences in thought processes linked to genetics, related to the male's task of growing the species, the childbearing role, motherhood, and all of that. But I don't think they are as responsible for as much of the difference as you do."

"I'd like to agree, to be more optimistic, but it just seems the agendas of men and women are so different...often contradictory, complex. Perhaps we haven't caught up with you on the evolutionary scale." Christopher offers her a warm smile.

"That's an intriguing thought, and one some of my friends

would love to hear."

"Well, Jesus, Juliette...we're animals disguised as people, you know, stalking, in heat most of the time. Your sex is calm, collected, sophisticated about it. Only when the mental and emotional level is sufficient do the crass, base physical urges seem to come into play for women."

"Other than Scarlet O'Hara, who can you possibly be talking about? Surely not me. Are you in heat most of the time, Christopher?"

"Well...yeah, I mean...hell yes. And it's like a drug for men. Or at least it appears that way. The 'affliction...or the fog' I call it. And when the 'fog' rolls over you...it can appear ten, twelve times on a quiet day when you don't wake up horny. When the fog invades every corner of your mind and body...it possesses you. It's like mainlining something. You get this immediate buzz, you know, the fog of arousal envelopes you...all your thoughts, sometimes your actions...they're controlled by the fog...the affliction...the buzz. And you do crazy shit. Cross a busy street and walk in the opposite direction from where you're going...to follow a woman in a short skirt with beautiful legs and a great ass. Heat. We're talking serious, immediate behavior modification."

"It's quite..."

"Hell, not only do you not know her intellectual capabilities, emotional makeup and propensity for affection and tenderness, you don't even know what her face looks like. And you're willing, at that moment, to sacrifice it all...beautiful wife, loving children, gigantic, long Mercedes, for one look at what could be a pimple filled ass and a few minutes of humping."

"Are you like that?"

He hesitates. "I'm exaggerating a little bit, but only about the children."

"I quite agree with you that women, universally, often view relationships differently than men do, and some of it is inborn. But I also believe women have the capability, and there is ample evidence of this, of developing an ability to enjoy different types of pleasure, and sexual relationships, based more on physical aspects, fantasies, visual stimulation...and less on the emotional. Somewhat similar to what you think all men are hopelessly addicted to. And this ability comes about mainly from the convergence of an inquisitive mind with liberated attitudes, upbringing, experiences and exposure." Juliette pauses, letting her words sink in. Then, her expression changing to inquisitive, continues. "But I wonder, Christopher, how many men are capable of providing the affection and intimate, emotional nourishment you think we crave, and I imagine you do, as well? How many...can you...were you able to provide that? Was that a problem with your marriage?"

"Certainly not the only one. We were too young and hopelessly naive...hopelessly stupid. But yes, it was a lot of it. I didn't satisfy her emotional needs and she didn't satisfy my physical ones. Or at least that's what we thought we boiled it down to, how we usually articulated the root of the mess. The irony, of course, is that we were both likely capable of providing what the other needed but withheld it as payback for not getting what we needed. It's all so mysterious, like wading into some bewildering swamp ...and then discovering...after the fact...you have to cross through it on one small, winding, hidden path before everything you believe you're entitled to, the good stuff you've dreamed about, can ever come true."

"So, Christopher, do you have an answer? How can it

work?"

"I'm not sure it can. The answer would seem to be for each person to try their best to drop their sexual or emotional inhibitions, fears of intimacy, their uneasiness with affection...to try to free or reprogram themselves. But of course, it's terribly difficult. You've been like that for all eternity...probably don't realize the extent of your problem. And if you have problems with intimacy, or affection, it's likely tied in with your sexuality. And if you have problems with sexuality, it's just as likely tied to your sense of...Christ, it's a bloody mess."

"You look dejected", she says, a flat expression on her lovely face. "Tell me what we can discuss that will make you smile?"

"Speaking of sex..."

"Yes, that might change your mood, is the 'affliction' suddenly holding you in its grasp."

"Jesus, no. The discussion we've just had. It's like a cold shower. But what did you mean by German?"

"German...I'm afraid I don't understand." Juliette answers, with an inquisitive expression.

"Do you remember when we were having dinner, and you were kidding me about not being able to speak a language other than English, or at least I thought that's what you were kidding me about, but you suddenly intimated you were talking about sexual cultures...a very deft switch of subject, you know, French, Greek."

"I do remember now, and it's interesting that you have," she says, with a touch of intrigue in her voice."

"Don't forget, we're always thinking about this stuff. Anyway, I never understood what you were referring to when you said German." His eyes remain squarely on hers.

"They seem to enjoy a few of the fetishes favored by my fellow Brits. But while it's usually played out here with restraint, a sense of elegance, perhaps in parlors... they march in jack boots into their dungeons, with hideous contraptions hanging from the ceiling and walls, and the straps have metal studs." Juliette stops speaking, staring intently at him.

"Go on," he says.

"From our earliest history, many English gentlemen, and a significant number of ladies, have appreciated the multiple benefits of the time-honored British tradition of the use of discipline." Pausing, she searches his eyes and expression for any clue. "To impress on one's underlings the importance of adhering to the British hallmarks of honesty, civility, restraint, and dedication to one's duties and authority."

Christopher hesitates before speaking, trying to digest what he has just heard. "And who are these underlings?"

"For years maids, students, wives. Students are not legal anymore, and with women's lib, you know...more than a few husbands. Actually, husbands long before women's lib."

"And why did they put up with it?"

"In the past, I suppose, many probably thought they had no choice. Was a trade-off in their situation. For what they did want. Or didn't want to lose. And...of course there were those who rather enjoyed it. Quite a few in that category. Many more than the uneducated and puritanical might think. That's what most of it is now, I would think."

"Are there many of these English gentlemen and ladies around now? Do you know any of them?"

"There are likely quite a few. And...I imagine I might. One never knows." Her steely, unsmiling eyes bore into his, and then the beautiful face slides into a slight grin, then a larger one. "I'd love to go to the ice cream shop for a chocolate sundae. I allow myself one a week and I've not had it yet. Would you like to go?"

The heat from the early morning sun's rays, slicing through the window and projected on the bed, has caused the thick down comforter to be kicked to the floor. Christopher's head rests at the top of Juliette's trim, soft buttocks, and he feels her back rise and fall slightly with each breath. An eye opens and peers down and back at him. "Do you really expect me to be able to sleep with your head there? I'm tired, Christopher."

"I'm sorry I had to wake you, but I have something to tell you, and I didn't want to wait. And besides, it's very comfortable here."

"For you perhaps."

"I think I know where Caroline Brockton is."

Jerking her hips away, she turns over quickly, sitting upright as his head bounces off the springy mattress.

"Where...who told you?"

"Let me start over. I may know where she's supposed to be in a few days. And I can't tell you how I found out. I had to swear on the life of my yet-to-be-conceived first child I wouldn't tell anyone."

"Well, where is she?"

"On a boat right now, supposedly headed for the Dutch West Indies."

"Has she been kidnapped?"

"I think so. But wasn't told so."

"When did you hear this?"

"Yesterday."

"Why didn't you tell me last night?"

"I was still trying to decide whether to forget the whole thing, and if I did, I wasn't going to tell anyone."

"Thank you very much for your trust."

"That's not it. If I had decided not to do anything with it, to stay out of it, I would have been betraying someone just to tell you. I can't do that. And putting you in danger. But if there's a chance I can help her I should. Or at least that's my position at this moment. Could change."

"So chivalry does live in southern men. What are you going to do?"

"Go to the authorities as soon as I can figure out who to go to. I was told it would be dangerous for her if I went to the local people. God, I can't imagine the questioning this time. I've thought about sending a note, but they'd know where to come first, and that would just prolong it, probably make it worse."

"Christ, Christopher. Don't you realize what this could mean for you. You want to write a book. And you're the only one who knows anything."

"Goddamn, Juliette, the girl's life is at stake. People don't drag someone from a hotel room after blowing their lover's brains out unless they're dead serious. Excuse the pun."

"I've not said a word about endangering anyone's life. You can always call the authorities, but why don't you see what you can find out first, from your contact in the states. And we can go there. A real adventure Christopher. And if things fall into place, fame and fortune, or at least the satisfaction of saving the damsel in distress. Which, you're right, should be the most important consideration of all."

There is silence for more than a moment. He's lying on his back, staring at the ceiling. "I've thought about all of it, from different angles...but it doesn't seem worth the risk. If anything happened and I thought I could have prevented it...Joe said nobody in the states seems to know anything solid except what's public. Her father hasn't been contacted or else he's playing dumb. I talked with Joe again yesterday."

"Christopher, have you thought about why he might be playing dumb?"

"Sure. If they contacted him and told him they'd kill her if he went to the police...Goddamn. And if I tell them. Of course, I've thought of that."

"Keeping it to yourself could well be her best hope, or at least until you know more and see what else happens. Whoever told you, can you get any more information from them?"

"I don't think so."

His adrenaline flowing now, his mind is so supercharged he doesn't hear any of what she says next. Her foot gently kicking against his shakes him only partially from his preoccupation. "What do you think?"

"About what?" he says, his voice sounding distant, unfocused.

"Christopher, I would appreciate it if you would listen to me. I think we should go to the islands, as soon as possible. We can't afford to waste any time. I must go back to London first. You can come with me, and then we will leave from there. Do you know when the boat is due to arrive?"

"A couple of days, that's all I know. Juliette, I've got to cover this last race, and then...well, I do have a couple of weeks with only the article in... But that's all insane to think about next to this. I've got to cover the race. It's in a couple of hours and besides I can ta..."

"You can what?"

"Nothing. Nothing. But I have to be at the race. I'll be missed if the story doesn't come in and that would cause more trouble than a few more hours is worth. Jesus, I've got to get going. I need to be on the mountain in an hour."

"What time will you be finished?"

"By three at the latest."

"I will meet you back here at three-thirty. Pack quickly. The travel arrangements will be completed by then and we will leave as soon as possible."

"Juliette, I can't believe we're really doing this."

"I think you have very little choice, Christopher."

"That's what I'm going to keep telling myself."

After showering Juliette looks for her personalized, leather date and address book as she is anxious to call her London travel agent and arrange the flights. Ten minutes into a fruitless search she remembers having it with her yesterday in Peter Molterer's suite. Dressing quickly, she picks up the two keys and rides the elevator to the top floor of the hotel. There is no reply to her rings on the bell for the manager's suite, so she slips the key in, pushes the door open, walks into the foyer, and turns into the elegant living room.

Her scream is only silenced by clutching at her mouth, as she stares, only twenty feet in front of her, at the blood drenched carpet and sofa where Peter Moltersr's body, neck slit wide open, eyes hideously agape, sits as if awaiting her arrival. As her knees go weak, it's all she can do to keep standing as she stumbles back to the door. But before going into the hall she hesitates, checks to be sure the door is locked, then leans back against the wall and slides down until she is sitting on the floor. Having trouble getting her breath, the sobs begin to wrack her, but she knows she must think quickly and clearly. A vice of fear crushes Juliette at the thought someone else might still be in the suite. She knows she must find the book. Wanting no more time to heighten her indecision and paralyzing fright, she rises and goes back into the room, scans the grisly scene quickly, then moves toward the small table and two chairs by the large window. The thick, black leather, zippered book lies on the seat of a chair, partially hidden by a wool throw. The incongruity of the crystal vase with three roses grabs her thoughts for the briefest of moments. Reaching down, careful not to touch anything, she lifts it by the small strap, pulls it from under the throw, and grasps it in her hand. Moving back to the door, she pulls her blouse from the leather slacks, rubs the material thoroughly over the door handle, thinks about what else she may have touched, then wipes the wall next to the door where her body slid to the floor. Opening the door, the tail of her blouse wrapped around her hand, she steps out into the hall. Glancing quickly around, she wipes the outside handle and doorbell, walks past the closed elevator and into the stairwell, descends three flights, moves through the door and into the hall, then to the elevator, and presses the button.

Christopher arrives at the top of the course twenty minutes before the scheduled start of the race, and scans the knot of racers, technicians, coaches and officials for the Austrian team, and Karl. He sees him on his knees, massaging the legs of Annamarie Stolz.

There is no time before or during the race when the Austrian trainer is not busy or surrounded by others. Christopher knows that to get his story he should move to the bottom once the first seed has finished and the results are all but final, but he's afraid he will miss Karl. For many minutes he stands not far from his friend, giving him ample opportunity to walk over, but he doesn't. The few times their eyes meet Karl looks quickly away. Finally, there is a slight break at the start house, Karl is left standing apart from the others, and Christopher moves quickly to his side and speaks in little more than a whisper. "I'm going to try to help her Karl, and if there's any other information you can give me..."

"I am very busy, Christopher, I cannot talk with you now." Karl interrupts him as he steps quickly away and back to a group of coaches. Christopher's instincts tell him there will be no more conversation...no more information.

After skiing down, getting the interviews he can and details from Billy McCormick of how the Swiss team swept the first three places, he decides to try one more time, and waits for Karl to arrive. He never does. At two-thirty he heads back to his hotel room.

As he enters, he steps on a piece of paper that is just inside the door. Stooping to reach for it, he reads the brief message before straightening up.

> Already enroute home. You must leave Zermatt immediately, the quickest way you can, and meet me there. Extremely urgent. You are in danger.
> 020 8473 6200

No riddle this time. Took a chance leaving it here. Obvious something happened. Jesus Christ, here I go. Christopher is changed and packed in fifteen minutes, checks out, looks at the schedules at the concierge's desk, and heads into the basement with the bag to pack his skis and poles. After a frantic dash to the train station, he rushes inside with just enough time to get to the platform and scramble on board before the train lurches forward for Geneva.

Within a few minutes he's stowed his gear, left a sweater and magazine to speak for his chosen seat, and carrying the portable computer, moved through the first of the loud, rattling, shaking platforms and sliding doors between cars, enroute to the dining car. His routine rarely varies. Grab a window seat on the side he thinks will offer the best views, then on to the dining car before the choice tables are taken.

As European trains go, this one isn't elegant; actually, rather spartan. But Christopher loves all trains and knows the scenery coming down through the mountains and along Lake Geneva will offset any lack of cushion in the seats, or excess noise. And he will spend most of his time in the dining car if he gets a good table. After yanking open perhaps five sets of doors, each time struggling with the swaying platforms make him lurch sideways as if dead drunk, he makes the dramatic transition to relative calm and quiet, passes the snack bar, and knows he has arrived. The car is almost empty, and he sits at a table that will offer a spectacular view of Lake Geneva once they are down out of the mountains. After activating the screen of his computer, he gets up to get a cup of coffee and croissant. Once back in his seat the desire for a more substantial meal crosses his mind before the stunning scenery captures his focus. The coffee is lukewarm, but he returns for another cup before forcing his attention away from the window and onto his story. Writing in this environment, to

Christopher, is almost as good as gazing out.

It's a formula, these stories, and he can put them together quickly. But his mind keeps wandering and after an hour he is still not finished. Juliette, Karl, Caroline Brockton, the islands, the wisdom…or idiocy…of what he's about to do…all grab his thoughts for a time. But what gradually floods his brain, settles there, as it so often does, is the emptiness, loneliness, the lack of purpose. And now…how this chaotic, dramatically consequential adventure will fit in. What's right…wrong. What he's doing, what he's not, what he should be…what's important, what he wants, or thinks he wants, how to tell the difference. The cozy house, warmth and security inside. Hedonism and excitement. Conformity or rebellion. The reasons…can he change? Should he? And always the sex, always the sex. The difficulty with relationships, the sabotage, things he can't seem to give. Wasted time, talent, and promise. His thoughts settle on his mother, his family, the quicksand ruminations on her death. And his, unfulfilled, alone? At this moment, in a train, moving through this stunningly beautiful part of the world, on his way to a gorgeous, wicked smart, intriguing woman and possibly a great adventure…why the hell is he depressed?

It's always been this way. His mind with so many thoughts of so many things, often connected…many with a negative slant. Then the change, the boundless optimism returns, but with the certainty it will change back. Only the timing of the cycle varies…how long up, how long down? Does he crucify himself needlessly, or not enough? Lately he's been thinking back to the years through early high school when it all seemed so promising. Music, sports, academics…and then it began to fall apart. But at the time never enough to cause much worry. Or enough worry. A resurgence of promise in the early years of college. Then the girl…and a commitment to short-sighted pleasure seeking. The ever-present awareness he was messing up.

The key seems a longing for meaning, purpose, respect, accomplishment, admiration, but with a humble goodness-of-heart. Contradictory? The sexual drive, the preoccupation, was endless then. But it was love, affection, companionship, possession, the status of having that in your life, that seemed so important, that he sought so desperately. The irony never escapes him. That so much of what he wants seems so difficult for him to give. The rebellion...often only internal, against so many things, including the family that offered him much of what he sought. He learned to break the emptiness with constant activity...sports, parties, alcohol...diversions. The serious, contemplative side he'd always had pushed more often into the background, along with the reality of goals, duty, and the future. Here, now, carving himself up again, the image is of a caricature emerging over the years, one that may have done irreparable damage to what's inside, hopefully the true core. To what has always seemed so different. And could be the only real worth.

Forcing himself to the keyboard, his mind makes the transition that allows him to finish, edit and rewrite, all within another hour. Satisfied, he folds the screen and returns to the snack bar. A large knockwurst, bag of potato chips, beer, and knowing his work is finished causes a relaxed, contented feeling to overtake him. Thoughts return of Juliette and what lies ahead over the next few days. Within minutes, after allowing himself to dwell, even fantasize, on some wonderful possibilities, into his third beer, excitement is pumping through his brain.

Chapter 13

"Jane, for God's sake, you've got to calm down. We've got to follow this through. It's our best chance."

"Why do you say that?" she screams through hysterical sobs. "How can you possibly know. How do you know they're not going to kill her as soon as they get the money? Why wouldn't they? And we won't have given anybody a chance to find her."

Joseph Brockton moves to his wife's side on the couch, but she quickly stands and steps away. "Don't you see, we're leaving everything up to a bunch of killers. You're letting them do whatever they want to. And the people who know something about these things, how these people think, what they usually do...you're not letting them help us at all. I can't take it any longer, Joe. If you don't tell them I'm going to. I swear to God I will." Jane Brockton starts to sob uncontrollably as she slumps back down into a chair, away from her husband.

Listening...feeling his wife's pain, his stomach knotted, tears slipping down his own cheeks, Joseph is silent for a long time. When she finally begins to calm down, he speaks very softly, slowly. "I'm sorry. But I'm doing the best I can. I'm doing what I think will give us the best chance of getting her back. There's no way to really know, but they've said what they will do if we tell anyone. I have a meeting tomorrow with Bob and the money should be there very soon. Please give me that much time. At least wait until we hear from them again."

"But that might be too late," she says, shaking her head as

her voice crescendos to a plaintive cry. "You may never hear from them again if they get the money."

Joseph starts to go over and hold his wife. He desperately wants to. But there have been many angry words in the last few days, and she has that distant, trancelike look in her eyes. "There's just no way to really know," he says, as he stands and leaves the room.

It's just before five thirty in the morning, still dark, when Joseph steps out of the back seat of the car and swiftly enters the building. Even at this time he expects someone to be waiting outside to shout one of the five or six standard questions he has refused to acknowledge, seemingly hundreds of times, over the past days. Once in his office he fixes a cup of coffee, his third of this early day, and a prelude to the many others that help him continue to function on the three to four hours sleep his personal hell allows him…on a good night.

For one of the few times since the first tape arrived, he's able to concentrate on his work with only a few short pauses for his mind to drift to Caroline. When he glances at his watch it's seven thirty. He's meeting Robert Wembley at eight thirty at the yacht club for breakfast, where he should learn the final details and time of the money transfer, and the thought of what will finally be set in motion causes the now familiar shiver, his throat to tighten.

The knock on the door startles him, and for an instant he doesn't acknowledge it. "Mr. Brockton, it's Richard Waite and David McCrary. May we come in please?" A few brief, irrational thoughts race through his mind, he dismisses them, then rises to let them in. "Yes, just one second please." As he unlocks and swings the door open he speaks in a slightly sarcastic, yet friendly tone. "I thought I might have a chance at some privacy and time to get some work done at this early hour. Obviously I was wrong. Come in. Would you like a cup of coffee?"

"Yes," McCrary says, "both of us. Thank you."

"I've moved a pot in here in case my forward lines of defense, and Amy Hawes, my last redoubt, ever give way and my office is completely overrun by authorities and members of the press. Then I can stay holed up here until I die of caffeine poisoning. Please flavor it as you like."

Even tired and on edge, as he constantly is now, Joseph feels a glimmer of good will towards these men he has been treating as adversaries; or perhaps it's a sense of what will best protect him. There is a moment of awkward silence he attempts to break by ushering them to the couch and chairs, away from the regal desk he sat behind in their previous meetings, and by speaking first. "So why so early this time, gentlemen?"

"Mr. Brockton, we have some information from overseas that has mentioned 'kidnapping' for the first time. And.."

"What have you heard, who did you hear it from?" Joseph asks, leaning forward in his chair, interrupting Waite.

"The information is very sketchy. And we're not sure of the source at this point," McCrary says very calmly as he enters the conversation. "But it's the first time we've heard the word mentioned by someone who might know."

"Well, what are you...?"

"Mr. Brockton, we don't have enough information of any kind to be able to do much of anything. But if your daughter has been kidnapped, and considering the circumstances, that must be at the top of the list of possibilities...you're going to be the first to know. If there's any validity to what we have you've either been contacted or you're going to be very soon. If you don't let us try to help your daughter, sir, you're going to make a very grave mistake. If you try to meet their demands...it's likely you'll never hear from them or her again. Statistics are on our side...we know that to be the case."

Joseph stares into McCrary's eyes as he speaks, mouth parting just slightly, words strong and measured. "I cannot not tell you what I do not know."

"I don't suppose you've heard from her again, because of course we would be the first call you'd make." There is a sudden hardening in the older agent's voice.

"No, I haven't."

McCrary stands up, turns his back on the other two and walks toward the large glass wall in back of Joseph, stops and stares out at the skyline. Joseph does not turn around. "I'm going to be perfectly honest with you, Brockton," the agents voice now booms from across the large room. "I think you're lying to us. Every newspaper in the world has the story, as well as T.V., and if she can't speak French or Italian, which I know she can, CNN is everywhere. She's been missing for the better part of a week, and nobody's seen her, or heard from her, except for that letter. And I imagine you've guessed how much I've wondered about that. You're one of the richest men on the planet. I mean it adds up, doesn't it? Now there are two possibilities, or at least the odds are ninety-five percent that one of these two things happened. Somebody kidnapped her, they didn't know Nygren was in the room, or maybe they did. In any case, they thought they should take him out. Or...somebody had a reason to kill this nice kid who happens to be a world-famous athlete, national hero, and loves the ladies...and found your daughter inconveniently with him. If that had happened, and there were no plans to kidnap anyone, any reasonably competent outlaw, once they realized who they had, would quickly add it to their plans. Or just as quickly let her go. Of course...there is one other possibility. One we considered a great deal at first. Maybe your daughter killed him."

"All right, McCrary," Joseph turns and starts to stand. "tha.."

"Calm down, Brockton. Aside from reasons you're about to give me, it was far too professional a hit unless she's been leading a double life. And if she'd had it done, she wouldn't be hiding. Everything tells me it was a kidnapping, and that you know it. And I'm only going to tell you one more time...well, maybe that's not true. We do keep trying when lives are at stake. You're fucking up, Brockton. You're fucking up real bad. And you're going to get your daughter killed. Now is there anything you want to tell me?" Finished speaking, the agent turns and fixes Joseph with a steel-hard stare.

"I don't know anything to tell you, Goddam it." Joseph's voice is louder now, with its' own hard edge. And there is one other possibility you're overlooking, isn't there? Or don't you have the guts to mention it to me? If they were after him, it might have made sense to them to get rid of her."

McCrary moves beside Joseph, still seated in the elegant chair, and fixes him with a stare as coldly hostile and contemptable as he can remember seeing. "I don't think your money can buy you out of this one. Why can't people like you understand that. After they have what they want they'll laugh at you and spit on your grave. Or her's." The room is silent for a moment. "You have the number." He starts toward the door, Waite jumping up quickly to follow him out.

Joseph fights as desperately as he ever has to keep his resolve from crumbling into total collapse...and calling after the two agents. He knows if he can hold on until they have had time to leave the building...*or are they leaving...are they waiting?. Maybe I should be chasing them...begging them. Maybe I'm fighting for her death instead of her life. Like he said.* "Dear God," he prays aloud as he drops to his knees, "please help me. Please help me to know...to know what to do. Please don't let me do anything that will harm her. Dear God, please keep her safe." He wants to lie on the floor, to curl into a ball...to weep, to let everything go. But he rises and begins to pace, considers the remaining options, the contingencies, the pros and cons, for what seems to him the thousandth time. By eight fifteen, when he must begin another clandestine escape from his office and walk to the yacht club, he feels stronger, again convinced he is making the right decisions, his record of successes when he has kept his own counsel fresh in his mind.

Robert Wembley is sitting in the model room of the New York Yacht Club, with his back to the door, on the couch under the front windows where he and Joseph usually talk. They have decided to meet here before having breakfast as they should be alone in the room at this time. Joseph's caution, or paranoia, has extended into what should be the impenetrable bastion of this elite, iconic New York institution, known worldwide for what once seemed the Club's unbreakable hold on the America's Cup yacht race.

As Joseph walks around the couch and greets his friend, he immediately notices the look of worry on his face. "You don't look like all is well with you."

"I think you're making a mistake, Joe. A very grave mistake."

"Has the money been transferred?"

"No."

"When will it be?"

"I'm not sure."

"Goddam it Bob, what do you mean you're not sure. We're down to a matter of hours. Jesus Christ." Joseph quickly catches himself as his voice begins to rise. "They got to you, didn't they? Did the Feds come to see you? Did you tell them anything?"

"Yes, late last night. I didn't say anything, but I stayed awake all night thinking about it. They're right. They've got the odds on their side."

"The hell with their odds. The only communication anyone has had with these scumbags states, clearly, that they're going to kill her if I either don't pay or tell anyone. If they're not bluffing...if I don't send the money...it's over. Do you understand, Bob, it will be goddamned over if you don't send the money. Caroline will die. We'll never hear anything else, or not until someone finds her in a dump or God knows where."

Joseph sees his friend's eyes mist over as he begins to speak. "Look, these people are vicious, we know that. But what will they have to gain by sending her back after they have the money?" He wants to go into more detail but can't bring himself to cross that line. "You're letting them dictate all the terms, Joe, you're letting them hold all the cards. That's not like you. And you're not giving anyone a chance to help her."

"Bullshit, this isn't a goddam business deal. I'm helping her by doing what I think will get her back. By doing what I've been told will get her back. If they're as coldblooded as you say, what's going to keep them from killing her if I cause them any trouble, if it looks like somebody might be able to get to them?"

"The money. Christ, Joe, that's what they want, and I don't think they're going to give up on it that quickly. We're talking about a hell of a lot of money, and they're already in really deep. I can't believe they're going to give it all up if the money doesn't show up exactly on time. Once they no longer have her, they have no leverage...nothing to deal with. And once they have the money you don't have any leverage to deal with."

"But we can't communicate with them, Bob, and no one has a clue as to where they are. If they get pissed off they can do anything they want to her, and still act like they have her. How the hell are we going to know? I don't want to give them any reason. I can't believe this. I can't believe you're going to let me down."

"What I think isn't the only problem. You don't have quite that much laying around in an account that doesn't require a lot of paperwork, signatures, and now that I'm being watched...I had it pretty well lined up, but it wouldn't be hard to trace."

"Once she's home I don't give a damn."

"Yeah, but I have to. It's the law, and my business, you know."

"Are you going to help me or not?"

"Christ, Joe, let's go talk to them. That's the best way I can help you."

Joseph stands abruptly and starts walking toward the door.

"Joe." Robert calls to him. He stops and turns around. "If you won't listen to what I think is damn good advice...I have a compromise that might work."

"Is this from the F.B.I.?"

"No. Just me."

Chapter 14

Snow and fog in Geneva forced him to stay overnight, and it's ten o'clock in the morning before there is finally an answer at the number she left. "Juliette, it's Christopher. I'm arriving at Gatwick at one o'clock. I tried to call a number of times last night but couldn't reach you." He tries to mask his irritation, to not give in to his desire to ask where she was as he remembers her cool response when he questioned her whereabouts in Zermatt.

"I was aware you could not get out of Geneva until today so I was not worried I would miss you."

"What happened? Why did you leave without me?"

"I will meet your flight and tell you about it then. What's the number?"

"Twenty-one fifty, British Airways."

"Ciao," she says, and as he starts to speak the phone clicks off.

Before heading for the gate he buys a copy of the Telegraph, then a cup of coffee and a croissant. Glancing at the front page while still at the food counter he feels his breath catch...his skin crawl. *Holy Shit!* The headline on the lower right of the front page is at least sixteen points.

```
MANAGER OF SKI MURDER HOTEL
   FOUND DEAD, THROAT SLIT
```

Christopher reads the first three paragraphs in an instant,

starts to turn to the continuation of the story, but instead lifts the steaming coffee cup to his lips and drains it in a series of short gulps that is all the heat will allow. Leaving the croissant untouched, he picks up the computer and small travel bag, then hurries to the gate. Once there, he finds a seat away from the counter, in a corner, finishes the story, then rereads it two more times.

Seated in the rear of the packed plane, he is one of the last passengers to exit, walk down the steep steps, across the tarmac and into the gate area. Juliette is standing just behind the ropes that cordon off the walkway, striking in a brown leather one piece jumpsuit, trench coat slung over her shoulder. Her tall, stunning beauty still almost stops him in his tracks when he has been a day or more without seeing her.

"Hello, Christopher," she says, her dark eyes sparkling as she embraces him, then gives him a quick kiss. "How was your flight?"

"Crowded, and the incredible shrinking seat seems to have evolved into a vice-grip pain-for-your ass. God, I'm glad to see you. I still want all the details, but I saw the morning paper, and...I guess that's why you left, huh?"

"Yes. Did anyone know you left when you did?"

"No. I was on the train within twenty minutes after I checked out. So how the hell did you..."

"I would like to wait until we are out of here. We'll get your bags. The car is just out front."

"I've got my skis, a lot of gear, you know."

"The Rover's being repaired. Some idiot ran into Marianne. We'll squeeze them in. Actually, we should put them into a locker. We'll come back through here before you need them again."

"Who's Marianne?"

"A friend of mine."

After collecting his luggage, sorting through it, and transferring what he'll need, he locks the boot and ski bags into an oversize locker, and they walk outside. She leads him to a silver Jaguar sedan, and they are quickly off.

"You know, it's hard enough for Americans to deal with the gripping fear of the first hour back driving on the wrong side of the road. At the speed you're going I may pass out."

"You are determined not to let me ever confuse you with the macho type, aren't you Christopher? And you are back driving on the right side of the road, and don't even think about saying 'no, the left'."

"So what happened, Juliette?"

"I left something in Peter's suite. I went to get it and found him. It was ghastly. I almost puked. I'm sure I was the first person who had been in the suite since it happened. I was so frightened. I thought I'd best leave as quickly as I could."

"Have the authorities contacted you? Did anyone know about your friendship with Peter?"

"No, they haven't. But that's one of the reasons I left. I imagined they might know, and they might try to make more out of it than it is. Or perhaps it's the others that know, whoever killed him. But after I left, I could not think of a reason the authorities would know. And then I became worried that by leaving...if they investigated the guests who left that day. It must be related to Nygren's death, don't you think?"

"You did say they questioned him after my story appeared,

didn't you?"

"Yes. But he didn't tell them anything."

"But he could have told the killers. What if Peter was in on it?"

"You're not making me feel any better, Christopher. Of course, I thought of that. I just can't imagine Peter being involved. Or if they would feel the need...take the risk...of harming me just for repeating what he told me."

"Maybe as a warning to others who are involved, or know something. Or maybe they think you know more than you do. Was there anything in the room that could identify you?"

"No. Well, I'm sure Peter probably has my name somewhere, along with plenty of others. Christ, Christopher, if they want to make a point by killing someone who passed along information they didn't like..."

"Yeah, well my sphincter tightened noticeably when I saw the headline. And I really think in light of what has now happened...I think we need to go to the police."

"It only reinforces what we agreed on," she says. "If Peter's killers are the same people who killed Nygren this proves beyond any doubt how vicious they are. They will surely kill the Brockton girl if something goes wrong, and the authorities finding out what you know could be that something. You're not trying to back out again on this great adventure and gallant rescue mission, are you?"

"Jesus."

There's a long silence in the car before they resume discussing the possibilities, the different angles, how it all might play out. "In any case, we have reservations on a flight to Saint Maarten at eleven in the morning," she says.

Deciding not to challenge her again just now, to wait, he nonetheless has an unsettling, growing conviction they'll be on the flight. It's a cold, damp day in London, the kind a person would swear was everyday if they only read the classics, but the kind Christopher has seen few of on his past visits. The traffic is horrendous and it's an hour and a half before they pull up to the apartment…in an imposing, period building, down a side street, around a corner from Hyde Park. An attractive young maid, primly dressed in starched mauve and white, greets and ushers them inside. It's large and elegant, with an appealing, eclectic blend of antiques and modern furnishings, Persian carpets, and art - modern, impressionist, sculpture, photographs.

"Anna, show Christopher to my room please. Take a few moments to relax if you would like, and to freshen up. But I am famished. It seems I am always famished when I am around you. There is a delightful restaurant I want to take you to for a late lunch. I must make a few quick calls and then we can leave."

As he follows Anna up the stairs he wonders if her dress is shorter than those worn by most proper English maids. He's sure her legs are better...much better. And he suddenly remembers something Juliette said, about parlors.

After washing his face and brushing his teeth he plops down in the overstuffed chase to the side of the carved poster bed, complete with lace canopy. Opening Michener's CARIBBEAN, which he bought at the airport, thinking it appropriate, he begins to read. Some time passes before Juliette enters the room. "Have you found everything you need?" she says.

"Yes, except you." Standing, he moves to embrace her, his tongue opening her mouth and slipping inside. His hand slides down across the soft leather until he can feel the jut of her ass, and he begins to gently rub the firm globes.

"We really need to leave now, Christopher," she says, leaning her head and shoulders back away from him. "I'm starved and would like to show you the gallery. We'll have time later."

"Women want to wait til' later. Men don't ever want to wait…ever…til' later," he replies.

"Oh, the enlightened ones do."

"Will you promise to make me enlightened if I agree to wait?"

"I suppose I could try." Juliette smiles that wicked little smile of hers, hesitates, then turns to walk toward the door. "But it might be a real challenge. Southern boy and all." Her mock drawl is impeccable.

The restaurant is charming, in an ancient building, but with huge, new, palladium windows, everything light and bright. The large salads and wine are delectable. "So what are we going to do when we get there?" Christopher asks. "Start snooping around like Holmes. We don't even know what island, we're not even sure about the area either. There are numerous islands referred to as the Dutch West Indies. This is crazy."

"It has to be where they are going. Are you absolutely sure you cannot get more information out of your source?"

"I told you Juliette, I tried. Wouldn't even talk to me."

"We know the name of the boat. That should make it easy."

"And what are we going to do if we find it? I've tried my best not to do anything to remind you of men that live to storm heavily armed hideouts filled with vicious murderers."

"Christ. We will tell the authorities when the time comes. Remember, this is the best chance to save her life. And the book...you must remember the book."

"I remember the fuckin' book. But I'm getting tired of these trade-offs. They're not going my way. Delayed sex for this salad. My life for the book."

She gives him a stern look, then breaks out in laughter. "Christopher."

"Sorry, just kidding. It's a great salad, great wine. I'll pour us another glass. And, of course, great company."

Later in the afternoon, after the bottle of wine is drained, they walk the ten blocks from the restaurant to the gallery. On the corner of the ground floor, in yet another grand building, there are large windows displaying the art and bustling crowd inside. "This show of Francis Bacon's work has been extremely successful for us," Juliette says, as they walk up the stone steps to the entrance. "It's the final week and I thought the crowds would have dropped off, but they haven't. And they are buyers."

"Do you usually leave on holiday when you have a major show like this?"

"As I said, it is the last week, and I have an excellent staff. The past month has been extremely hectic, and it seemed exactly what I needed. I haven't been doing enough of it lately."

She introduces him to staff and acquaintances who are inside, seems to know quite a few of the people browsing through, and gives him a tour of the small, elegant gallery, and Bacon's amazing work. Excusing herself to take care of some business, Christopher goes back for a closer inspection of the paintings that most interested him and soaks up the considerable ambience of Juliette's place of business. Highly polished hardwood floors, gleaming white walls with light flooding in as the gray day has brightened, red roses in crystal vases strategically located on occasional tables, champagne served by a young, very handsome, tuxedoed waiter, and a pianist playing Chopin on a small grand. An eclectic, prosperous looking, intriguing mix of people milling about, talking softly, examining the works with seemingly strategic precision. Christopher has always been attracted to small, chic galleries. There's a certain feel...clean, cultured, sophisticated. And this might be his favorite. He spends more time stealing looks at the people than at the art, trying to imagine what they do, who they are, what the different niches of London society represented here are like, which Juliette fits into.

By the time they leave the gallery and start the walk back to her apartment the sky has again darkened, and a light rain is falling. Within minutes it begins to beat down hard, and for shelter they huddle together under the awning of the nearest shop. A gusting wind blows a considerable amount of water sideways, into them, and they scurry inside for refuge. Christopher finds himself in the midst of thousands of old items, antiques...but mostly curios, small pieces, rather than furniture or larger pieces. An incredible, cluttered assortment. "A great place to be stranded," Juliette says. "Never a lack of things to look at."

As they wander their separate ways Christopher is fascinated by the variety, the unique nature, the quality of these things British. He inspects the collection, scattered about, of old pub signs, something he has a weakness for, while also paying particular attention to items having to do with the horse and nautical sets. And the odd, old book. A large brass urn swallows an assorted collection of umbrellas, walking sticks, and two exceedingly slender, crooked handles. His mind wanders. Suddenly aware that she is watching him, he glances back at her, then back into the urn.

"See anything of interest to you?" Juliette asks.

Christopher places his hand lightly on one of the crooked handles. "Not sure. Probably not. How about you?"

"A bit harsh for my taste," she replies, looking straight into his eyes…as he stares back into hers.

Turning her back, she steps away, his eyes lingering as he thinks of her long, slender, perfect legs and gorgeous bottom. Another image slips into his mind's eye. One that titillates…and disturbs him.

Once back at the apartment, Juliette busies herself with packing, again brushing off his advances. He's had sex on his brain a good bit of the day, and with the high wearing off from the wine and champagne, the cumulative effects of her rejections pinball from frustration, to anger, to depression, to doubt. He doubts her sincerity, her affection for him, himself, the wisdom of coming here, certainly of taking the flight in the morning. Feeling cross, irritable, confused…he can't decide whether to confront her, ask what the hell's wrong, read, go out for some beers, or leave for good and go to the police. Grabbing his book, he fights through ten or so pages, his mind only occasionally allowing the words to sink in, while constantly wondering if it's her, or him. Laying his head back, he closes his eyes, and within moments starts to doze off.

Her warm lips on his, the gentle touch on his neck… seems at first thought to be a dream. They snuggle, then make love…soft, gentle, luxurious love. Afterward he gets a bottle of beer, lays close to her, and with his mood now at the zenith of the arc…talks, plans, and questions. Doing his best to keep the conversation alive, they giggle and nuzzle against one another until she insists he let her go to sleep, then turns out the light. Still wired, laying on his back, eyes wide open, he thinks of all that's ahead.

Chapter 15

"That son-of-a-bitch. Goddamn, I'll teach him not to even think about fucking with me. He may never know my name, but he'll goddamn sure know he's fucked with someone he shouldn't have. Just like the world will know. Two more weeks, the whole goddamn world will know...goddamn will they know! We need to do it, Brian, let's get it done and get the son-of-a-bitch his little gift."

"Ian, we have at least another twelve hours before we can get anything on a plane. Let's not rush this. There is time before the deadline...and don't you think there's the chance the transfer might have to be made in two or three separate transactions?"

"Hell no, I don't think that at all. What's wrong, losing your nerve? I'll see it gets done even if you don't agree. Maybe you're becoming a little too attach...." The yacht, fighting at a steady twenty knots through the heavy, rolling seas, slams into a huge wave on her forward quarter, buries her bow in the trough and lurches back up, sending the two men grasping for a handhold in the huge, elegant, main salon.

"What the hell's the idiot doing?"

"He told you we should reduce the speed some more. Go have a look, Ian, the seas have really built up. A few more hours isn't going to make much difference."

"Fuck it, it isn't that bad, and this baby's supposed to be able to take it in stride. I'm anxious to get there. I don't care who does it but be sure we have the package ready as soon as we get close enough to drop the Zodiac over the side and take it ashore."

Brian walks forward, leaving Ian alone. He sits for a few minutes on one of the leather couches, then gets up, walks down the steps and into the hallway that leads to the aft cabins, and looks through the bullet-proof, double paned, small window set into the heavy, second door on the right. Caroline Brockton is lying on her side, asleep. Staring at her blond hair cascading off the pillow onto the sheet...he thinks of arguments he can use with Ian, until the motion of the boat makes it difficult for him keep his balance.

Slowly walking to his cabin, he lays on the bed and closes his eyes. It must be personal...has to be, he thinks. *It can't be the violence, not in the context of this whole thing. That would be ludicrous. But maybe not. It's her and not them. It's all justified though. That's what's important.* Taking the small, dogeared King James version of the Bible from the drawer under the berth, he begins to read.

Chapter 16

Sam giggles out loud as the wind rushes up her legs and over her exposed loins, the cotton batik skirt billowing around her waist like a giant mushroom. Removing and tying it securely into the rigging of the trampoline, she lays back down, naked, and watches the night sky fly by above her, its sparkling billions starting to fade in the light of the rising moon. Her body relaxed like a ragdoll, she lets it rise, fall, and sway with the luxurious rhythm of the trampoline as 'El Tigre' screams toward the deserted island of Ille Fourche. She hums the theme to the final movement of Dvorak's 9th, 'New World Symphony', raises her legs, spreads them, lowers them, rolls onto her stomach, scissors them in and out so the delicious breeze caresses her sex, stops, then explodes against it again.

The sound of the turning drum wrapping the headsail tells her they are getting close. The big cat's speed begins to drop. And then she sees Andre, naked, standing over her. Looking up his tall, dark, muscular body from his feet is a spectacular sight. The silver, tropic moonlight illuminates and softens parts of him, shadows or sharpens others. His considerable manhood sways, sleek and magnificent. "I have the autopilot on," he says, "and I've slowed her down a bit. We have some time before we have to anchor."

Their kisses are electric, his touch and caresses gentle and tender. Starting on her ears and neck, he moves to her breasts and nipples. Brushing, rubbing, circling, tickling. His tongue. Hot and wet. Barely perceptible bites. Across her stomach and into the red thatch of hair, then to her feet, and toes. Back up her legs, slowly, lingering on the inside of her thighs, moving even slower now, higher, her legs spreading for his fingers and mouth. When he reaches her loins, in the wind, with the sky flying above, on the moving trampoline...and probes, caresses, licks...she feels a sublime crescendo build until she reaches the edge. She stays there, as he stays there, for what seems a long time...then he pushes, enters and fills her. Their movements are slow, fall into rhythm with the smooth plunge and rise of the yacht through the seas, lessening as they come into the lee of the island. She wishes it could never end. And then he suddenly pulls away.

"We're here."

"Jesus, Andre, you've got to be kidding."

"No, but it'll only take a minute."

"Dammit! Dammit!" she screams in mock dismay...then again giggles out loud with delight.

Anchoring in what she guesses is record time, he returns to her side, and now she attacks his body with a vengeance, determined to win the battle of fingers, tongues, and orgasmic brinksmanship.

Andre opens his eyes in the first, faint light of dawn, startled by the roar of enormous diesel engines at high rev, and sees the mass of a gigantic, ultra-modern yacht, with no lights, pass no more than a hundred yards south of El Tigre. Startled at her speed, he stares in amazement at how quickly her stern grows small. Then the wake reaches, rolls under, and rocks them, lifting and dropping the pontoons a good four feet or more. Sam bolts upright beside him. "What's wrong? What's happening?"

"If she was black, I'd say Darth Vader's personal yacht just blew by here at warp speed. Man, I haven't seen a boat that large move that fast since I've been out of the Navy."

The rocking motion has calmed to gentle, and they cuddle and kiss in the double sleeping bag lined with a silk sheet, then lay back and watch silently as the tropic sun makes its swift leap from the horizon into the morning sky. After a few minutes of quiet contemplation Andre goes back into the cockpit and returns with two steaming cups of coffee.

"So what's the latest from Captain Hardy on when Zulu Warrior's going to leave for points down island, or north and the Med?" he asks.

"Well, everyone seems to be having a great time around here. Lots to do, lots of beautiful women, and that alone could keep Alan and his band of horny, merry Aussies in a place for life. Actually, I expect they'll be ready to leave within a week or so. I've heard some grumbling about the casino's getting old or taking all the crew's money. And that more than a few of the women are spoken for. They may have to go back to sea to lick their wounds. They're taking Zulu to Anguilla today to do some diving and drink at English bars."

"Didn't you want to go?" The squint of his eyes and sly grin are telling.

"I thought about it." Lifting her head off the pillow, she rolls onto her side, positions her face just above his, and breaks into a wide smile, her green eyes sparkling. "No, actually I didn't think about it. I'll never regret for a minute opting for this little nautical camping trip with you. Besides, who better to go diving with than an ex-frogman."

Andre is still staring up at her. "Ye mon, definitely time for an early morning swim. One of the real treats down here, getting in this incredible water first thing. But right after the first cup of coffee and before the second, that's okay too."

"Agreed."

"There's a little reef just off the point. I'll get the masks. Do you want fins?"

"Sure, if you have them."

The cool shock feels delicious, and after a few seconds she falls in behind him, fighting to keep up, as they begin the short swim to the rocks. She watches his sleek, naked body, the muscular perfection, magnified through the crystal-clear water and mask, move swiftly and effortlessly in an elegant, powerful motion combining a rhythmic rocking of his torso with strong kicks. Sam is sure he is moving much faster without fins than most people could with them. He stops for a moment to let her catch up.

The reef is shallow, but there's a beautiful assortment of coral and numerous species of spectacularly colorful, small fish. Climbing rapidly, the sun is high enough to give a bright, wondrous illumination to the red fire coral, the fan coral's purple filigree, and the yellow clumps that resemble, and are the namesake, of the brain. Andre points to different fish as he swims among them, chasing one and then another over and around the large rocks and coral as if he were the largest among equals.

Sam is infatuated with a group of emerald green and black striped angel fish, and when she looks back up he's motioning to her. Swimming towards him she suddenly notices the sleek, silver body hovering some ten feet from Andre, its' steely eyes staring directly at him. Covering the last few feet to his side slowly, cautiously, after making a quick check to be sure she doesn't have anything on that's shiny, she laughs to herself as she realizes she doesn't have anything on, shiny or not. She's seen a few barracuda, never feels too safe around them, and this one is big. Next is a school of bright blue fish, maybe a hundred or more, each the size of a large hand. Andre goes down ten feet to swim just behind them, causing the school to speed up as they move in unison, synchronized in a darting dance.

Back on El Tigre, they rinse off with the freshwater shower, then lie in the sun to dry their bodies.

"You should be a diving instructor. God, you can swim like the natives under there," she says.

"I'll leave the instructing, or teaching, to you, professor. It's such a worthwhile thing to do with your life. Don't give up on it. Besides, don't you think I'm a good captain?"

"Of course I do, the best, but couldn't you could take special dive trips? What a combination, sailing on El Tigre and then diving with Andre the human fish. Anyway, my guess is I'll end up teaching at some point, but something a little less esoteric, more practical, than philosophy."

"Jesus, Sam, I'd love to have the opportunity, the time to learn about the great thinkers, their thoughts. So what the hell if you can teach somebody how to write an advertisement, or to be an accountant. The other stuff's enduring, man, and maybe a better understanding of it would really help us with all the damn problems we have."

"I wasn't thinking about advertising or accounting. But I still want to know why you don't teach diving. It seems to be a really big deal down here, and with your background...you must love it."

"Maybe I got enough of it in the service. Tell me what you'd like to teach?"

"First I want to know what problems you think we could solve by understanding the 'great thinkers', as you put it?"

Andre pauses, lets out a sigh. "I mean, it seems people

don't know how to apply the basic principles of human dignity, rights, equality, opportunity....and maybe that's because there's not enough agreement on what they are. Philosophers deal with the plight of man, how he fits into the overall environment, the best way for people to interact, don't they?"

"Many of them try."

"Nobody wants to believe anybody today. I know there are people saying the same things, things that make a lot of sense, that have the same basis as what the great thinkers of the past said...things that are really the truth, the way things should be. But man, because everyone assumes everyone else is out for themselves, or their company, or their political party, nobody'll listen, or try to understand. It's like...everybody's competing to be heard, or to get something, not to do what's right."

"And what about the problems with your race?" she asks.

"Well, I don't know, what do you think about it?"

"I asked you first."

"Yeah." He's silent for a while.

She turns onto her side and snuggles up to him, her voice soft now. "Is that a bad question to ask you?"

"No. I was just thinking. The problem is getting the kids out, you know. We're going to need help with that. The kids don't see any hope, any reasons to do what it takes to get out. It's such a vicious cycle in the projects, ghettos, any place a whole bunch of poor people live together. Don't have to be black. But often are. Once you're out...I mean we don't have the same opportunities as whites, but there are enough now that all of us have got to start being responsible for our own fates, our own lives. We've been told, and a lot of us have come to believe it, that discrimination is what causes all our problems. And it does cause a hell of a lot. No doubt. But it's also become a crutch. The reason I'm here on this boat instead of studying to be a lawyer, or a businessman...it isn't a lack of opportunity. It's me. Nobody but me. And I'm one of the lucky ones. I got out."

"But don't you think if your father, or mother, had been lawyers...maybe both had been lawyers, or doctors...that the path for you to become one would have been easier?"

"Yea. I'll give you that. But maybe the easier way isn't always the best way. For everybody. Are you Jewish?"

"No. Why do you ask?"

"I've always admired the Jewish people. I mean from what I know nobody's been discriminated against as much as they have. And they've seemed to overcome it so many different times. I guess they're just tough as hell...focused, as they say. Their military's awesome, unbelievable."

She raises up, lays her breasts across his shoulder and chest, and kisses him lightly on his lips. Her skin, fired from the sun, feels deliciously hot and smooth to him. "You know what I really want to do right now?" she asks, her voice only a whisper, her green eyes sparkling, the main of red hair falling around his neck like a scarf.

"I know what I hope you want to do," he says, slowly, lightly tracing his fingers down the small of her back and across a firm, perfectly rounded buttock. "And I damn sure know what I want to do."

"I'm starving, Andre. I've got to eat right now." Her voice is flat, her face expressionless for a moment, and then there's a slight giggle to go with the small, wry smile. "Why do you have such a pained look on your face?"

"Pure hunger, nothing but. It's amazing how much we think alike, and at the same time." He rolls his eyes. "Mental telepathy, is that it?"

"Sounds right to me."

"Man, on top of everything else, hanging around you is helping me use big words," he says.

"What did you bring for breakfast?" she asks.

"Pineapple, plantain, and some of that bread from the French bakery on Barts."

"Will you promise not to get your feelings hurt if I'm very honest with you about something?" Her face now takes on the serious, concerned, intense look of someone about to make a pronouncement that will greatly alter the whole course of a life.

"Promise."

"It was so sweet of you to bring such a wonderful, healthy breakfast for us, but I would literally give my life right now for some eggs, pancakes, syrup, bacon. I get these cravings. Only occasionally, you understand, but unless I satisfy them...well, it's too horrible to even think about."

He tries to stare at her without expression, giving no clue to what he will say next. "Compromise. The food I have will be a snack, something to hold you over. When we get to town I'll have you at a restaurant where the view and food are fit for a princess, possibly even for you. American princess, of course. Pancakes, bacon, eggs." White teeth sparkle as he releases the huge grin.

Up in a flash, straddling him with her feet, she looks down. "Well...that's a hell of a compromise. You're on."

"There is one other thing, Sam. Again, we're so much

alike. I also have cravings that can cause me to go absolutely crazy if they're not satisfied." His eyes leave her face and pan, slowly, the luscious body rising above him. "We'll keep you from going crazy with the healthy stuff, then keep me from going crazy…then head to town and your breakfast."

An hour later, after another quick, rinsing plunge into the sublime temperature of the turquoise water, they are flying with El Tigre toward Bay Saint Jean.

Chapter 17

"You have a message to meet Bob at the yacht club tomorrow at eight for breakfast." These are the first words his wife has spoken to him that weren't in anger in the last three days, and they are disturbing.

"Did he call?" he asks, but she ignores the question as she retreats out of the bedroom. Joseph thinks it odd that Bob Wembley would call his house with that message, knowing the phones are tapped, and as careful as they have been to hide their meetings and conversations. He wants to go to Jane and ask her again about the message, but decides against it, as their relationship has degenerated into the all-out war of silence, broken only by harsh, biting remarks. She seems to have only contempt for him, and in turn he's become angry, resentful, yet still believing she must feel the sympathy he does, experience periods between the anger, the confusion, when he cares so deeply for her. When he understands her actions, her pain, what she's going through. Her last civil words to him began with a final, calm, but tearful plea, then ended with hysterical threats when he again refused to give in and cooperate with the F.B.I. To his knowledge she hasn't compromised him, at least not yet. Maybe now though. Bob would have no reason to be cautious anymore if they knew.

Joseph gets off the bed and heads downstairs to the guest bedroom that Jane has moved into. The door is locked. He knocks. There is no reply. He feels the heat rise in his face. "How did you get the message? Did you tell them? Goddamn it, did you tell them?" He is shouting now, jerking on the door handle. Turning abruptly, he rests his back against the wall, tries to calm himself, then goes back to his bedroom, begins to dial Bob Wembley's number, and realizes the mistake he's about to make if they still don't know. Lying back on the bed, he knows he must wait until they meet to find out. It's eleven o'clock, six hours until he will get up, and he knows at least three of those hours will be spent without sleep...tossing, walking, trying to read, to find anything to occupy his tortured mind.

Joseph has George, his driver, drop him off at 64th and Fifth Avenue, and he enters the park. A cold, clear early morning, dense clouds of frozen breath spurt from the horse's nostrils as a mounted patrol passes him. Looking forward to the twenty-block walk to the club, he hopes it will clear his drowsiness and lift his spirits. He's determined not to think, or at least try not to think, of the chaos, the foreboding of tragedy entangling him. Instead, he will soak up the early morning sights and sounds, the sweet pungent aromas of the great city as it prepares for the day. Let them transport him from his particular misery, blend him into the human mass attempting to forget their smaller problems, or larger ones, and make it through another day.

From habit, at the beginning of his walk, while still in the park, he glances over his shoulder, scans the area to the left and right of him, to see if he is being followed. But he decides to give that up too, knowing it may not matter anymore, or if it does, to hell with it if it's going to ruin his escape.

Crossing 59th he walks past the Ritz, makes the turn onto 5th Avenue at The Plaza, and again heads south. The cold cuts into him, feels good...clean, invigorating, and he never thinks of the sanctuary of a heated room. At Rockefeller Center he's drawn to the smell and steam rising from coffee and bagels on a cart. Wishing it was later so the ice rink wasn't empty, he walks down and leans against the rail above it anyway, draining the cup in short sips, trying to savor the uplifting sensation as it slides through his mouth and into his throat. As he looks down on the frozen surface, an image appears to him...of he and Jane skating, and Caroline, between them, holding their hands, seven or eight years old. He lingers for only a second, then turns and walks quickly back up to Fifth and toward the Club, pulling the collar of his coat tighter around his neck.

"Good morning Charles, is Mr. Wembley here yet?"

"Good morning, Mr. Brockton. No sir, I haven't seen him come in yet, but there's a package here for you."

Joseph's mouth goes dry, his chest begins to pound.

"The man who delivered it said it was very important that you have it as soon as you arrived."

"Who...uh...thank you, Charles, tell Mr. Wembley I'll be in the model room," he says, trying to hide his anxiety as he takes the small Federal Express box and turns for the stairs.

"Would you like me to take your coat sir?" Howard calls after him.

"Uh... no, I'm fine, thank you."

Moving quickly to a corner of the room, he sits with his back to the door, and begins to tear at the package. A smaller package covered completely in silver duct tape is inside the outer box, a Styrofoam container under the tape. As he pulls the container apart, he sees a clear plastic bag rolled over multiple times, begins to unwrap it, then hears himself gasp out loud. Retching, the vomit surges up into his throat. Clasping his jaws and teeth tightly together, he sits for a moment, not moving, then quickly gathers everything up and walks to the restroom half a floor below. Once inside he goes into the last stall, falls to his knees, and throws up violently, until he can only heave. Tears come. And sobs. After a time of not moving, his back pressed against the inside of the stall, seated on the floor, he knows he must look again. He stares at the finger, severed well below the second joint. Her little finger, with skin, bone and tendon, dried blood…and on it a tiny signet ring…her signet ring, with the family crest. Looking frantically through the package he finds a folded sheet of paper.

```
FOLLOW DIRECTIONS PRECISELY
OR NEXT TIME THE BOX WILL BE
LARGER. NOT PART OF THE MONEY -
ALL OF IT. SOON. TIME IS RUNNING
OUT.
```

Leaning his head back, Joseph closes his eyes. His mind feels like it's going blank…his physical strength, all emotion, every thought draining from him. But he knows he must get up and outside. Suddenly he senses the anger arrive, feels it rise. Within seconds it's raging.

A quick glance back into the model room confirms his conviction that Bob Wembley is not coming for breakfast. Inside one of the polished mahogany telephone booths he makes a call he hoped he would never have to make, and in another ten minutes is inside a cab for the long ride to Belmont Park.

Joseph locates Carmen Taglia inside the stall area, watching a groomsmen pamper a beautiful filly after her morning workout. He introduces himself and within a few minutes the two men have moved away a few paces and are talking quietly. Taglia takes the small slip of paper Joseph offers, the conversation takes little more than ten minutes, ends with nods instead of a handshake, and Joseph is back in the cab, headed back to the city. He is now sure of one thing. The twenty-five million dollars that Bob Wembley would not send will be in Grand Cayman... without delay.

Chapter 18

Ian and Brian wait until the crew has loaded the bags and gear into the Zodiac for the short trip to the dock. Then they help lift the large, six-foot-long ice chest, air holes punched discreetly in the back, Caroline Brockton's limp body curled inside, onto the lift attached to the davits, then attach it securely with straps. Watching closely, intently, their eyes never leave it as it is lowered. Once in place, they scramble quickly into the thirty-foot RIB and sit on either side of the cooler, placing their arms across the top.

The idling engines suddenly rev, the deep-throated throb jumps in pitch, they lurch forward, and the ice chest shifts and pins Ian into the corner of the back seat. "You fucking idiot, slow down," he screams. "You know what I'd like to do. I'd like to shoot every fucking man in this whole goddamn crew, this ship of fools, and find a new one for the trip back. Jesus. I told you. Slow. Quiet." His face glows beet red against the white-blond hair. "Son of a bitch."

The sleek craft slows until barely moving forward and begins to bob and roll through the seas just outside the small passage through the reef. "Goddamn it, I don't mean you have to go so slow we don't get there until tomorrow." Ian is no longer screaming, but his voice is still loud, steel hard. The crewman driving the boat, badly shaken, hesitates, almost flinching, as he tries to ease the throttle, ever so slightly, forward.

They are met at the dock by Michael, and after quickly securing a bow and stern line around the large round pilings, he begins to help unload what is necessary to allow Ian and

Brian room to maneuver the ice chest so it can be lifted onto the dock. Cautiously, gingerly, it is hoisted and placed on the wide planking, and as soon as the two men scramble out of the boat behind it, is lifted again, carried across the wooden walkway leading from the dock, and placed in a waiting van. Ian and Brian jump in alongside the cooler, Michael closes the two back doors, climbs into the cab, drives away from the dock and onto the road, turns left, then immediately back right and up a steep incline. In the back Ian again checks to be sure the doors are latched shut as the angle of the climb now presses the full weight of the cooler and Caroline Brockton hard against them.

When they come to a stop on level ground the men quickly unload the cooler and carry it across the pebbled drive to the entrance of the stone house. The doors open as if on command, a man greets them, then leads them down two short series of steps and through two large, tiered rooms, their wooden shutters pulled back and open to the sea. The group of four men, now carrying the ice chest between them like a casket, head down a hall on the lower floor to a room at the end. Inside, a fan turns overhead to create the breeze blocked by the thick shrubs outside the iron-barred window. The double wrapped duct tape on the cooler is stripped away, the lid opened, and Caroline Brockton, blindfolded, left hand heavily bandaged, folded into a fetal position, unconscious, is lifted out. The robe falls partially away from her body as she is carried to the bed and placed on it. As he stares at her beautiful, pale skin and the perfect triangle of hair between her legs, Ian is tempted, as he has been more than a few times over the past week…to discard caution, reason, and any slight hint of decency he might feel. With a sense of annoyance and relief he watches Brian quickly pull her robe back around her. "Be sure this room is secure. She should be out for another hour," Ian says as he turns and walks back through the door, followed by the other men.

Brian, now alone with their captive, gently removes the blindfold, pulls back the covers on the double bed and lays them over her, checks to make sure the water pitcher on the table is full, and everything she will need is in the in-suite bathroom. Before leaving her alone he stands for some time at the foot of the bed and stares at her motionless form. His thoughts, some longing, melancholy, many deeply troubling, are far different than Ian's.

There was Kathleen, the girl of his dreams...pure, noble dreams, whom he desperately and clandestinely loved throughout his school years. And then Jenny, whom he forced himself to steadfastly pursue until she humiliated him that awful day at the cricket match. He had wanted to give up on it all, crawl away, do something that would take him from it, could be a substitute for what it seemed he might never find. But only for a while. Then he began to look again, to always look.

Finally forcing himself, Brian walks through the door, pulls it shut behind him, and closes the large padlock with a heavy, metal click. He descends a short stairwell at the end of the hall that leads to another hall in an underground basement. There is another small glass window in a heavy steel door just a few steps away that he peers through. The reality of the scene startles him. A small figure in head-to-foot, yellow hazmat garb is bent over a large table cluttered with racks of vials, beakers, and what appear to be small aquariums. On the floor of the room gleaming, silver metal cases the size of suitcases are stacked, one of them open to reveal numerous small, heavily padded foam compartments. Empty vials fill the compartments.

The figure suddenly turns as he hears the knocks, sees Brian's face against the window, and raises a finger in a "just a minute" gesture. Brian watches as he moves through a door into the adjourning room, where the laborious process of removing the protective gear will take place.

"Hello, Doctor," Brian says, as Dr. Gerard LeFont finally moves through the door into the hall. "How has your stay here been so far?"

"Adequate."

"And do you have everything you need here in your lab?"

"Yes."

"How does the schedule look at this point?"

"I will be finished as planned. Precisely as planned."

"Well, if there is anything else I can do for you, please let me know."

"There is one thing."

"What is that?"

"The girl, Mora. She would like some company, I believe. Another girl. And I would like that as well. And you must instruct her."

Brian hesitates before he speaks. The loathing he felt for Lefont when they first met, when he laid out his conditions, is quickly back with him. He steadies himself, thinks of the ultimate goal. "Yes, Doctor, I will see what I can do."

Back upstairs he finds Ian sitting at the bar, with Mora standing beside him. Her long, slender bronze legs taper downward from the white embroidered shift that ends just below her hips. Brian sees her raw, sensual beauty, feels a stirring, and is ashamed. He knows what she is about, what she will do, and it is those like her that his dreams are contrasted against.

"Have you seen LeFont?" Ian asks as soon as he sees him walk up?"

"Yes."

"How is the weasley little bastard? Is he getting any work done?" He looks at the girl with his peculiar, sneering grin, then laughs out loud.

"Everything seems to be fine." Brian starts to relay Lefont's request right there, in front of Mora, but quickly decides he doesn't want to appear to be any part of it to her, doesn't want her to know he would stoop to take part in this whole sordid task of keeping LeFont satisfied and diligent. "I need to speak to you for a moment, Ian."

They walk to the corner of the room, out of earshot, next to the open shutters where the breeze and scent of hibiscus is strong. "He wants another girl. In addition to her," Brian says, disgust clearly in his voice as he nods in the direction of the bar.

"That scumbag. Jesus," Ian says, then suddenly laughs out loud. "I'll take care of it, sure, sort of a last request. But you tell him I want another day off the schedule for it. The fucking little bastard."

"You tell him. It makes me sick to be around him."

Ian turns and walks back to the bar. Brian watches him brush by Mora, stop, his hand touching her thigh and sliding under the material of the shift. She leans forward and kisses him on the cheek, then on the lips.

Brian walks down the hall and into his room and gathers his toiletries. After showering, he goes back through the house and open breezeway onto the back patio and lawn. Picking up one of the chairs from the flagstone, he carries it across the lawn until he is only twenty feet from the cliff that plunges straight down to the sea. Sitting, he gazes for a long time at the distant, mountainous islands and deep blue water, sparkling under a clear, bright sky specked with puffy white clouds. None of the beauty and tranquility of the scene is lost on him, but neither is the irony of this setting for what is going on here, what he's helping to orchestrate and set in motion. He feels the depression, fright, a familiar flash of panic start to come on. Opening the small, black leather Bible he has been holding on his lap, he begins to read.

Intersections

Book 2

Chapter 19

The customs agents have decided that Christopher and Juliette will be their sacrificial offering from the flight from London, and the contents of their suitcases, opened to the prying eyes of anyone who happens to wander by, are causing considerable interest. Particularly the filmy, tiny bits of lingerie and postage stamp swimsuits. They look at the suitcases, then at her, then at him. Christopher is only slightly embarrassed...mostly damned proud...to be with this drop-dead beautiful woman whom these middle-aged, overweight men are drooling over, trying to imagine in her underwear or less, before doing God knows what with her.

"Bastards," she says under her breath, but perhaps loud enough for the agents to hear, as she and Christopher move to one side of the long table to try and stuff the tangle of garments back into their luggage. Of course, it doesn't fit, takes up far more room than it did just a moment ago before it was rifled through, and again he hears her raspy whisper - "Fucking bastards" - just before she raises up on her toes and throws practically all of her weight back down on the suitcase. It snaps shut.

They are silent until out of the terminal and into the luxurious air...air one is aware of your body passing through, displacing. A brisk, steady breeze mixes the scent of flowers, warmth, and humidity to perfection.

"Christ," Juliette says, exasperation still in her voice. "What a life. They actually get a thrill out of that. Rummaging through luggage, displaying your lingerie, slowing everyone else down, making damned sure you know this is their little kingdom. I was close to offering the short one, the one who was sweating and kept staring at me, the panties I have on. I would have loved to see what he would have done when I took them off right there and handed them to him, told him I wanted to be sure he didn't miss anything." She laughs.

"Why didn't you do it?"

"A weak moment."

The ride in the taxi to Philipsburg, the Dutch side of Sint Maarten, is bumpy and fast, with each of them alternately holding on to their door to keep from landing on top of the other as the driver takes the turns as if racing around pylons on an obstacle course. With the windows open, it's also dusty. He explains the air conditioning is not working and there seems to be construction everywhere. Christopher is sitting on the side of the car adjacent to the sea, and the only views worth looking at are across it. "Why is this place so torn up?" he asks.

"Progress spurned by commercialism, much of it from your country," Juliette answers. "God, people in the tourist business know just how to screw up a place for tourists. And there was a major hurricane. I was here a couple of years ago and it was much the same. I suppose they will stop building when there is no shoreline left to build on."

"Damned shame," Christopher says. "The other islands I've been to in this part of the world are really nice."

"It's much worse here. I imagine it is the access, the airport is quite large for the Caribbean, and of course there are the casinos. Once it's started all sense of reason seems to vanish. The other islands in this area are probably more like you remember. Far more restrictions on development. The French side here is nice...an improvement on this. I thought we'd best stay here first. This is the main harbor and should be a good place to start our search."

"So, are you a gambler?" He has abandoned the view to gaze directly into her eyes.

"Well, I think it can be terrific fun for a time. But no, not a serious gambler. Although I have on occasion lost more money than I should have. What about you, Christopher? I would guess it's not your favorite thing either."

"Actually, I like to gamble, just not for much money. It takes the fun out of it for me when I begin to sweat having to move onto the street if I lose. When I was young I used to gamble on everything, and for a while I was quite a poker player. But only for nickels and dimes. You know, a bunch of guys sitting around playing red and black and baseball, all the games with three wild cards, drinking beer, smoking long, fat cigars."

"Baseball? I don't understand."

"It's the name of a card game, a poker game. Do you play poker?"

"No."

"Well, if you're not using serious money there are a lot of crazy games with wild cards that make it more interesting. The purists only play straight poker, draw and stud, nothing wild. They look down their noses at the way we played. And they play straight in the casinos. But it was great fun."

"Will you teach me to play poker?"

"Sure."

"Perhaps we can play in the casino tonight."

"That might not be such a great place to learn. There's a hell of a lot more skill involved than other games in a casino.

And serious psychology. The atmosphere around a table can be pretty intimidating if you don't know what you're doing."

"I think I can handle it, Christopher."

He smiles at her for a moment. "Yes, that was a dumb thing to say. Of course you can."

"You can stand just in back of me, watching carefully, as they do in the movies, and if I forget any of the instructions you've given me we can have some type of clandestine sign or gesture, so that I'll be sure not to make mistakes."

"That could be challenging. And risky. Huge, mean men deal with cheating in casinos. And I'm sure I can't teach you enough this evening to guarantee you'll win enough to fund your retirement."

"I have enough to retire Christopher. It will be splendid fun."

After being shown to their cottage on a hill rising from the beach, they strip to their underwear and lie on the bed in the breeze of the overhead fan, stretching and resting after the twelve hours of travel from London. Only mid-afternoon due to the time difference, Christopher thinks of shutting his eyes, sure he would immediately fall asleep. His next thought is of touching Juliette, of a session of slow, low energy sex to further relax him, and is about to roll onto his side and slide his hand across to her when he feels her weight lift from the bed.

"Get up, Christopher, we must get started. We should at least go to the harbormaster before the office closes to find out if PURITY has cleared customs here."

Reluctantly pulling himself to a sitting position, he fights to keep from reaching up and attempting to draw her down beside him.

"God, where have I seen this uniform before," Juliette says under her breath, her voice oozing sarcasm and contempt, as they walk through the door of the customs building and toward the desk. "Excuse me, we are looking for some dear friends on board a yacht that is due into Phillipsburg sometime this week. The name of the yacht is PURITY. Could you be so kind as to tell us if they have registered and cleared through your office?" Her tone is light, friendly, and Christopher notices how she fixes the man with her smile.

The customs officer stares at them both for a moment before answering, then his eyes come to rest on Christopher. "Have you looked in the harbor?"

"We haven't seen them, but we don't have a boat and it's quite large. There's also a good chance they've moved on to another anchorage, but they were supposed to clear at your office. If we know they have arrived on the island, we can begin to look for them, or wait until they do. It would be a great help." Juliette's voice and smile, to Christopher, take a slight turn toward seductive.

"What type of yacht is it?"

There's a moments' hesitation that Christopher speaks quickly to end. "We're not sure exactly, but a large motor yacht."

"How large?"

"Hundred feet or better."

"I do not know of any yacht that fits that description that has cleared in the last few days. I cannot give you more information than that"

Juliette leans forward, hands and weight now on the desk, her loose-fitting blouse open and hanging off her body, and

Christopher sees the man's eyes dart quickly and lock on what is surely a clear view of her braless breasts. "It would help us a great deal, it could save us a lot of time, if you could please check and just tell us yes or no." She speaks slowly, softly, her head down for the first few words, his eyes not moving as long as hers do not confront them. He is now oblivious to Christopher's presence. She looks up and straight into his eyes. It takes him a split second to recover and when he does, he looks off to the side. "We do not want to waste our time on your lovely island looking for them if they have not arrived. We would rather relax and enjoy all you have to offer here. The name of the yacht is PURITY. Surely you can do us this one small favor."

The customs officer says nothing for a moment, never looking back at them, then walks into a back room. Christopher glances at Juliette. Her face is impassive as she returns his look, then there's a lightning-fast wink, and she turns to stare at the door the man has disappeared behind.

"There is no record of the yacht clearing here within the last week," the officer says upon his return to the desk.

"Thank you so much for checking," Juliette says, her voice again smooth, sensual, and rich with appreciation. "Do you have any way of knowing if it could have cleared on the French side?"

"No."

They jump into the first of two taxis waiting outside the building, their drivers sitting under a tree in the shade, and Juliette smiles at them to try and hasten their return. "Island time," she says. "Wonderful if you can ever get into it, bloody exasperating when you need to get something done. I hope we will have time to get to Marigot, on the French side."

"Juliette," Christopher says, "don't you think these people

might forego customs considering what they're up to."

"Yes, I have thought about that, but if it's a very large yacht, it would seem they would have to clear. It would be hard to hide. And very large yachts are often looked upon with curiosity…even suspicion…around here. Were you guessing about the hundred-foot power yacht?"

"Hell yes, but if they crossed the Atlantic in close to a week. She's got to be big. And fast."

"Marigot, please," she tells the driver as soon as he slides into the seat. "We will go over and at least look in the harbor and ask some questions. We'll go to Grand Case if we have time; if not, we'll go in the morning. It's just up the road and there are a few superb restaurants there, for either lunch or dinner."

They hire a small boat to take them on a cruise of the harbor at Marigot and pass behind the transom of the last of the three large yachts that turn out not to be PURITY as the red sphere of the sun, dramatically enlarged, slips into the sea. At an open-air restaurant overlooking the harbor, over grilled Mahi-Mahi, ice cold Heinekens, then a bottle of white wine, the effects of being up for twenty hours and traveling thousands of miles accelerate quickly. Their conversation slows to short sentences and monosyllabic words. Christopher, trying to at least stay even with Juliette's lead and aggression in their investigation, forces himself to ask a few questions of the waiter and bartender. No one knows anything. She falls asleep in the taxi on the way back to the cottage. He wants to, but with his head back against the seat his mind, though in slow motion tandem with his exhausted body, focuses, refuses to quiet. Thinking of the gravity of the situation they're trying to be a part of, the possibilities, he feels sure he understands it as well as he can at this moment. He wonders once more if she does.

The scent of fresh flowers and a brisk, luxurious breeze welcome Christopher as he comes awake. Glancing at his watch he sees it is only six thirty, knows the flat light outside is because the sun is still hidden below the horizon, pulls the sheet back up, wraps it around him, curls into a fetal ball, and soaks in the sublime feeling of being in bed, rested, with no reason to have to get up.

But within minutes he's restless and anxious to get started. Maybe it's being in the islands, the excitement of returning to one of his favorite parts of the world, and the memories. Or the excitement he still feels when arriving in a new place, even after all the travel. Or perhaps his mind has made the shift to eagerly anticipating what, just a few hours ago, it seemed to dread. The thought of all of it stimulates him now. Scenarios run in and out of his thoughts like lightning - visions of emotional rushes, gallant actions and rewards. Suddenly scrambling out of bed, into the bathroom, he hurries to brush his teeth. After a quick shower and a shave, he fixes a cup of coffee, walks onto the porch, sits in one of the wicker chairs, and watches the sky light up and turn blue as the sun begins its climb.

After the first cup he goes back for another and sees Juliette's alluring form under the thin sheet. Tempted, as usual, but he instead heads back to the porch with his refill. Before the cup is half empty his adrenalin sends him back inside. Dressing, gathering what he will need, he heads to the small building that acts as the office for the group of elegant cottages.

It takes some time to talk the man at the desk into opening the rental car booth at such an early hour, handle the paperwork, find a detailed map of the island, then study it in the lobby. He is back in the room by eight and she is still asleep.

"Juliette," he whispers, his hand gently brushing the hair back from her face. After there is no response, he speaks louder, shaking her shoulder. She still appears comatose, so he slips his hand under the sheet, traces one long, silky leg until his fingers feel the curve of her bottom, then slips it gently into the soft thatch below and begins stroking her lightly, slowly. She begins to stir and rolls onto her back, her eyes batting open.

"What a wonderful way to wake up, " she says, her voice hoarse with sleep.

Christopher kisses her on the forehead and pulls his hand from under the sheet. "Time to get up, we've got to get going."

"That is a miserable trick to play on someone so early in the morning."

"It's not that early. And remember it. It's probably the last time in your life you see me demonstrate this kind of erotic restraint. At least with you."

"The fog must not be with you yet."

"Wrong. It's just that we've more important things to do. Solve a murder, a perplexing mystery, and save a fair maiden. Actually, I'm sure over the last few days, even hours, I've finally reached full adult maturity, I've learned to control my base instincts when it interferes with reason. Juliette," his voice suddenly leaps an octave and more than a few decibels, "Its happened. A major evolutionary milestone has taken place. I've finally learned to think with my mind instead of...well...you know." Stripping the covers away with lightning speed, he leaps onto the bed beside her and begins frantically licking and sucking one of her breasts. Within a few seconds he is standing again, pretending with a grand gesture to wipe his mouth with his sleeve, and smiling sheepishly down at her. "Well, perhaps I was wrong...still have a little work to do."

She laughs out loud as he turns, walks across the room and sits down in a chair. "Can you be ready in thirty minutes. We really do need to get going. The timing is critical. Remember, you said that."

The single, narrow main street in Grand Case, with its quaint, brightly painted West Indies cottages, is a welcome relief from the unsightly construction and helter-skelter architecture on the Dutch side of the island. No matter that many of the houses are now restaurants and shops. This may be as authentic as a town with a view gets on this monument in paradise to commercial excess. They move from bars to restaurants, to shops and the docks, questioning everyone that gives any appearance of having been here for more than a day or so. No one has seen or heard of the yacht PURITY, and no one wears a look that indicates secret knowledge or danger when they are questioned. After stopping for a beer at a delightful, lively, 1940's style cafe with a covered terrace and a splendid view of the lovely harbor, the sea, and land-spit island of Anguilla to the north, they head back to Marigot to check with customs.

The answers are all the same, as they are later at Simpson's Bay and other possible harbors Christopher has selected where a boat the size they assume PURITY to be might rest at anchor.

The game of poker occupies the conversation in the car on the last two legs of their reconnaissance outing, and by the time they are back in their cottage Juliette is convinced she has it down. She still insists Christopher stay close by her side, but he's convinced it's because of the Bogart-era romance and adventure of how they will look, his passing clandestine instructions with a nudge on her chair...rather than any help she thinks she might actually need.

All but the hard-core losers or winners take notice as they enter and go on a brief tour of the small casino. Juliette, on his arm, is stunning in a low cut, loose, sheer white silk pants suit, with the jeweled accoutrements of wealth, though understated, that could be expected to adorn a woman of her exquisite beauty and privilege in life. Christopher has on his best...his only... sport coat, a treasured silk and wool number from Polo beginning to show a little wear around the edges. But his shirt is freshly starched, everything fits well, and he feels like a king as he soaks up the envious stares. *Who was it that said the ultimate power trip for any man is to be seen with a beautiful woman? And the most powerful man in any room is not the one with the most money, but the one with the most beautiful woman.*

There is only one poker table, catering to mostly Americans. *Texans*, Christopher muses. When she starts to play the crowd gathered around isn't reminiscent of the elegance and intrigue he imagines Juliette would prefer. The baccarat table at Monte Carlo this is not. Many T shirts. No tuxedos. She takes her lumps at first but displays no lack of resolve or cash. Sure enough, when he looks around after a particularly long stint of trying to count cards and discreetly nudge the leg of her chair, there are people two deep. Then she begins to win.

Texas Hold'em is definitely her game, and her steely expression and unwavering, deliberate moves during the hands would do credit to any legend in Vegas. While the dealer shuffles, she smiles and talks easily, and Christopher is certain ninety percent of the men around the table would gather to watch this creature stack cow dung instead of chips.

There are never more than three other players, and for the last hour, when Juliette's beginner's luck starts to wane, only two. The fidgety, loud, obnoxious man in the white linen shirt takes obvious pleasure, likely affirmation of macho superiority, when his stack begins to grow at the expense of his gorgeous adversary. But the last hand, played with considerable courage, gall, or recklessness by Juliette, only holding a pair and an Ace, combined with a shocking level of stupidity by him, changes the final tally by more than ten thousand dollars. To Christopher, the coup de gras, applied with the touch of an anvil, comes when they stand, her arm in his, she nods toward her opponent, says "Thank you," gathers what for the most part were his chips only minutes before, and the two of them walk out together to all sorts of unimaginable pleasures of the flesh. He resists the urge to look back over his shoulder and wink.

The ride back is filled with laughter and joy at her triumph, then silence as the length of the day and number of drinks take over. After a nightcap for each of them inside their cottage, some half-hearted conversation, and a last beer for Christopher...he heads, unsteadily, for the bed, all thoughts of unimaginable pleasures tabled for the evening.

After an early morning flight into St. Barthelemy and the usual rounds of customs and immigration, Christopher enlists a tall, reed-thin young island boy to take them on a tour of the lovely harbor of Gustavia. There are two large motor yachts riding at anchor well out from the entrance, another two tied stern-to to the quay. The boy calls himself Cosmos and within minutes of pushing off from the quay Christopher is mesmerized watching him row the small, brightly painted boat with alternating, bicycle-like strokes that are as elegant and powerful as anything he remembers seeing from any athlete, anywhere. The hull slices rapidly through the water. Cosmos speaks enough English to enable them to communicate, but for the detailed instructions on which boats to pass aft of the stern, to stay well away so as not to cause suspicion, Juliette speaks to him in French.

Again, there is no yacht bearing the name PURITY, and after thanking Cosmos and giving him enough of a tip to elicit a broad, shy grin, white teeth flashing against his flawless, dark complexion, Christopher and Juliette climb back onto the cement pier and stroll through the town. They question each shop owner they encounter, and after an hour of hearing nothing encouraging decide to head to highly recommended Bay Saint Jean to look for a hotel and spend the afternoon on the beach. The Mini-Moke they rent is a joy to Christopher, and he takes the keys from Juliette and hops in the drivers' seat.

"Damn I love this car," he proclaims in a tone of childish joy, an excited smile covering his face. "The ultimate in functional transportation, a cross between a go-cart and a jeep."

"It's rather basic, don't you think?"

"Yes, and that's the beauty of it. Small, but enough room, a back seat, tough, no gadgets, and no top. No car can be truly enjoyable unless the top comes off."

"It's quite obvious you have never lived in London, or too far from the temperate zones of the world. The weather in the south must be divine."

"Most of the time. But you can always put a top up." He stomps on the throttle as they leave the town, roar and bounce along the rutted road by the harbor, then head up the series of steep switchbacks leading to the spine of the island and the drop to the eastern shore.

"I would rather not have to depend on the top on this vehicle," Juliette says, raising her voice just short of a shout to be heard above the roar of the wind and the engine at high rev.

"Well, it's perfect for here anyway. I've always loved sports cars, roadsters. Owned a few when I couldn't afford them. Another one of the kinks in my personality. I love the basic functionality of something like this. Simplifies life. If it's going to be simple, though, it's still got to be fun, have some sense of romance to it. This does. I've never been attracted to small, simple, basic Japanese sedans." There's silence between them as they crest the ridge, slow to a crawl, look back down onto an incredible view of the harbor, then ahead to the sparkling, multihued bay. "Do you have any thoughts on where you want to stay?" Christopher starts the Moke down the plunge paralleling the dramatic pitch of the runway and toward the bay as he speaks.

"Filao Beach Hotel if we can get a room." I think you will like it."

After a quick stop at the airport to collect the bags they stashed, they arrive at the hotel desk. Juliette again speaks French, and after what seems an inordinately long time to check in, she walks over to where he has collapsed into an overstuffed rattan chair.

"We are quite lucky. One of their guests had to leave early due to an illness in his family. Apparently someone who stays here regularly. So we have a room, but only for the next two nights. Every hotel on the beach is fully occupied."

Juliette, topless, with only a tiny triangle of fabric below her waist, spends the afternoon reading and working diligently, with a complex series of lotions, on a tan.

Christopher has a book but spends much of the time staring at the spectacular, bronzed, topless women lying in the sun or flashing by on brightly colored sailboards. If there's a more beautiful beach with more beautiful people, he hasn't seen it. *Sort of like culling the creme de la creme from St. Tropez, restricting the crowds, and dropping them all into this gorgeous bay.*

Partly because it looks like great fun, and partly because one of the instructors is a particularly lithesome blond, he decides to take a lesson on one of the little wind-powered rocket ships. He's told in a very thick accent that it will be twenty minutes until she is available, so he walks the length of the crescent of white sand and back while waiting for his turn.

As the gorgeous instructor explains the basics to him while they stand on the beach, he must fight two thoughts to concentrate on what she is telling him - the embarrassment and humiliation the next thirty minutes could bring if he has no more luck than he did the one other time he tried this, and how he's going to keep his eyes and mind off the beautiful, pert, firm breasts that she displays nonchalantly just inches from his eyes. *Good exercise in mind and ego control.*

Both concerns prove warranted; but then, just before the lesson ends, he finds himself flying along at probably 15 knots, back and arms straight, pulling down and moving the angle of the sail to increase his speed. It's glorious, he wants to scream with the exhilaration, and stays out another thirty minutes, flashing back and forth, again and again, just off the beach.

"You look absolutely exhausted." Juliette rolls onto her back to address him when he returns.

"Yeah, but God is that fun." His words come in short

bursts between gasps of air. "When I tried it before I decided it was the hardest thing I had ever done. I mean...I'm a decent athlete, a pretty fair sailor, and I usually don't have much trouble picking things up. But I never did get any real feel for it. It was awkward as hell."

"Did you have an instructor like that?"

He laughs out loud. "I've never had an instructor like that...for anything."

"Maybe you perform better in the fog, Christopher."

"Juliette!" His voice drips with mock disgust. "My mind never slipped. Total, one hundred percent concentration on the technical details of sailboarding."

"Your tongue was hanging out. Before you got on the board."

"And I guess I know what you would say if I asked you what you'd do if you took a lesson from that tall, ripped, curly haired guy while he was naked with a hard on."

"Yes you do. I would laugh. That is the difference you know. We women hardly ever seem to have an interest in that sort of thing." She looks over at the tall Frenchman, not more than fifty feet from them, stacking the masts and brightly colored sails on a rack. When her eyes return to Christopher's there is a devilish look in them, and she slowly licks her tongue across her upper lip.

L'Hibiscus is perched high on a hill above Gustavia, just below what the maître de explains is a famous Swedish clock tower. A small hotel with an open-air restaurant, it offers a magnificent view of the harbor. They watch as the sun's disappearance spreads across the horizon, creating an exploding backdrop of varying, changing shades of orange, red and purple. Lights flowing down the hills begin to emerge and cast their sparkling reflection on the oval of water below. The lobster bisque is exquisite, the wonderful bottle of wine creates a relaxed glow, and Christopher slumps down in his chair and looks at Juliette.

"Okay, what do I have to do to be able to live like this at times when I'm not involved in a major international crime with an incredibly beautiful, bright, intriguing, wealthy woman?"

"There are a number of people who do," she says.

"Inheriting it like you have is out. My father could cut me out of his will, but even if he doesn't, we have a history of serious longevity in our family, he's still relatively young, and the ornery type that will be around forever. And he's only well off, not wealthy."

"Your book, Christopher. It's going to make you rich and famous. You'll be able to buy a house here."

"Right. You know, maybe if I could determine what the problem is. Sometimes I think I don't have what it takes, the drive, that dogged pursuit, the ruthlessness to make a lot of money. Then I think it's because I'm not doing anything I like enough to cause me to be that dedicated. Then on days when I'm being kind to myself, I write it off to all my interests. That I just like to do too many different things, that life's too short, to put in the time it takes working to make serious money. But God do I love to live like I have it."

"Most of the people I know who have made a great deal of money on their own are true bores. I'm not sure if it is the affectations they take on while trying to become successful, feel they need to fit in with the wealthy after they have arrived. In any case it never works. It is quite obvious. Many seem so one-dimensional. Perhaps because all they do is work. Of course, when I think about it, a great many people who have inherited it are not terribly intriguing personalities either."

"In the U.S...wealth or at least a significant amount of money and its trappings...has become the only measure of success that seems to matter to a lot of folks. On the one hand it seems perverted, but on the other I guess it's because so many of us aspire to it. Is it like that in England?"

"Given enough years in a capitalist system I imagine it will always come to that. But it is different in England. Our system is not as developed as yours, and our history is much longer. Much more associated with traditions, causes and heroes outside of entrepreneurship and amassing wealth. Does it bother you, that you're not wealthy?"

"NO. Not real wealth. But enough to be secure, successful, or maybe appear successful. Or maybe it bothers me because it bothers me. Is there anything you regret about inheriting all that money?"

"No."

Walking arm and arm down the steep hill from the restaurant into the town they agree it's too early to turn in for the night. They enter a small courtyard and what appears to be a lively, raucous pub, take a battered table under a slowly rotating fan, and Christopher goes to the bar and orders a Heineken and her second Grand Marnier of the evening.

"I don't think that's the drink of choice in this place," he says as he returns to the table. "Yeah, I like this. Salty, isn't it. I mean this is a real bar. Sailor's bar. There must be a few of these on the Isle of Wight, in Plymouth."

"England has no lack of authentic pubs. Wherever you happen to be."

"Yeah, but the nautical flavor, a sailor's bar. It adds something, don't you think?"

"I suppose."

As they continue to drink and talk, he is aware of three men at a table to the side and back of Juliette. Alternately they stare at her, occasionally at him, turn their heads towards each other, talk and laugh in loud, crude voices, then stare again. One is stocky, thick, with a beard, the other two tall and lean with long, stringy black hair, thin faces, and days of unshaven stubble. Possibly brothers. Two are dressed in the chambray work shirts of seamen, the other in a grease-stained tee shirt. Angles and hollows fill their dark faces, and their eyes, when they catch his, are cold and menacing. Christopher thinks they are speaking Italian, doesn't understand a word, but recognizes the universal body language and inflections of drunk, uncouth men in heat. The longer they stay, the more directed their behavior becomes, the more Christopher's sense of danger rises. When they try to get his attention, by very obviously calling to him, he starts to suggest to Juliette that they leave, then doesn't for fear that might incite them further. On his third or fourth beer, he needs to urinate, but again hesitates, afraid to leave her alone at the table. He feels a hot flash of anger at the position he's been put in, enraged at these men for what they are doing. But his fear dominates, and that disgusts him. Hypothetical situations churn through his mind, images of how he will react.

"Christopher, you are not listening to me. What is wrong?"

"Uh, sorry, I....there are three men at the table behind you. I think they may be trouble. Have you heard any of what they are saying?"

"Yes."

"Why didn't you say something."

"It's so incredibly ridiculous. I just don't let it bother me. When it does then I will say something." She looks at him with a serious, flat expression. "Or perhaps you will."

He starts to joke about his avowed aversion to macho acts, thinks twice, and remains silent. With his stomach tightening and his throat dry he decides he'll risk everything this time. With total abandon if it comes to it. Then he sees one of the tall men slide his chair forward, reach for Juliette's hair, and fear slams back through him.

Turning the instant she's aware of his fingers, she glares at him, their faces no more than a foot apart, then speaks in a very slow, steady voice, in Italian...words that Christopher can only assume from her tone are curt, to the point, laced with venom, sarcasm. The man quickly spreads his palms open, his expression changing to one of mock apology. He speaks softly to her for a few moments, her steely expression never changing, then leans his face a little closer to hers, smiles and continues to talk. He glances at Christopher, his grin sharp and sinister, then back to Juliette, says something else and laughs. In a millisecond Juliette has spit in his face and he is on his feet, saliva running down his cheek from under his eye. As he draws his open palm back to strike her Christopher is out of his chair. "Leave her alone goddamn it."

The cruel face, now tortured with seething rage, turns, and there is a frozen instant while they stare at each other. A sudden, gutteral snarl...and Christopher feels spittle splatter into his eye. Hidden for so long, an impulse explodes with lightning speed, and his fist shoots toward the glaring face. Lunging forward as he mostly misses, he feels an anvil like blow across the back of his neck that sends him sprawling across the table, then bouncing off onto the floor. He scrambles quickly to get to his feet as he hears a stream of unintelligible words just above him, expecting another blow as he rises. Suddenly there are several men, shoving, shouting in different languages, and he sees the man that spit at him being held back by two of them...straining, neck veins bulging, screaming to get at Christopher. He is pulled toward the door, his two companions arguing loudly with three other men. Juliette is at Christopher's side now, her arm around his waist, her head pressed close to his shoulder.

"Please accept my apologies, monsieur. I am Jean-Paul, the owner of Le Select. We do not condone that kind of behavior here. Are you all right?"

"Uh, yes, I'm all right," Christopher replies as he looks into the sparkling blue eyes of a tall, heavy set, muscular man with close cropped, sandy hair and a swarthy complexion.

"Your evening here will be with my compliments. Please stay and have something else to drink with us. I have a private stock of exquisite scotch and rum, and perhaps you could use a double after that," he says, a warm grin spreading across his face.

"Thank you...but," he looks at Juliette.

"Please, madame, you would honor me, and make me feel less guilty if you would not leave on such a sour note."

"Thank you very much. You are most kind," she says, as Jean-Paul straightens the table and chairs for them, then leaves to fetch their drinks. Once the beer is in front of Christopher, he drains half of it in one gulp.

"I never for a moment believed all that rubbish about your aversion to manly acts," she says as Christopher stares off at nothing.

"A weak moment, I assure you," he says, turning to face her. "Or maybe a weakness for you. Most women don't inspire me to such levels of courage."

"That was true chivalry, Christopher, and you would have done the same thing for any lady."

"Bullshit, the guy spit in my face. But it doesn't really matter to you, does it?"

"What do you mean?"

"I mean I really do care about you. A lot. And I get the feeling that you're...just...indifferent. Seems superficial."

"You know that's not true."

Her tone and expression are flat, and he searches her eyes, her body language. "I mean, there just doesn't seem to be any depth of feeling. Perhaps that's a better way to put it. Are you afraid of commitments?"

"We've had a wonderful time together, and we get along quite well. I find it ironic that you would ask me about commitments after all you have told me about yourself. Remember, we are different. We have certainly established that. There is no reason that what just happened should make you attack me. We need to forget it for the moment and plan what we are going to do tomorrow. We have been here two days and have learned absolutely nothing."

Juliette is only halfway through the glass of rum from what Jean Paul described as an exclusive, small plantation in Barbados, and Christopher is thinking of ordering another beer. She is not sipping slowly. The excitement sobered him quickly, but now the two Heinekens he has just inhaled have reactivated the effects of the evening's drinks and he is again quite high. "Why are you trying to change the subject?"

"Really, Christopher, do we have to deal with your insecurities now?"

"Well, you certainly don't inspire a great deal of confidence with someone trying to establish a relationship."

"Maybe you are trying too hard. Relax and enjoy what we do have. Now I think we need to rent that seaplane tomorrow. We can cover all the harbors here as well as those on Anguilla, Saba, Nevis and St. Kitts in one day. We should have a much better chance of finding her if we do that."

"If it's anywhere around here, which I really doubt..." His voice is laced with cynicism, his mind still somewhere else. "There are a hundred reasons why it's not here now, or she's not on it, and that's if the information I got was good."

"You have said your source was good. You've said that again and again, that you believe them."

"Yeah, but things could have changed, or it could have been a smokescreen...you know, maybe it was just for my consumption, or everyone involved with it was told that and they're really in fucking Finland."

"You said you do not think your source was set up."

"Christ, Juliette, I told you that I can't imagine any connection at all, that he must have overheard it, because there's no way he could be involved."

"So it's a man."

"Uh oh...well, you're pulling it out of me now, aren't you? Hot on the trail. That narrows it to about two and a half billion suspects." His face breaks into a slight grin and he reaches under the table and lays his hand on the silky skin of her thigh. "Look, I belatedly agree, let's forget all this until in the morning. I promise I'll have renewed vigor for the whole adventure by then. But I've been stomped into the ground by a horny, spurned, berserk seaman, I'm a little drunk, and I'd like to go back to the room with you and enjoy the rest of the evening."

She doesn't smile, doesn't speak for a moment, then replies. "I think I would like to finish my drink and then I'll be ready to go back. I am quite tired and a good night's sleep sounds wonderful."

A familiar, hollow feeling washes over him, goes to his core. He thinks about staying and getting really drunk, then that he shouldn't, then wonders why in the hell it matters. Turning the bottle up, he drains the last of it in three large gulps, then orders another.

He offers only half-hearted responses to her conversation until she suggests they leave. The uneasiness and fear return, but are tempered by the alcohol, and he decides to say nothing.

As they walk through the courtyard and into the narrow street Christopher is conscious for only a moment of the warm, flower-scented air that envelops him like a luxurious, feathery blanket. His heart begins to pound as his eyes dart from shadows to corners, intensely trying to pierce the darkness, his mind racing. They have only another block before reaching the Moke. Turning, he looks past her, back over his shoulder.

"What's wrong, Christopher?" Her voice is soft yet carries a sense of urgency. He doesn't answer. "Christopher!!" The fingernails stab into his arm the instant her voice rises.

Wrenching his head to the front, he sees the three men standing, blocking their path, not more than twenty feet away. He knows they should run, yell, but he is frozen, makes no move as the tall, slender figure, the man he fought, steps forward and spits out a stream of vicious, vile sounding Italian.

The origin of the sharp click registers a split second before his eyes catch the glint of steel. His body takes a sudden step forward as his arm pushes her behind him, as if being moved and manipulated by an invisible hand, with no conscious decision from his brain. His arms spread out in a way they have never been trained to do, and he goes into a crouch.

"No Christopher," she shrieks, her hand pulling at his shoulder and the back of his shirt.

Swiping his arm back to push her away, he watches the man take a few quick steps forward, then lunge. Eyes glued to the hand and blade, he instinctively jumps back and to the side, pushing against her. Confused motion is suddenly all around him, the sound of a heavy impact, the weight of the man's body pushing him down, pain in his side. As he struggles back to his feet he is aware of yelling from where the other two men were standing, sees someone swing a club, someone crumple in a heap. Suddenly a large, burly shape is on the back of the man with the club, knocking it from his hand, but the shape is thrown off with lightning speed. Two kicks to his midsection and a blow across his neck send him sprawling.

"All right, motherfucker, get the hell out of here." The voice...deep, clenched-teeth coarse, gravelly with anger, resonates along the street and through Christopher. Coming to his senses, he glances down and moves quickly back as he realizes his attacker is unconscious at his feet.

"Are you all right?" A tall, slender, imposing black man steps to within a few feet of him as he speaks.

"Yeah, I uh...think so." He sees the baseball bat back in the man's hand, then turns to look for Juliette, standing a few feet behind him, staring, motionless.

"You're bleeding. Let's have a look at it," the man says,

moving closer as Christopher sees blood on his shirt and pulls it out of his shorts, now aware of a stinging pain.

"Nothing but a little slice, doesn't look very deep. You shouldn't even need stitches if the bleeding will stop. We'll go back inside and clean it up."

They follow him in a sort of trance, single file, Juliette and Christopher just in back of the baseball bat, gripped about a third of the way up the handle, pointing down as if an extension of the long arm, swaying in concert with the man's long, sleek, unhurried strides.

Jean-Paul meets them as soon as they step back inside Le Select, then ushers them back through a curtained doorway and into a small office adjacent to the kitchen. "You were right, Andre. It looks as if you were lucky, Christopher, or perhaps by now you are thinking how very unlucky you are for having walked into Le Select. Again, my sincerest apologies. There is seldom trouble here."

"Hey, don't believe a word he says. Happens every night." Andre's voice is still deep, but soft now, and with the wide smile, warm and comforting. He gently slaps Jean-Paul on the back, then looks at Christopher, then over at Juliette. "Please join me for a drink, or coffee, or whatever you may feel like after Dr. Jean-Paul gets you fixed up." He turns, props the bat against the wall, and walks out of the office.

The sharp sting from whatever Jean Paul cleaned the wound with has subsided and now Christopher only aches as the three of them walk back into the bar. His eyes quickly search the room until he spots Andre at a table in the corner, facing the crowd, a woman with a thick mane of red hair sitting across the table, facing him. As they approach, their rescuer rises to his full, considerable height, and again the smile is warm, inviting.

"I don't believe we've officially met. I'm Andre. This is Sam."

As she turns her head and brushes her hair back, the sparkle in her eyes and beauty of her face rivet him. Recovering quickly, he replies. "I'm Christopher and this is Juliette. How can I ever thank you?"

"Only by joining us for a drink. And of course you won't have to pay." He extends his hand toward Jean-Paul, once again behind the bar. "This man refuses to let anyone who has been set upon by blood-thirsty thugs in his establishment ever pay for anything again. At least until tomorrow."

"Where did you come from?" Christopher asks as he pulls the chair out to sit down. "It all happened so fast. For a second I thought you were one of them."

"Well, you left very quickly, but I wasn't too far behind you. I saw everything that happened in here. I just had a feeling."

"Where in the hell did you get the bat?"

"They keep it behind the bar. But I really was just kidding Jean-Paul. This is a pretty safe place, a great bar, but it can come in handy. The sight of it's usually enough to straighten up the odd drunk who has visions of the Barbary coast."

"Where are you from?" Sam asks, while glancing first at Juliette, then at Christopher.

"I live in London." It's the first words Christopher can recall from Juliette since he assured her he was all right in Jean Paul's office. "He's from North Carolina. And you?"

"I'm originally from New Mexico. Andre lives here, says he's from St. Louis, but as many people as he knows I'm suspicious. I suppose it's possible he could have been born there."

"Maybe you can help us out if you live here," Juliette says. "We are looking for some friends who are in this area on their large yacht, but we have not been able to locate them."

Christopher feels his anger rise quickly.

"The name of the yacht is PURITY. Have you seen it over the past week?"

Andre's face is impassive, gives no clue to Christopher. After hesitating a moment, he answers Juliette. "No. Can't place it. There are so many big boats that pass through these islands…especially St. Barts."

"Are you familiar with the surrounding islands?" Juliette asks.

"Yes."

"He's familiar with everything around here, and everyone," Sam chimes in, smiling and turning her head to look at Andre.

"We have looked around St. Maarten and here on Saint Barts. Again, it is a large yacht. Likely at least one hundred feet. What other islands in this area have harbors that might attract them"?

"Let's talk about this another time," Christopher says, breaking suddenly into the conversation while looking at Juliette. "Andre has done enough to help us tonight. What do you do here?" His eyes shift to the man he is beginning to feel very comfortable with, with whom he senses an immediate, though shallow, bond.

"No. It's fine. I'll be glad to help you if I can. But I'm curious. Didn't your friends tell you anything about where they were going to be."

Juliette answers immediately, with no hint of hesitation.

"They do not know we are here. It will be a surprise. They are dear friends and will be quite excited to see us. We were only told they were going to be in the Leeward Islands."

"Well, that's where you are, but within eighty miles there are a number of islands with numerous harbors or deserted anchorages that could accommodate a large yacht. Sixty miles to the west are the Virgins, and once out of the Leewards there is an unbroken chain that runs south, then west all the way to South America."

"We are going to hire a small plane tomorrow to cover as many islands around here as we can."

"That might work. What does she look like, what kind of boat is she?"

This time there is hesitation from Juliette, and Christopher is sure Andre, looking directly at her, picks it up.

"We are not sure. It is a new yacht. We have not seen it yet."

"Well, you better have some good binoculars and a pilot who likes to make low passes if you're going to have to read her name or port of call off the transom. A lot of large boat owners still have the class not to plaster it all over the sides. Where does she hail from?"

"Ah...actually, we are...ah, not sure of that either. But somewhere in England."

Christopher, irritated, drunk again, and convinced Juliette's out-of-character hesitation has caused suspicion, suddenly leaps over all barriers of caution. "Look, Andre, I wish the hell she hadn't brought this up. But now that she has, there's more to it than that." The pain is sharp as fingernails dig into his thigh. "There's someone on that boat who we think might be in danger, who might be there against their will. It's a very delicate situation, but it could be urgent."

There is a long silence as Andre stares at Christopher, his expression flat, his eyes probing. "Sounds like you might need the help of the authorities more than mine."

"Like I said, it's a very delicate situation. Believe me, we've given that a lot of thought." Christopher's response is without hesitation.

"I'll make some calls to a few people I know. But I won't be able to do it until I get back here around noon tomorrow. I've got to take the boat over to St. Maarten early in the morning and do a trip."

"Do you live on a boat?" Christopher asks.

"No, but I'm the skipper on a catamaran that makes runs between Saint Barts and Saint Maarten.

Christopher suddenly feels very drunk. "We'd better go now," he says, rising and extending his hand to first Sam and then Andre. "Again, thank you so much."

"I'm only glad I could help. I'll be on the quay by El Tigre…that's my boat…about three thirty tomorrow afternoon. If you come by, I'll tell you if I've been able to find out anything."

After exchanging farewells once more, Christopher and Juliette again walk out into the night. "Christ, Christopher!. Goddamn it! Why did you tell them? Don't you realize where they might go with it?"

"I sure do. And I'm hoping. I'm fucking hoping."

Andre and Sam lie in bed in the small room his friend Winston lets him use on the occasions it's not occupied and he's staying over in Saint Barts. In return Winston gets personal delivery service to and from the larger island. Andre stares at the fan turning slowly above his head, unable to fall asleep, deep in thought. "Sam, are you awake?"

"Yeah."

"The boat. That was it."

"What? What are you talking about?"

"The boat. Remember that huge yacht that blasted by, woke me up, and rocked us around when we were at Ile Fourche. You know, when we were sleeping on the trampoline?"

"I never saw it."

"PURITY. That was her name."

The left wing tip of the small plane drops, the nose drifts down, and they roll into a dive. His body tenses, the tug of fear pulls on him, and queasiness grabs at his gut as they are now nose down and dramatically increasing speed. His eyes instinctively close until he feels the return of gravity signal they are leveling out. Opening his eyes, Christoper's perspective immediately shifts to the thrill of the strafing-run-height pass over the horseshoe- shaped body of water, multi-hued and crystal clear. Pulling negative g's, that helpless, out of control sensation of falling…when it happens…is the only thing about flying he doesn't like. And he's convinced Montana, their pilot, was an anal-fixated dive bomber in his previous life. Or perhaps a crop duster earlier in this one. They pull into a steep climb, flashing above small, brightly colored houses climbing the hills, then level out above the ridge, all eyes looking for another place to search and let Montana do his ritualized, hell-for-leather, drop-from-the-sky-routine. The plane has buzzed numerous bays and harbors on Saint Barts and the adjacent islands of Saba, Saint Kitts, and Eustacia, all without any sighting of a yacht named PURITY.

"Those are all sailboats, too small," Christopher says, his voice hoarse after yelling the last three hours to be heard above the ear-filling roar of the plane's engine. "It's about time we started back anyway. I don't want to miss Andre."

Neither Juliette nor Christopher speaks on the thirty minute ride back to Saint Barts. The landing there requires essentially another dive to lose altitude quickly enough to remain on the swath of concrete that tilts down severely toward the sea. But Christopher likes to watch approaches, this one is unique, and his excitement overrides his usual uneasiness when Montana pushes the nose down. *Just a state of mind susceptible to change. God, that bay is beautiful.*

Pacing back and forth alongside EL TIGRE, Christopher looks wistfully at her sleek hulls, large, self-tailing winches, and coiled sheets. His eyes travel up the lofty, thick mast. Everything about the catamaran says power and speed to him, and he tries to imagine what it must be like to fly along on her, spinnaker bulging and straining as the force of the trades scream into it from the aft quarter. He looks back toward the bench where Juliette is sitting, reading a newly purchased spy novel while her tongue slides slowly and seductively up an ice cream cone.

"If I owned a boat like this would you spend the rest of your life exploring the world with me?"

She looks up slowly, after finishing a sentence, or paragraph. "What did you say?"

"I said would you spend the rest of your life exploring the

far corners of the globe with me if I buy this boat?"

"Absolutely not." Her eyes quickly return to the book.

"Christopher, how are you today?" The deep, booming voice catches him off guard as he is locked into a daydream involving exotic yachts, passages, good books, and a sexual predator for a companion.

"Hello, Andre."

"I hope you haven't been waiting too long. We're a little behind schedule and I don't have much time, but I do have some information for you." Andre motions for Christopher to follow him and they walk to the end of the quay, away from his passengers, now lined up and stepping onto El Tigre for the trip back to St. Maarten. "I've found your yacht. She's lying in Admiralty Bay in Antigua. Hundred and twenty-footer, super high tech... a real machine. PURITY. Portsmouth's her port o' call."

"Thank you so much, Andre. I wish there was some way I could repay you for all the help you've been."

"Maybe there is. I don't usually pry. But what you said last night...the way you said it. If this is really serious stuff, don't you and the lady mess up trying to be heroes."

Again, Christopher feels a strange closeness, a connection with this man he hardly knows. "Can we talk?"

"I've got to get going so I can get these people back in time to feed the casinos their evening meal. Why don't you ride along. Do you like to sail?"

"My mouth's been watering ever since I first saw El Tigre."

"We can talk after we get there. Get Juliette, I do have to leave now."

199

"I'd like to talk alone. I may go solo" Christopher says, evenly, staring directly into Andre's eyes.

"Well, handle it however you want to, but be on board in ten minutes if you're going to go."

Walking along beside Andre, Christopher notices for the first time that Juliette is not still seated on the bench reading. *So that's why she wasn't over listening to what he was telling me.* Unzipping his passport case, he scribbles a note on a small piece of paper, glances quickly around, then pulls the piece of gum from his mouth and sticks the note with it to the back of the bench. Running back to El Tigre, he steps down off the quay, into her large cockpit, and meets Andre's warm smile from behind the wheel with one of his own. *All right, let's get the hell out of here before she gets back.*

"Everyone say hello to Christopher," Andre bellows. "And Christopher, say hello to the crew and world class revelers of the fastest sailing yacht in the Caribbean."

Two hours later, as he sits at the bar waiting for Andre to make a telephone call, Christopher feels as good as he has since arriving in the islands. The spinnaker run back to St. Maarten was spectacular, he is enjoying his new friend immensely, and the excitement laced with foreboding of learning the whereabouts of PURITY, and the implications of that information, has begun to set in.

"Where is Sam today? Or are you two not the item you seemed to be when we met last night."

The tall, black man chuckles softly as he pulls out a stool and sits down next to Christopher. "She's back on board Zulu Warrior, doing some chores. That's the yacht she arrived on, and I imagine the yacht she'll leave on. And that may keep us from being an item for much longer. If we ever were one. She's terrific. Some guy's gonna' get real lucky one of these days. So, my friend, is there any way I can help you with any of this?"

"Can we move to that table in the corner?" Christopher asks as he leaves a five-dollar bill on the bar for the two-dollar beer. "I get the feeling I don't need to ask if I can trust you."

"No, you don't. But if it will make you feel better, go ahead."

As soon as they are seated, Christopher looks straight into the dark, intense eyes, and asks, "Have you heard anything about the skier who was killed at the World Cup ski races in Zermatt?"

"Snow skiing wasn't big in my inner-city neighborhood... a true hood...when I was growing up, so I don't follow it too closely. But I think I did see something about it on the news. Something about some heavy-hitter rich guy's daughter being involved, missing or something. Holy shit!" Andre pauses for a few moments, his eyes narrowing as if trying to pierce Christopher's skull. "She's on PURITY?"

"I think so."

"Just how sure are you?"

"Pretty sure. My information should be good. The circumstances...when...how I received it...the source. I'm pretty damned sure."

"Then why the hell haven't you been to the authorities? Man, this doesn't sound like the kind of thing to play inspector Clouseau with."

"I was also told if there was even a hint the authorities knew she would be killed."

"Yeah, I see. The old proverbial rock and hard place. Do you mind me asking how you got involved in all this?"

"I'm a writer. I was in Zermatt, Switzerland, covering the ski races and knew someone who knew something. They asked me to help."

"And you're too much of a good Samaritan to turn them down?"

"Not exactly. I was ready to go the authorities, have been a number of times. Even with the threat I think it may be the best option. But Juliette talked me out of it?"

"What does she have to do with it?"

"A lot like me. She was just there and knew someone."

"So why didn't you bring her with you?"

"She's stubborn, hardheaded as hell. And I'm not sure her motives are as pure as they should be. A bit of a thrill seeker. I'm sure you get the implication."

"Are yours?"

Christopher pauses, looks down at his beer and twirls the bottom of the bottle on the table. "I don't know. But I do know the most important thing to me right now is doing whatever gives Caroline Brockton the best chance to get out of this alive."

Andre slides his long frame down in the chair, crosses his arms over his chest, and gazes out at the large bay just below them. There is silence between the two men for some time. Then without turning his head, or moving a muscle, he speaks, in a soft, almost resigned tone. "I would like to think of myself as a good Samaritan too, or at least that I should be one." He turns to Christopher. "I guess we need to figure out a way to get this done. Our next move."

"God, thank you," Christopher's flat stare at Andre masks the enormous sense of relief, even jubilation that suddenly washes over him.

The puzzling mirages of distant landfalls from sea, particularly in the faint, first light of dawn, have been replaced with an unmistakable sighting of the headwalls of Antigua. Juliette and Sam are both still asleep, from sheer exhaustion, as Andre hands a cup of steaming coffee to Christopher, now two hours into his three-hour watch at the wheel.

"You haven't slept much at all," Andre says, "I'll take over for you now if you'd like me to."

"I can sleep later. I wouldn't give up a minute of sailing this rocket ship for anything. And last night was so glorious...I didn't want to waste it."

"Glorious for sure. And with a big measure of luck. That wind shift to the northeast is a bit unusual, and sure saved us hours and a lot of tacks."

"Do you think they can hear us?" Christopher says, almost in a whisper.

Andre looks to the back of the cockpit at the two women wrapped tightly in blankets, curled into fetal positions on the oversized air mattresses. "Naw, they're out."

"I was surprised when Sam was on El Tigre. I thought you weren't going to bring her."

"I wasn't. But I've always been a sucker for beautiful women, particularly when they beg. She said Zulu's leaving in a few days and if she didn't come she might not see me again. She'll fly back out in a day or so if we're still down here."

"Does she know what's going on?"

"Not much more than she picked up from you in Le Select. I didn't really have time to explain, go into detail, before we left. It was a last-minute decision.

For her sake, in case things go south, the less she knows the better. But she's here, so that's not going to work."

"Well, the fewer people who know. But you're right... she's here...already a part of it."

"Yeah, well, she's cool...smart as hell. Would have some good ideas. We'll tell her the whole story."

"Juliette's who we probably should have left," Christopher says, shaking his head and smiling. "Surely you've noticed she's paying me absolutely no attention. Hasn't spoken but a few short, very basic sentences to me since I got back to Saint Bart's this morning, and they weren't pretty. I haven't known her long enough to guess how long it will take her to get over me leaving her there."

"She's beautiful, seems like a real classy lady. Is there a future in it?" Andre's deep voice has lowered to just above a whisper.

"I don't know, though I guess I doubt it. I like her a lot, but I'm not sure if she's too serious about anything, particularly me."

"Do you really think the Brockton girl is still alive?"

"That's a tough one. I've thought about it a lot, and if I had to bet...yeah...I think she probably is. Guess if I didn't think so, this wouldn't make any sense. If her father pays them and then doesn't get her back, we'll probably hear something fairly quickly. That kind of news doesn't stay hidden. It seems they would keep her alive until they are paid in case they need a way out of it. But once they're paid, or convinced they aren't going to be...then, well, the odds would change."

"What do you know about her old man?"

"Rich as hell. A couple billion I think. But he never has been in the public eye much that I know of. I've heard he has the reputation of being a decent guy, low-key, a family man, though she's his only child."

Christopher looks directly ahead past the forestay and straining genoa and sees the boat he could barely make out just to starboard a few minutes before is now almost dead ahead of them. In the faint light of early dawn, raising the powerful glasses to his eyes, the position of the craft's bow and wake tell him she is on a course that could bring them close. But the distance is still too great to consider any kind of course correction. Besides, he has the right of way under sail, although he knows that often means nothing out here.

"Would you like to be worth a billion dollars, Christopher?"

"Sure, I've always thought I'd be an overwhelming success at handling wealth. You are talking about it being given to me, aren't you? I'm quite sure I don't want to work hard enough to earn that much."

"Yeah, I'm talking about it being laid in your lap, baby. No strings."

"I don't think it happens that way very often, but in any case, I'd sure like a shot at it. And you know what I think I'd like the most about it?"

"I'm waiting."

I'd probably have the Ferrari and all, one of these, a place in the Alps. But what I'd really like is giving it away. I mean, I'd be really good at that, selecting worthy causes, creating all sorts of philanthropic programs."

Andre looks at Christopher a moment without saying anything, then speaks. "Why do you say that?"

"Because I really enjoy giving, always have, comes from my mother I suppose."

"Do you give much of what you make, or your time now?"

Christopher looks down at the deck, then back up into Andre's eyes. "No. At least not enough."

"What makes you think you'd change?"

Again, there is silence between them.

"Jesus...that son of a bitch must not see us! Where in the hell did he come from?" Anxiety fills Andre's voice as he has turned his body away from Christopher and is looking forward.

Christopher looks ahead and is startled to see a large boat bearing down on them. For a moment he is confused, then realizes it is the same one he saw in the distance only minutes before, closing at a high rate of speed. Out of the corner of his eye he sees Andre reach for the binoculars.

"I can't see anyone on board. Let's tack."

Within seconds the port genoa sheet is unwrapped to one turn and handed to Christopher. He watches as Andre moves with lightning speed to the starboard side, pulls in the slack, yanks the sheet into the teeth of the self-tailing wench and looks back expectantly. Christopher quickly pushes the wheel to the right, the bow comes across the wind, and the winch sings with the fury of Andre's power as he cranks the sail in.

"Keep her high. I want to get a close look at these bastards," Andre says, stepping out from the shield of the main to the port side of the cockpit. "Well, I'll be damned." His words are slow, drawn out, the tone of anxiety and steely purpose of a few moments ago now replaced with one of surprise.

Christopher's eyes lock on the towering bow, no more than a hundred yards from them, and the enormous volume of water being thrown from its path. "What do you mean?"

"There's your yacht."

The sudden, shattering roar of enormous engines and churning water fill his ears as the huge, sleek vessel passes off their port side. He looks quickly over at Andre, binoculars raised, then back to see the stern has come into view. "Jesus Christ!!" he screams, although the roar has quickly subsided. "Purity." That's it, let's go after her."

There is no reply from Andre as he continues to look through the glasses. Then he steps back and glances at the compass, then back at PURITY, then at Christopher. "El Tigre's fast," he says, chuckling, "but that's a whole different animal. Besides, if anyone were looking and saw us turn around."

"What did you see through the glasses?"

"Nothing. They must all be inside, not paying a damned bit of attention to what they're doing. She's got to have radar, but no one must be monitoring it."

"Hell, maybe they were trying to run over us."

"They could have if they wanted to. Believe me."

"What's going on?" Christopher turns to the back of the cockpit to see the tousled main of red hair and gorgeous face of Sam peek out from her tightly wrapped wool cocoon.

"What these folks have been looking for all over the

Caribbean just nearly ran right over us." Andre turns toward Christopher. "Based on their heading, I'd guess they're on the way to Barbuda. The best thing we can do is go into English Harbor and talk to Charles."

Charles Overton is a tall, angular man with short, greying blond hair, the jutting chin and chiseled features one might see on the face of a Norwegian seaman, a sea bag over his shoulder. He was Andre's commanding officer for a time in the Navy, and Christopher's feelings stir as he watches the easy conversation and open familiarity between the two men.

Charles runs a yacht repair and hauling service in a yard tucked in the rear of English harbor, and according to Andre, had a lot to do with his own migration to the leeward islands after leaving the military.

As they continue to talk at the bar, Christopher, Juliette, and Sam take a table on the other side of the room. They make small talk, but Christopher's eyes continue to glance toward Andre and Charles, wishing he could be a part of their conversation, but reluctant to join them for fear of intruding.

When the two men finally come over to join the group, Andre introduces everyone, they pull up chairs, and the conversation immediately turns to PURITY.

"Charles doesn't know anyone who has met any of the crew or passengers from your yacht," Andre says.

"Surely they come ashore at times. How long have they been here?" Juliette asks.

"They arrived in the harbor day before yesterday. A few of the crew have been in, but they're a pretty formal bunch, uniforms, spit and polish, seem to stay to themselves. Apparently, someone flew in with a part of some sort, went on board for most of the day, then flew back out. "

"Charles." The call comes from the bartender as he holds a telephone out.

"Excuse me," Charles says, rising from his chair and walking to the bar.

"How much did you tell him?" Sam asks, her eyes sparkling with the excitement of having heard the details just hours before?"

"What I needed to."

"Surely he asked. I mean it must all sound so clandestine," Juliette adds.

Andre turns his head and stares flatly into the eyes of the English woman. "He won't ever ask. And what I do tell him, you'll have nothing to worry about. He'll only help us."

"What else did he say that might help us?"

"There are always guards on deck, and they're armed."

"How long will it take us to get to Barbuda? Juliette asks.

"Four or five hours."

"Are we going to leave this afternoon?"

"No," Andre says, "We couldn't get there before dark, and it's tough to anchor there without light, even in a cat. So much coral. Shallow"

"I think we have no time to waste," Juliette says sharply.

"We'll get some sleep, then leave here about two and be there at first light."

Charles has returned to his chair when Juliette looks first at Andre, then at Sam. "Do either of you scuba dive?"

"You're in the presence of a frogman, an underwater

commando," Sam says perkily, nodding her head toward Andre. "Actually, I guess two frogmen," she adds, smiling at Charles.

"Really?" Juliette looks straight into Andre's eyes. "I also dive and think we should take some tanks. Charles, is there a place in the harbor Andre and I can rent equipment?"

Christopher notices a lightning fast, almost imperceptible glance between the two men before Charles replies. "There are two dive shops here."

The island of Barbuda is little more than a large sand spit, has no elevation and only one small village with very few lights…all of which make approaching it safely in the dark a serious challenge. Andre has plotted a course that has them within a few miles of shore as they wait for first light. If she is where he thinks, the only possible anchorage for a boat of PURITY's size on this side of the island, there is no glow from lights. Either meaning she is not there or is blacked out. For El Tigre to remain out of sight, their line of sight into the anchorage is hidden from their position.

"All right, as soon as it gets light, we'll anchor and go see what we can find out," Andre says from behind the wheel, sailing EL TIGRE about as slowly as possible with only a loosely trimmed jib up.

"Can't we just sail around the island until we find them?" Juliette asks.

"It's a long way around, and a long stretch would be upwind. It would take too long. They might see us first. This is the most likely anchorage."

"We definitely don't want them to spot us," Christopher says. "It's hard to believe no one saw us yesterday. If they see

EL TIGRE again...it makes more sense to find out where they are and then decide how to get to them."

"It should be light in about an hour. Wake me up when the excitement starts," Sam says.

Christopher moves over to Juliette and takes her hand in his. "Want to go up and watch the stars?" They climb forward, lay back on the trampoline, and gaze at the sky.

"So, we might have them in our sights very soon. Then what are we going to do?"

"Well, we are going to have to find a way to get on that yacht," Juliette replies.

"And what if she's not still on it?"

"We have to find out first, and that means going on board. Unless, of course, you have a better idea."

"Look, I'm really sorry about the other day," Christopher says, in a soft, sheepish voice. "It bothers me that we seem so distanced from each other."

"I can assure you I have forgotten about that. There are too many other things to think of now."

"Well, if you have forgotten about it, why are you acting so cool to me?"

"Christopher...." Juliette snuggles up against him, kissing him lightly on the lips. "It's your imagination, or your expectations. Relax."

Pressing his body tightly against hers, his arms hold her close. He feels her breasts through the thin cotton shirt and the familiar stirring. Placing his hand on the warm, silky skin of her thigh, he slides it slowly upward.

"Do you know what?' she purrs, eyes sparkling

seductively as she gently wraps her hand around the rapidly growing bulge in his shorts.

"What?"

"There is no place to do this." She kisses him again, then quickly rises and returns to the cockpit.

Desire and elation race through Christopher's mind before confusion and resignation settle in.

He comes suddenly awake, not sure for a moment where he is, his mind confused, before the sight of Andre kneeling just in front of him clears his mind.

"Hell yeah, it's got to be," the black man says under his breath.

"What is it?"

"Take a look," Andre says, never turning his head, as he reaches back and hands the glasses to Christopher.

After a moment of intense concentration, of trying to see images in the hazy, grayish cast, one suddenly takes form. "Damn right. Should we back off before they see us."

"The main and jib are down, and without sails there's not much they can see of us in this light. I moved us farther out once we had a line of sight. We're so low...the spar is about the only thing. But you're right. We'll move back around the point until we've decided what we're going to do.

The looks of groggy sleeplessness dissipate quickly as they begin to discuss their next move; a current of excitement permeates the cockpit.

"If we stay around the point so they won't notice us, you and I can swim in."

"Juliette....please don't take this personally, but as well armed as these people probably are, and with what they've got to lose if they've done what you say...I just don't think I feel comfortable with your scheme." Andre's voice is flat, emotionless.

"How else do you suggest we get on board."

"Maybe we don't need to."

"Look, we have been over this again and again," Juliette says, her voice carrying a distinct edge of frustration. "Unless you're going to call the authorities, and we've come this far because we do not want to do that...we must get her out. You and I can dive, Christopher can take care of the boat and keep it where we need it."

"I can dive. I'll go with Andre," Sam says, looking directly at Juliette.

"How many dives have you had?" Juliette's tone is sharp, and her question comes almost before Sam has stopped speaking.

"Uh, four or..."

"Look, this is crazy as hell," Andre says, cutting Sam off. "This isn't Hollywood where a rich, beautiful woman joins up with an island boat bum and rescues the princess, killing the bad guys along the way."

"I just do not think we have a choice."

"We might," Christopher says, looking at Andre. "Andre has a device that can tell us exactly where the boat is...a tracking device. If we can attach it we'll be able to track her, we'll know we won't lose her."

"We know where she is...Christ, we are looking at her," Juliette says, her voice laced with frustration.

"Would you please wait until I finish Juliette."

"He also has something to insert into a through hull fitting that will start a small fire below, or at least what looks like a fire, with a lot of smoke. Enough that everyone might get off, or at least come up on deck. We should be able to see if she's there."

"And then what?" Juliette says impatiently.

"We're going to contact the authorities," Christopher replies quickly. "They can take over, provide some man and firepower if the boat does have to be boarded."

"I cannot goddamn believe it. Christopher, after all this."

"It's the way it's going to be. We don't stand a...

"If you were a commando...surely they trained you to rescue hostages, to do these kinds of things." Juliette's eyes are on fire now as she stares at Andre.

"Yes, with a team of highly trained...the best...special operations people in the world. And they also taught me when the odds are too great to go to plan B. Besides, we might have a shot at getting to her if they get off, or even if there's a lot of confusion in the fire. We'll be watching, and ready."

"Where did you get these devices you're going to use?"

"Don't ask," Andre says quickly.

"When will we go to the boat?"

The tall black man says nothing for a moment, then speaks softly, but with a riveting edge to his voice. "I will go, alone, and it won't be until tonight."

"But..."

"Surely you realize swimming up there in daylight in water this clear would be suicidal."

At one-thirty the following morning, two hours after El Tigre, totally blacked out, has stolen back to within a half mile of Purity, still anchored in the same spot, Andre begins checking his gear for the final time. *Five years since I've had a tank on. Seems like yesterday.* His mind seizes on that day, the day his career as a SEAL effectively ended, but also a day he easily could have died. He's never been able to fathom how Charles got him out of the pipe alive, how he sensed enough to follow him.

Silently Andre chuckles, as for the first time in a while he considers the irony of overcoming the claustrophobia through the hell of BUDS training, graduating, completing his first mission, then falling apart during a training exercise with the Brits.

Suddenly realizing he must wait no longer, he slips the goggles over his head, opens his mouth, bites down on the mouthpiece, slides under the lifelines and rolls off the hull. The rush of cool water envelops him, he straightens his body, and two powerful kicks start him forward. As he sucks air from the tank into his lungs…it all feels so natural. *Five years. Hard to believe.*

He slowly kicks down, to about twenty feet, just off the bottom. Stars are visible through the crystal-clear water when he looks up, stops for a moment, hanging suspended, breathing slowly. Falling into a rhythm, his breaths are slow, methodical, his concentration focused so narrowly they become as steady as a metronome. Shooting forward again with a few powerful kicks, he angles away from PURITY, knowing if he makes a wide enough arc he can reach the beach without his trail of rising bubbles being visible.

His proximity to the surface enables him to make it to the

beach without ever having to break the top of the water. As his legs and belly scrape the soft sand, he lifts his head and glances back. PURITY is only a few hundred yards away, everything is still dark. He stills himself, listens intently, and hears no sound other than the gently lapping surf.

Andre has decided he will swim to the boat without the tank and regulator, to eliminate the telltale bubbles on the surface and any chance of metal hitting and reverberating through the hull. Slowly, just under the surface, he will come up for occasional breaths. He will free dive to attach the tracking device and insert the fire charge. Holding his breath long enough could be a problem, particularly since he doesn't know the exact location of the fitting, but he's stayed down almost three minutes in the past, and he is confident he can make it all work. The timing on the device should allow him enough time to swim back to the beach, and through the night vision scope get a clear view of the deck.

After leaving the tank, regulator, and scope out of sight behind a couple of large rocks on the beach, carrying only the two devices and knife in the sheath on his calf, he sinks silently beneath the surface and pushes off from the sand. Moving forward, only a few feet under the gentle ripples on the surface, his strokes are slow and quiet but still powerful enough with the large fins to propel him at a rapid pace. Stopping dead still before raising his head to breath, there is no sound and practically no break in the water as his nose rises just above the surface. He moves and stops, moves and stops, until only a hundred feet separate him from the boat. His eyes and nose stay above the surface for a longer time now, scanning the deck for any activity, trying to judge the location in the hull of the fitting he must find.

Swimming slowly the rest of the way, head up, continuing to watch for any movement, he determines where he will dive with the charge, where he should be able to locate a thru-hull from one of the heads. Suddenly his body is close, almost touching the towering freeboard of the white hull, so that eyes scanning the sea from the deck will miss him. He inches along the starboard side.

Reaching the sleek, knifelike bow, he stops, turns, moves twenty feet back down the hull, quickly pulls the backing off the tiny tracking device, positions it two feet below the waterline and pushes it slowly but firmly against the hull. The adhesive will turn to paste, then harden to the consistency of cement, all within two minutes. Convinced it is attached, he moves back toward the beam of the yacht, then slightly aft of it. Drawing a long, slow, silent breath, he reaches for the knife on his calf, pulls the slender round cylinder from where it is wedged in the sheath, sinks below the surface, then rolls his body and kicks strongly to push himself down. The crystal clarity of the water allows light from the night sky to show him the mass and bottom of the hull, fifteen feet down, and his hand is quickly searching above it. Nothing but smooth, gel-coated fiberglass. Confused at not finding the opening after covering at least twenty feet, he's aware of the first burning sensation in his lungs. He continues to move aft...still nothing...wants desperately to come up but doesn't. Knowing he can hold on longer than he thinks, he steels his mind, locks his jaw, begins searching with the fingers of both hands. *Five seconds to get up, a quick breath, it'll be loud, then back down and away.* His chest screaming now, he knows he must go. Then the feel of the round ring, the opening. Frantic, he struggles to line up the cylinder, to push it through the hull. *Hold on!!* A sharp pain splits his chest, water explodes into his lungs, and Andre knows he's a dead man.

"We've got to go now. If he's seriously injured, he could

die if we don't get to him soon. He could be lying on the beach, bleeding to death."

"Sam, I realize how worried you are, but we could put him in greater danger if we go in and he's hiding, waiting to come back." Juliette's voice is soft, has a comforting tone.

"Why would he possibly wait until it's light to come back out?" Christopher is sure he can see the redhead's eyes flash, even in the dark, as an edge rises in her voice when answering Juliette. "He knows what the hell he's doing, I guarantee you that, and swimming back in daylight would be too damned stupid for him to even consider."

"He could have made his way to another beach, out of sight of PURITY, and be resting." Juliette's voice is again gentle, in response to the fire in Sam's.

"Andre said he would get back as soon as he could. You know that," Christopher says flatly, his head down, eyes staring at the deck. "I wouldn't have guessed it would take this long...but I still don't think we should search, try to find him just yet."

"It's been three hours, Christopher. We've got to do something." Sam pleads.

"Another hour and a half and it'll be light. If he's not back, we'll do something then. We should be able to see if anything's happening on board with the glasses. We'll go in and come up closer to them on shore."

"There is a better chance they will see us if it's light. We need to go now." Sam is not about to give up on her urgency.

Christopher replies again. "We'll have to take that chance, be really careful. Look, I'd like to go now too. But it could get crazy in the dark. We'd never see him unless we bumped into him."

"He'd see us. And what if we do wait, go in, and can't find him?" Sam asks.

Christopher hesitates, looks down at the deck again. "We have to go to the authorities."

Juliette's reply is instantaneous. "Terrific, Christopher. Now we're going to get Caroline Brockton and Andre killed."

"God no..."

"Look," Christopher cuts Sam off. "We're in over our heads." He raises his eyes, stares over at Juliette. "I've tried to be patient, but..."

"We should go back and get Charles if we can't find him," Sam says. "He'll be able to help and he'd want us to do that. They're very close."

The sudden, thunderous roar of huge diesel engines revving quickly to full throttle slams into them. Immediately on their feet, they frantically search the darkness. Christopher can make out nothing and turns three hundred and sixty degrees as the direction of the roar, now deafening, confuses him. He sees the large shape only an instant before he's blinded by the blast from the spotlight searing El Tigre.

"Jump, jump," he screams, mouth stretched wide, then his arm is around Sam and he jerks her, tumbling, into the water. Buffeted, tossed wildly about under the surface, he holds tightly onto her small body. Knowing he must breathe, the turbulence finally easing, he pulls her to the surface. They both cough water, then separate and float for a few moments in silence.

"Juliette...God, dear God." Christopher's scream is half panic, half despair. No reply. Scanning the surface, still choppy from the wake, he sees only debris, two large sections of the hulls, bobbing, pointed toward the heavens. An eerie silence settles over the scene, broken only by the distant, fading sound of the engines.

"Are you all right?" Sam asks.

"I think so. How about you?"

"Yes."

"Christopher."

"Juliette!! Juliette!! Where are you? Are you all right?"

"Over here." Her voice sounds week. He starts swimming toward it.

"Where are you? Say something so I can find you!" He's shouting now, trying to sense the direction.

"Christopher!" The voice is just in front of him. Suddenly she's there, draped face-down across something, floating, not moving.

"God, are you all right?"

"My head, I think I'm bleeding badly."

He sees the side of her face is covered with blood, brushes her hair gently back, but it's too dark see the extent of the wound. He looks toward the beach, then at the sky, then back to be sure of the direction.

"Sam, see if you can find a piece of the hull or something to hang onto and follow us. We're going ashore."

As he begins to kick his legs, the five-foot-long piece of teak, which had been El Tigre's bar and now holds Juliette, begins moving slowly through the light chop. Its full-length fights and waddles against the water as Juliette's upper torso and head lay across the width of it. Small swells begin to wash over her face, and he slows his kicks until they are only creeping.

"I'm going to be sick Christopher." She retches immediately, then two more times, and he stops until she lays her head back against the wood.

The journey to the beach seems to Christopher to take longer than it should. When they finally reach waist-deep water, he helps Juliette to her feet, and they slowly scramble up onto the sand.

Crouching over her after she lays on her back, the faint, early light allows him to see the gash, caked with dried blood, just below her hairline. An angry, purplish blue colors the surrounding skin, and he's sure it is quite deep, probably to her skull. But it's not very long. Remembering concussion victims should stay alert, he shakes her arm. "Juliette."

Her eyes are immediately open, gazing up at him as she speaks. "Are you all right?"

"Yes, but how about you?"

"Unless you tell me my skull is crushed, I think I will be."

"Andre! Andre!"

"Sam. Wait. Stay with Juliette."

"How far are we from where Purity was?" Sam looks frantic as she questions Christopher.

"Probably a half mile down the beach, around that point, then out in the bay."

Christopher and Juliette watch as she begins running, her stride awkward as her bare feet slip and grope for a hold in the thick, soft sand. Her desperation is easy to sense.

"Do you think he's alive?" Juliette whispers.

"I don't know. But it doesn't look good."

"If he's alive they must have captured him. It's quite

obvious they knew we were out there."

"I'm not so sure. That's what I thought at first. But if they were really trying to kill us...I mean for a reason, they would have come back to be sure we didn't survive."

"If he is alive, if they captured him, certainly they would know about us."

"I doubt it. He was a commando, remember, a Seal. They don't talk. Besides, it just seems like he'd find a way to try and protect us."

"I think Sam is right. We should contact Charles." Juliette says.

"Well...I don't want to talk about it now. I'm going to try and clean your head up and then go and find Sam...help her look. But it's going to be hard as hell to talk me out of getting some official help."

Before she can answer, Christopher is up and walking toward the water. He takes off his soaked, clinging tee shirt, squeezes it out, wets it again, then comes back and kneels beside Juliette. His fingers gently push back her hair and he begins to wash the blood from her face and neck. The flow has stopped and when the wound is clean he sees it is, in fact, deep, but the bone is not visible. Kissing her gently on the cheek, he rises quickly. "My Mom always said salt water was good for cuts. I'll be back soon. Try to rest, but don't go to sleep. In case you have a concussion, you need to stay alert."

"I'll be fine. I want to come with you."

"Any exercise will make your blood pump and you'll bleed again. Please stay here, quiet for a while, but awake." Giving her no time to react, he moves quickly away.

As he steps over the rocks and rounds the point that separates the two long stretches of white sand, he can see for another quarter mile or so in the growing light. No sign of Sam. Continuing along the water's edge, his eyes try to pick out anything that might indicate Andre was on this beach, in the water, anything that might be a clue.

Walking the entire length of beach until it stops against a row of gnarly, scrubby trees, rocks and brush, Christopher pauses. Here the coastline turns back in and is uneven, with a small band of sand under a low hill covered with more brush, rocks, and small, cactus-like plants. Checking his position again, he is sure the beach he has just covered is the one PURITY was anchored off. He has seen nothing unusual, no sign of Andre having been here, nothing in the water close to the beach. Starting back, retracing his steps, he again lowers his eyes and tries to concentrate. Periodically he glances inland, trying to scan the fifty feet or so of beach up to the brush. After a few minutes he looks up, ahead, and sees Sam, sitting just beyond the water, arms hugging her knees, face turned out to the sea. He quickens his pace and in a few moments is beside her. She doesn't acknowledge him.

"Where were you when I walked by?"

"I found a trail off the beach and walked down it."

"Have you seen anything?"

There's a long silence. She still looks straight ahead. "No."

Christopher waits for her to continue...waits...

"Do you..."

"He's probably dead, isn't he?" Her voice is flat, drained of emotion.

"I...I don't know, but I don't think...we just don't know enough about what happened. I mean...I think there's a good chance he's still alive."

"But if he is, they probably have him. And that may be worse." She turns her head slowly, looks up at him, tears sliding down her cheeks, her eyes red.

"You really love him, don't you?"

"I think so, but I'm not sure what that means…after only a week. I was probably going to get back on Zulu and not see him for a long time. Maybe never. He's just…" She lowers her head to her knees, and Christopher hears her begin to sob, watches her shoulders shake.

Raising her head, she sniffs two or three times, wipes her eyes and face with the back of her hand. "He's just such a wonderful human being."

"I haven't known him as long or as well as you have," he replies, in a soft, gentle voice. "But from what I do know…I couldn't agree more."

"I'd like you to wait before going to the authorities," she says. "At least until we can talk to Charles."

He wants to object, knows he should disagree, but knows he won't. "All right."

"How far out do you think she was anchored." How far off the beach?" She looks up and into his eyes.

"Probably not more than a hundred yards. Andre said the anchorage was close to shore, an open area after you thread through a field of coral heads. But a boat that size would need some relatively deep water."

"I'm going to swim out and take a look," she says, standing up.

"I'll go with you."

They wade in until the water is waist deep, then push off and begin stroking steadily, side by side. She is a strong swimmer, and Christopher has to exert himself to keep up. When they are far enough off the beach they begin swimming in lazy circles, peering down. Without goggles the bottom appears hazy, even with the crystal clarity of the water. And their eyes can only stay open until the burn of the salt is too much. Anything of significance might be spotted, but nothing is, and they continue circling, moving away from the beach.

Suddenly he sees the flash, a reflection off steel, stops and hangs in the water. *What...the knife. Should I tell her, try to go down.* He looks around. She is right beside him, motionless, staring along with him. They both lift their faces from the surface.

"I'll go down and see if I can reach it," she says.

She flips over, kicks, and slides down. Then he goes back under. She is well below him, but still with a lot of distance between her and the glint on the ocean's floor when she starts back up.

"It's...too deep." Her words come in gasps. "Must be twenty-five feet, maybe more. If I had fins."

"I'd try. But I can't come close to getting down that far and then back up."

"Let's move into shallower water and keep looking."

For another fifteen minutes they comb the bottom, seeing nothing of interest. The salt is now burning so badly in Christopher's eyes that he can only look down for a few seconds. He wants to go back to the beach, knows they will see nothing else this close to shore.

When they finally give up Sam walks out of the water ahead of him, her thin white cotton shirt and shorts clinging to her body. Without underwear every curve and crevasse of her legs and bottom are accentuated by the wet, transparent material. Feeling his heat rise, he is sickened by it, then forgets his guilt when she turns and he is staring at the perfect breasts.

After walking to the small village on Barbuda and locating a phone, Sam uses the number for Charles Andre had her memorize. She explains very little before he tells her a plane will pick them up shortly. Within a couple of hours, the three of them are in a small, four-seat seaplane half-way back to Saint Barts. Slumping in his seat next to the pilot, staring out the window at nothing, Christopher wonders if he's ever felt worse than he does at this moment. Since the Interpol agents broke into his room that first morning, he has been anxious, nervous, but with an edge of excitement. Now he's scared. Sad. Exhausted. Confused. And indecisive. Looking for help, comfort, but seeing none anywhere. Dropping his head, he wants desperately to sleep, to escape his misery, but the drone of the engine and pitching of the small plane bring him back each time he starts to doze off.

All three passengers are too tired, listless, mired in their own troubling thoughts, to look out the window as they cross the coast of St. Barts. A couple of thousand feet below and off to the right a large yacht sparkles white in the bright midday sun, riding alone at anchor just outside the surf and reef that guards a small cove.

Pitch black darkness greets him when he awakens. Before looking at his watch he gets up and peeks through the curtains. Also dark outside. Flipping on the light switch he sees it is 9:20 P.M., five hours since he collapsed across the bed in their room. Severe hunger pangs knaw immediately, he realizes more sleep will be impossible, and Christopher decides to go into town, to eat alone, so he can think. Juliette and Sam are still asleep.

The hot shower feels luxurious, but he pulls himself away after only a few minutes of standing, eyes closed, head tilted back, water cascading over his face and down his body. Deciding not to shave, he dresses quickly and walks outside. Leaving the moke in case the two women want or need it, he walks across the street to the black, 70's vintage Mercedes taxi with the dice hanging from the mirror that seems to always be parked in the same spot, and enlists a ride to town. On the way he thinks for a few moments about the large cheeseburgers and fries at Le Select before it occurs to him that Jean Paul might question him about Andre's whereabouts. He decides he'll walk through town and try someplace new, and if he doesn't find anything to his liking, continue up the hill to Le Hibiscus and the beautiful French waitress. By the time he has asked the driver to stop and let him out he has opted for the hike up the hill. The view down over the harbor will set a proper mood for serious decision making.

A gentle breeze caresses his face as he stares at the surrounding arc of lights, spreading down and sparkling below him, reflecting in the black water of the night. It's as beautiful, maybe more so, than he remembers. As is the waitress. The stuffed Grouper is divine, an almost creamy consistency of rich, spiced flavor that dissolves quickly in his mouth, flooding every taste bud with ecstasy. The ambience is extraordinary; perhaps for him, he decides, the ultimate, and he spends the time over two beers and the first half of his meal trying to enjoy it. His thoughts shift constantly, but avoid dealing with the critical issues at hand, drifting from melancholy memory to amused perspective, to another memory.

As his plate and third beer are almost empty, his thoughts become less expansive, quit pinballing, and come to rest squarely on the work that lies ahead. *Charles could be on the island by now. What the hell's he doing if he's here? Asked for a day at most. Commando stuff. Is it really like the books? Seemed like it with Andre. Jesus...maybe he can do something, at least find out. What about Sam? Tomorrow night. That's the latest. I'd better call Joe. Should wait till the last minute. The book. He laughs to himself, a smile spreads across face. Should I be keeping a journal, writing stuff down? Christ, if I can't remember this...*

After another beer, definite, irreversible plans of action now settled, Christopher decides to rest his mind. The transition from tired, relaxed state of melancholy to one of energy driven optimism is complete. The decision he now faces is whether to continue stealing looks at the gorgeous waitress or move down to Le Select for more beers. Alcohol has rendered questions from Jean-Paul about Andre no longer a problem. Slightly annoyed at this indecisiveness, he acts quickly, leaves more money on the table than he should, and heads toward the door.

Momentarily sheltered from the breeze, the heat feels sticky and he's glad his route is downhill. The syncopated rhythm and lilting voice of Bob Marley, or perhaps Jimmy Cliff, flows up to him, lifting his mood another notch. Christopher whistles along the last fifty yards to the entrance to Le Select. As he starts to walk into the courtyard, he sees her, a block away and across the street, at the intersection, by the moke. Even at this distance, the height, black denim shirt tied at the waist, thigh length black tights, short black hair are unmistakable. Changing direction, he starts to yell, then notices the man in the shadows. An internal alarm, something causes him to dart behind a tree. For a few minutes he doesn't move, looks back to see if he's being watched, tries to listen, to look. He sees him step out of the shadows, and the two of them begin to walk, across the intersection and up the street. Christopher lets them move about fifty yards, then follows.

The scooter is a block away and they both climb on, the man in front and in charge. Cristopher peers from behind the side of a shop until he hears the whine of the motor and sees the scooter move slowly forward, then runs as quietly as he can toward the entrance to the quay and the two or three waiting taxis. His eyes stay locked on the scooter's route while he gives the driver instructions. They back up, swing around, and take out after the tail- light receding into the distance. *Just like the goddamned movies.*

The chase winds up over the spine of the island, past the top of the airport's runway and onto a fork to the right. They wind back down, then up again. Christopher leans toward the front seat. "Not so close. Do not get this close. Stay far enough back that we can just see their light, just so we don't lose them." The taxi drops back slightly, then attempts to rejoin. Certain he's not being understood, he reaches across the front seat with both arms, points ahead, spreads his hands, brings them close together, shakes his head. "No. No good. Slow. Slow." Spreads his arms again. The taxi falls back.

As they reach the peak of a particularly steep grade, Juliette and her companion slow to a stop, then turn left. Christopher checks his watch. Twelve minutes. He puts his hand across the driver's shoulder and pulls back until they slow to a crawl. After the taillight disappears, he pulls harder on the driver's shoulder as he says "Stop." Christopher reaches across the driver's body and turns off the lights, eliciting a hard, cold stare. Pulling some rumpled bills from his pocket, he drops them in the driver's lap without looking at them, and puts his finger to his lips, his hand again on the man's shoulder.

They sit in silence for a few minutes, then Christopher reaches again into his pocket, pulls out another wad of bills, sees the twenty, quickly hands it to the man, puts his finger to his lips again, and gets out of the car.

After standing still for a few moments, he motions for the driver to turn around and leave, then starts toward where the scooter turned left. A gravel drive tilts uphill toward a number of white villas, and he creeps slowly and as quietly as he can up the hill.

The scooter is parked outside the third villa he comes to, or at least a similar silver scooter. Moving as silently and with as much stealth as he can, he slowly moves to the side of the building, where the ground slopes down and offers more room to hide. There is only one window on this side of the villa and it is dark inside. Continuing around the corner and to the back, crouched low, there is another window, and a low light behind the glass. As he inches up, moves close enough to peer in, he quickly lowers his head after catching a glimpse of Juliette sitting on the bed, facing the man, sitting in a chair, facing her, his back to the wall to the right of the window, his upper torso hidden by the angle. Waiting a few moments, Christopher slowly raises his eyes to look again. They're in the same position, talking, not loud enough that he can hear.

Over the next few minutes Christopher's mind whirrs at a new speed. Then he hears a raised voice, a man's voice, and again he raises up to look.

Standing, her back is now toward him. Naked from the waist down, the creamy skin and gorgeous lines of her buttocks and legs flow from the black material of the shirt, cinched snugly around the tiny waist. Christopher feels his eyeballs bulge. She bends forward until her head and chest are resting on the high, four-poster bed, her bottom is arched over the foot, legs slightly spread, and her toes are on the floor. Behind her the man steps up, a leather belt hanging from his hand. Slowly raising it, he hesitates for an instant, then slashes it forward. She twists her body just slightly, pushes up on her toes. A light, barely perceptible pink mark runs across the smooth, pale flesh. Christopher never thinks about lowering his head, taking his eyes off what he is watching...until the man turns sideways...until he sees his face.

Chapter 20

B rian tries to cover his head with the pillow to kill the sound of the low, muffled groans. Groans of ecstasy. But how could anyone, he reasons, enjoy having sex with a monster like Ian; a monster he reluctantly calls his friend. There are three of them in there. Ian and the two girls. Two young, beautiful girls. And they, like so many others, seem to like him immensely. In spite of, or perhaps because of, the horrid way he treats women. Taking what he wants, daring them not to play along, not to hang on him and his every word. How can something that should be so pure, so beautiful, certainly one of God's greatest gifts if it is practiced in his name, by two believers, committed to him and to each other - how can it be blasphemed in this vulgar way? Yet still compel him to think...and yearn. He tries to stop the thoughts, cleanse his mind. But it is important to think, and wonder, about Ian. To Brian, during the time since they started across the Atlantic, the knicks in his crusading Christianity have become great wounds. Without Ian their noble quest would be impossible, could never have moved past conception, but his actions and personality go beyond merely raising questions as to the sincerity of his motivations.

Chapter 21

Putting the phone down after his first call, he hesitates a minute, steps to the refrigerator for another beer, then turns the small address book back to the page with the tabbed M. The process of getting an international operator is once again nerve rattling, but finally there is the odd, jangling buzz he has come to recognize.

"Hello. Hello. May I speak to Karl Mueller?" Christopher pronounces the words carefully, slowly, loudly. There is unintelligible language from the other end. "Is Karl Mueller there? Karl Mueller."

"Yah. Karl Mueller."

"May I speak with him please?" Silence. "May I speak with Karl Mueller?"

"Yah. Karl Mueller. Yah."

"Talk. Talk with Karl Mueller. May I talk with Karl Mueller?"

More German, all a complete mystery to Christopher. Then silence.

He slams the phone down in frustration, starts once again with the ritual and long wait for an operator, then rushes to the refrigerator and back with another beer. He has not missed the voice when he picks up the receiver again; this time it seems to take even longer.

"Yes. I was trying to make an overseas call to St. Anton, Austria. The person I reached speaks no English. I have an emergency for someone at this number. Could you please locate a bilingual operator to leave a number and a name. Again, this is an emergency."

His request takes very little time, amazingly little time compared to what he was expecting, and as he thanks the operator he hears footsteps just outside the door. The clicking sound of the key. It swings open; she walks in.

"Hello". Juliette has a momentary, surprised look on her face. "I thought you might be catching up on sleep." Silence. "What is wrong with you, Christopher?" Silence. "Why are you looking at me like that?"

"I followed you from town tonight." He searches for her reaction. She stares at him, not moving, no change in expression. "To...I guess it was his villa."

"And?"

"I....uh, saw the two of you. I watched what you did." Still no change in her expression...flat, eyes directly on his.

"And? Spit it out, Christopher?"

"Juliette...I don't..." He turns his head away, looks at the wall, at the ceiling. "I don't know...it looked like he was hurting you, but you didn't look afraid, like it was bothering you that much." Looking back into her eyes, he continues. "You never asked him to stop."

"It sounds as if you watched for quite a while. Why did you watch for so long, Christopher? What were you thinking as you watched?"

"Did you enjoy that?"

"Not with him. God no."

"But you enjoy it with other people?"

The sudden glare from her eyes seems to burn through

him. "Yes! I can. Christ! And I thought you were bright. You might also, you know, or perhaps it is something else with you. Everyone has a fetish or two lurking somewhere, waiting to be set free."

"Why Thatcher? He's a damned Interpol agent. One of the guys that broke into my room after the story was published. How did he know where...? Why...why is he here?"

Her expression softens, the fire gone from her eyes, the tension from her face. She walks to the wicker chair, collapses into it, body slumping, sliding down, her legs crossed. "I was not completely honest with you, Christopher. I'm sorry. It was a difficult decision. He showed up at the gallery the evening you were in Geneva, waiting to fly out." Her voice is low, her head down. For a few moments she is silent, then her eyes rise, and again meet Christopher's. "Part of the reason I didn't return your calls. I needed time to think. He knew about Peter. About my relationship with him. And you. He told me straight away he also knew about my little...secret, shall we say. And a few of my acquaintances who share my kink. Some rather prominent people on his list. Must have done a hell-of-a-lot of research over twenty-four hours. He made it impossible, at least to my thought process...impossible not to at least act like I would cooperate with him."

"And tell him what you knew?"

"Among other things."

"So did you tell him everything I'd told you?"

"Only what I had to. Enough to cover myself."

"He's been here the whole time, hasn't he? And a lot of others too?"

"No. He arrived this morning."

"And how many...?" His voice rises, then he thinks better of what he wants to say. "Why haven't they done something, once we found the boat?"

"He is the only one, and he is waiting. Look, he had enough on me, enough information to make me the object of a murder investigation and reveal my little kink and my friends. Some serious leverage, although the world wouldn't bat an eye if it learned a rich, globe-trotting, English heiress and another few celebrities and captains of industry occasionally like a little dominance and submission with their sex. An old story in my country."

She pauses, a wry smile creeps across her face. "It was obvious I also needed a bit of leverage, and I recognized his body language and voice said more about interest and arousal than revulsion when I answered a few of his pointed questions. So I seduced him. Not for sex. But to experience my take on my kink. And what I had discovered was his as well. Your male "fog of sexual arousal" was a guiding principle. My limits were non-negotiable. No sex, he would come to my apartment in one hour, and only stay for one hour."

Pausing, Juliette looks hard into Christopher's eyes. "I have a room. It can be set up for.... In any case, within the hour he was there...and thanks to a hidden camera, I acquired serious leverage of my own. Enough to set more hard rules and limits. I called him an hour after he left; a call I had promised to make to give him more information. My favorite thought now is imagining the look on his face when I described my leverage."

Juliette pauses again, waiting for Christopher to respond. Silence. Finally, he says, "Go on."

"He would tell no one, and allow us to find out what we

could, up to a point. I would keep him updated on our progress, anything I learned, but he would not come in with Interpol or any other agencies unless I asked him to, or we hadn't learned anything significant within a reasonable amount of time. So, you see, Christopher, we have it both ways. The authorities know, but only one of them, who will give us room and time to operate…but can be there quickly with reinforcements if we need it. Think of what you saw as my sacrifice for our plan."

"Why didn't they come to me again, try to squeeze me like they did you?"

"I convinced him your contact was, ultimately, their best chance. That they could not take the risk of your contact backing off if he knew they were involved. He didn't have leverage over you."

"What about the F.B.I., other agencies, do they know? Jesus, half the men on this island might be watching me. Come to think of it, I've seen a lot of white legs, black socks and Bermuda shorts."

"I don't know."

"Well, ask him next time, will you?" Christopher's are the eyes that now glare. "Now that I think about it, the bastard's probably too selfish, doesn't want to share the glory." There's a long period of silence, Christopher shifting his eyes from Juliette to the floor. She continues to look straight at him. "Well, at least when I go to someone…and that might be damned soon, I won't have far to go. By the way, how many more sacrifices are you obligated for?"

"None. He was furious when he found out about the camera, knew I had him. But aware he had not lost all his leverage, negotiated one more "punishment", because I had been a "bad girl" to film it. It didn't seem worth more argument. That's what you watched. And that's it. Over. Period."

Christopher walks toward the door, then stops, looks back. "Are you sure what I saw only happened because of blackmail, or as you say, leverage?"

"Don't ask stupid questions that I've already answered, Christopher. It's not becoming to you."

As he walks across the courtyard, he wishes he had asked about Sam. Thinks of a couple of reasons not to, then why he should.

Back at the door, he opens it and speaks loudly without coming in. "Where's Sam?"

"I don't know. But I suspect she may have arranged to meet Charles."

It's almost midnight and only a few of the local hard cores remain in Le Select as a bearish, bearded man with a lot of tough years on his ruddy face bends and sweeps around the empty tables.

"Is Jean-Paul here?" Christopher asks, walking up to the man with the broom.

"No." The answer comes without movement of the enormous head from its' eyes-down position, no change of expression from the face of red splotched skin anointed with a craggy, bulbous nose laced with tiny red veins.

Christopher stands close to the man, doesn't move or say anything else, hoping his silence and proximity will elicit another response. It doesn't. "Do you expect him back?"

"Doubt it." The man says, turning his back toward Christopher to work on another section of floor.

"Uh, look. I'm really worried about one of Jean-Paul's close friends. He may be in trouble, may be injured. I really need to find him."

"Walk to the top of the hill. Le Hibiscus. Ask for him." The man shuffles across the floor and behind the bar, never looking back at Christopher. The huge head and beard bend over and out of sight. Bottles clink.

As he steps outside the wide open, heavy wooden door of Le Select, Christopher's senses are razor sharp. Eyes darting, he listens for any hint or sound foreign to the tropical, night concert of insects and creatures. His thoughts flash to the attack by the drunken sea dog, and a smile crosses his face as he realizes how trivial a danger that seems now. Starting up the hill, a vision of the waitress appears in his mind, the soft, lilting French and pouting lips. While allowing the image to linger for a few moments, he is aware his sensory alert is still on. The image fades and his focus again sharpens. Two-thirds of the way up the steep climb, his eyes lock on two men in the shadows, leaning against the side of one of the small bungalows nestled close to the road. Christopher's stare is strong and unwavering, he senses these are innocents, and wonders about his steely cunning, resolve and courage. Will it carry over, or crumble when the true danger arrives? Has it always been there - but only when needed?

His breaths begin to come hard as his long-strided, rapid uphill pace brings him to the wooden steps leading to the door. After passing through the entrance, he questions the first person he sees, a young man with a tall chef's hat perched at a backward, after hours, at-ease angle. The quizzical stare reminds Christopher once again of his need for more mastery of the local language.

"Jean Paul. Jean Paul. Owner...uh...uh, Le Select." He points down the hill. "Jean Paul. Jean Paul. I must talk to...Jean Paul. Important.

"Oui." The chef holds up a finger as he turns and walks through a door.

The wait seems longer than the five minutes Christopher's watch shows. And then the sweetly accented "Christopher" causes him to turn and face the smile of the Frenchman. "How can I be of service?"

"Have you seen Andre within the last twenty-four hours?"

"No."

"I think he may be in trouble, maybe serious trouble."

"Come. So we can talk." Jean-Paul leads Christopher through the door the chef disappeared through, through the kitchen and out a back door. He lights a cigarette as they reach a walkway and asks, "So what do you know?"

Chapter 22

Joseph Brockton slumps down into the leather chair behind his desk. Trying to relax every muscle in his body and quiet his thoughts, there are only a few short minutes before his mind jumps back into gear. *Well, the money is there. Dirty money, maybe laundered money. I'll pay dearly for it, 20% for no more than a couple of weeks. Do I feel better... worse...the same? Relieved...more frightened and anxious than ever? A bad choice, but the best choice. Never thought I'd have to go there...but did what I had to.* Looking at his watch, it's 9:00. Lost in thought for the past hour, he gets up, grabs his briefcase, and calls for his car. Staying late at work has become the normal lately, as he dreads the distance, even open hostility Jane greets him with when he arrives home. It was an easy decision to keep the money transfer completely to himself. Only Carmen knows, and nobody Joseph knows, knows Carmen. *Come on. How many of his gang...the family...knows?* Tempted to stay in the office all night in case they try to communicate, he has decided they will wait until they can get a delivery, during business hours. And since he's being watched, an all-nighter might raise suspicions.

Chapter 23

Dr. Gerard LeFont stumbles down the steep gravel driveway in the pitch-black night, his hand on the shoulder of the man ahead of him for balance and reference. No lights, complete blackout. Just behind him a man carries two large, metal boxes, wrapped in black duct tape. Ian is ten yards further back, eyes and ears on high alert for any sights or sounds other than those of a routine Caribbean evening. When they reach the dock and the Zodiac, the three men help LeFont into the boat, stow the boxes and LeFont's bag, and begin to move at slow speed, with very little noise and no wake, toward Purity, anchored just outside the reef.

"Why didn't you say something earlier? Your yacht has been on the other side of the island," Jean-Paul asks Christopher, a serious and frustrated expression on his face.

"The last time I saw you I didn't know enough to ask. And if you'll remember the circumstances, I had just met Andre and barely escaped my own death." He pauses, the two men staring into the others' eyes. "Juliette and I, purely by the luck of the draw, are involved in looking for someone who may be in grave danger. Andre agreed to help us. It all must be done in secrecy...under the radar. He found out the boat was in Antigua, we went down overnight on El Tigre, followed them to Barbuda, and that's where we got in trouble, where we lost him. We haven't seen or heard from him since."

"Come with me. You can tell me the details when we're in my car," Jean-Paul has already started down the hill as he finishes his command.

The diesel engines are humming at low rev as the powerful lift brings the Zodiac, the men, cases and bags onto the deck of Purity. Each man moves with caution and concentration in the pitch-black night, and the first two out lift Lefont over the hull. Within minutes, the Zodiac is secured in its' cradle above the aft deck, the anchor is raised, the yacht executes a sharp turn, and heads toward the open sea at a crawl, silent and totally dark. Once she is a couple of miles offshore, Purity turns onto a northwest heading, and gradually increases her speed to a quiet, slow 10 knots.

As Jean-Paul's jeep carries them over the ridge of the spine of St. Barts on the east end of the island, Christopher finishes filling him in on what happened off Barbuda, and enough of why they were there to satisfy his questions. Cutting the lights as they descend the steep road into a bay, Jean-Paul slows them to a crawl, then stops on the side of the road and gets out. Christopher learned on the ride that Purity has been anchored in this bay, on and off, for much of the past week. There is a dock associated with the only house above the bay. A property available for rent or lease. A large Zodiac has been tied up there while Purity was anchored outside the reef. Jean-Paul's plan is to get to the house without being seen and learn what they can. Motioning for Christopher to follow, he grabs a flashlight and crowbar from the backseat, pulls a semi-automatic pistol from under the seat, stuffs it in his waist, and begins to walk, quietly, down the steep slope of the road. After perhaps two hundred yards they reach a gravel driveway that rises steeply from the road. Crouching, he starts up, walking just off the gravel to silence his steps. Christopher follows. When they are halfway up the driveway, Jean-Paul stops, turns, pulls a small scope from a pocket, and while still crouched down, looks out toward the bay. They quickly resume their uphill climb.

The house it totally dark and the entrance door from the main parking area at the end of the driveway is cracked slightly open. Jean-Paul hands the crowbar to Christopher without a word, pulls the pistol from his waist, then the flashlight, pushes gently on the door and steps slowly inside. Total silence. A beam of light from the flashlight suddenly illuminates the far wall. They creep through the house, room by room, until they are sure it is empty, then start a close inspection, with only the flashlight, back through each room. Jean-Paul breaks the silence. "Yacht's gone."

The strong smell of disinfectant and spotless surfaces, even in the kitchen and bathrooms, indicates a serious effort to remove any evidence of whoever was here and what they were doing. Back outside, they walk, upright now, down the middle of the driveway, cross the road, and stop at the wooden walkway to the dock. The beam from the flashlight comes on, and they look closely at every plank, the surface of the water, as they move slowly forward. Again, they find no clues. Christopher is following Jean-Paul, about to step back off the walkway onto the ground when he notices something small, white, in the dim moonlight, in the water. Bending down, he grasps a small piece of white plastic and pulls. From the water's edge, lodged mostly under the walkway, a small, white garbage bag is freed and in his hand.

Back at Le Select, behind the bolted door in Jean-Paul's small office, they carefully go through every item, any scrap of a possible clue, contained in the garbage bag Christopher found under the dock. A few dirty paper towels, gauze, Kleenex. Plastic wrappers, a single, yellow, hazmat-type heavy rubber glove, and the bottom half of a broken test tube. And a piece of lined paper torn from a small, pocket-size notepad with a water-blurred six-letter word and a number.

The number is completely indecipherable. The first three letters of the word look like Rec, the last three so blurred that only a long-odds, lucky guess would solve the riddle.

Chapter 24

His chest aches, throat feels raw when he swallows, and he's confused. Vision blurred. Disoriented. As he feels the motion and his mind begins to clear he realizes he's on a boat. Trying to remember, still foggy, he drifts back off.

A loud sound brings him back to consciousness, and a large man with blond, spiked hair is standing over him, staring down at him.

"Wake up, nigger. We need to talk. Who are you? Who the hell are you working for?"

Quieting his anger and flattening any expression, he again fights to clear his mind, with more success. "Andre."

"Andre. That's your name?" Probably not but let's move on. Why were you trying to blow up my boat? Who sent you? Who do you work for?"

As his memory kicks in he takes a couple of deep breaths. "It's hard to talk…to breath…can you give me a minute?"

"I ain't got much time, and neither do you. You better level with me or this will be your last conversation. Ever."

"I don't know who sent me or who, as you put it, I'm working for."

Rage flashes in the man's eyes. "I'd just as soon disembowel you right here," he says, pulling the large knife from its' sheath on his belt.

"I'm an independent contractor. I get a communication with instructions, usually not even a conversation."

"And why are you such a bad-ass that you got hired to blow up my boat?"

"I'm ex special ops. I hire out as a contractor. Independent. For private companies, individuals, sometimes governments. And I wasn't trying to blow up your boat."

"Then why were you trying to stuff a bomb up the ass of the through-hull?"

"I was told to find the boat and disable her for a couple of hours. Would only have been a small flame with a lot of smoke. Then you'd have been on your way."

"So what did they tell you…why you had to slow us down? Or blow us up?"

"I have no idea. Don't get those kinds of details. Just the instructions to do what they want me to do."

"OK, Mr. commando. Who's they? You must know something about who sent you."

"No. I work through an agency. They contact me on behalf of the client. I never know unless I guess."

The man…tall, thick, towering over Andre, who is sitting on the bed…is silent, his eyes boring into Andre's. Finally, he speaks. "Well, what the hell's your guess?"

"Can't guess. Just woke up on this boat hurting like hell. Mind, thoughts foggy as hell. Barely remember trying to find the through-hull."

"I don't believe a fuckin' word you're saying. But if you want to ever get off this boat you better level with me…or convince me you are. One more dead nigger would suit me just fine. I'm getting ready to kill more that you could ever count. In a week." He turns abruptly, puts the knife back in the sheath, walks through the door. Andre hears two bolts and padlocks close.

As Ian climbs the stairs to the open deck, he is aware of the yacht slowing from its' already slow pace. In the dark he barely makes out land with elevation, but as his eyes adjust PURITY continues closing and he watches the faint image of the point as they will round, then tuck in behind on the lee side. Before the grating sound of the heavy anchor chain running out stops, all of the crew and Brian are starting to unpack and spread the large rolls of dark grey duct tape, two and four feet wide. The Zodiac is lowered until it floats, but the two large outboards remain raised. Two men scramble into the boat, attach adjustable lines to the bow and stern, then to the deck of Purity, and begin to unroll the tape and apply it to the sides of the yacht, starting at the deck and working down to the water line. Brian and another crew member start on the rear deck, covering every inch of white surface, teak and metal on the hull, decks, and superstructure with the tape, cutting it to fit as they go.

Ian directs the transformation of all the surfaces of the yacht above the waterline that would be visible from a distance, or the air. He knows it won't withstand scrutiny up close, but he's convinced it likely won't have to. At night it will be practically invisible. In light, at a distance, it should look like a dark gray military vessel. He helps where he's needed, or to correct the mistakes of the others. For the most part, as planned, they maintain silence as they work.

Brian knows they will be finished with the tape within an hour, then leave quickly before the sun rises much above the horizon. Tired, hungry, thirsty, he walks down and into the kitchen area for a quick break, then decides he will check on her. He promised himself, from the beginning, he would be responsible for her well-being, and as much comfort as possible under the circumstances. Once he reaches the lower hallway and the heavily bolted cabins, he passes the first and gently knocks on the second. "It's Brian," he says. Within a few moments there is a return knock from the other side and he begins to open the padlocks and bolts.

Andre hears the locks, then barely audible voices. Moving quietly to the wall separating the cabins, he presses his ear against the polished wood. *Female voice, pretty sure.*

Caroline Brocton looks weak, tired, disheveled, but Brian once more notices the strength in her eyes. She tells him she needs more water and would appreciate a cup of coffee. Walking back through the door, he is careful to close the bolts and locks. As he turns there is a weak, scratchy voice, soft, from the adjacent cabin. "Please help me. Help me. I can't breathe." He decides to call Ian...then decides he needs to know what kind of shape their other prisoner is in. Not comforted by Ian's story about the man, he wants to find out more. Their success may depend on it.

With a different key he quickly opens the locks and pulls the bolts open, slowly pushes on the door, and peers inside as it opens. A steel vice clamps his arm.

With frightening speed, Brian is pulled inside, a kick across his midsection and a chop to the back of his head leave him in an unconscious pile on the floor, and Andre is through the door and into the hall. Moving quickly toward the faint light, he breaks into a sprint as he starts up the stairs, crosses the saloon, and heads for the starboard rail across the open area on the aft deck. Hearing shouts, then rapid gunshots, he launches, missile-like, with an explosion of speed, into a head-first dive.

"Don't shoot, you idiot," Ian yells. "Goddam...you'll wake up half the island. Go after him in the Zodiac. And don't kill him unless you have to."

Andre, still underwater and moving rapidly away from the direction of the island and the boat, turns to look for rounds entering the water, and sees none. Slowly raising his head just enough to clear his nose for a breath, he glances quickly to get his position. Back under, he moves in the same direction, coming up for occasional breaths, for at least fifteen minutes before adjusting his course for a distant point on the shore. Another twenty minutes and he is in shallow water off the point he has targeted. When he can stand on the bottom to rest, he stays in water deep enough that only his nose, eyes and the top of his head are above the surface. Andre remains still, taking slow, steady breaths, totally silent, until he finally watches the men climb into the Zodiac well down the beach and head back toward Purity. Once they round the point and are out of sight, he moves quickly onto the beach, crosses to the scrub, rocks, and palms beyond the sand, walks into the brush, tears off a palm frond, turns back to the beach, covers his tracks for fifty yards, then across the beach to the water. Once more he starts to swim, heading farther around the island.

"Goddam it, Brian. What the hell happened?" Ian is livid, his face twisted in rage. "Why the hell did you open the door?"

Still woozy from the blow that knocked him cold, in severe pain from what he thinks are broken ribs, Brian doesn't answer…just continues to sit on the bunk and bend forward with his head in his hands. Ian turns and storms out. "Fucking idiot!" When he reaches the open deck he yells, "Goddammit, goddammit, we gotta move. Get the hook up…now! It's light."

Andre is capable of swimming for miles, but all he has been through in less than 24 hrs., the ache in his chest, the zig-zag distance he has already covered…cause him to tire, slow his pace. Making it to the point on Tintamarre Island that is the closest distance across the water to St. Maarten is his goal, but he decides to angle back toward the beach and rest. No longer concerned about the crew from PURITY, he collapses onto his back in the soft sand not far from the water's edge. He's confident he's no more than a half-mile from the point, then just more than a mile across the water. Knowing the passage is a favorite with charter yachts, private and commercial craft going to and from the popular tourist destinations of Bay'Orient, St. Barts to the west, and Anguilla to the east, he's sure he can hail a vessel and a ride to civilization rather than have to swim the whole distance and end up on a rocky, lee shore in the middle of nowhere. *I'll get a log, piece of wood that will give me some flotation and I can raise to hail a boat.* Still flat on his back, he laughs at the thought of how attractive to a yacht full of white tourists a black man hoisting a small log in the middle of the sea will be.

Closing his eyes, he lies perfectly still for a short time, then with renewed energy scours the beach until he finds a limb large enough for flotation but light enough to raise with one arm. Heading back into the water, he begins to swim the rest of the way to the point. Conserving energy, in no hurry, he kicks as he pushes the floating limb ahead of him.

Coming even with the point, only a hundred yards off the shore, he sees a small boat with brightly colored horizontal stripes in the passage, angling in front of him from the east. *I'll be damned! The perfect craft to rescue a black guy floating in the sea with a log.*

Raising the limb as high as he can with one hand while treading water, he yells and waves it back and forth. Long before he needs to pull the limb down to rest his arm, he sees the bow of the island fishing boat turn toward him, and the black man driving it stand to get a better look.

Chapter 25

It's been two days since the money was deposited, and Joseph has heard nothing. Frantic, frightened, enraged, he must act as normal as a man can whose daughter has been kidnapped by killers...as no one else in the loop knows about the money. Jane has been crying more than yelling at him, and he senses she may be closer to going to the authorities with what she knows.

Fifteen minutes after Joseph arrives at the office, having finished a particularly long morning walk, Amy Hawse knocks on his door. After telling her to come in, she walks across to his desk with a package in her hand...and his heart feels like it has stopped. Other than a 'good morning' from each of them, no words are exchanged as she places the package on his desk, turns quickly, walks back through the door and closes it behind her.

Tearing into the package, he pulls the video cassette free, spins around in his chair, plugs in the earphones, and places it in the machine. Snow, a blank screen, more snow, then his daughter's image appears. She starts to speak in a soft but steady voice.

```
"Thank you, Daddy, thank you so much for
cooperating. Please, please continue to
cooperate, do what they tell you to do…
and I'll be with you and Mom soon. I
I love you…I love you."
```

Joseph's tears flow freely. His body goes limp with relief. But quickly it occurs to him to look for any indication of a date. Was the video made after the money was deposited? Or before? As he watches the video over and over, he finds no clue. His daughter looks tired, pale, anxious. But alive.

Losing track of time, deep in thought and consumed with watching her image and listening to her voice, Joseph is suddenly aware of another knock on the door. He quickly pulls the video from the machine, places it in a drawer in his desk, hides the box and wrapping in another drawer, closes the cabinet, then says, "Come in."

Amy again walks toward his desk, this time handing him a large, sealed envelope. Their eyes meet for only a split second, and again she quickly leaves him alone. Finding only a small, folded piece of paper inside, his body and eyes remain frozen after he reads the two lines of type.

```
Keep your silence.
We'll be in touch.
```

Chapter 26

Christopher, Juliette, Sam, and Jean-Paul are sitting at a table in the corner of the courtyard at Le Select, each with a beer in front of them, when the bartender walks up and calls Jean-Paul away for a phone call. It's only a few minutes before he walks back toward the table, sits down, leans forward on his forearms, and says in a soft voice, "He's alive. That was Andre."

Sam looks stricken, her green eyes wide with shock and instantly moist. "My God. Dear God. Where?" Tell me it's true?"

"He's on St. Maarten, headed to his apartment to get some clothes. I'm going to arrange a plane to get him back here." Jean-Paul's face softens as he looks at Sam.

"You're leaving on Shadow this afternoon to go back to Zulu, aren't you? She leaves in the morning, right?" Christopher watches tears roll down her Sam's cheeks as he finishes his question.

She says nothing, wiping her cheeks and eyes. After a few deep breaths, she answers. "I'm not leaving on Zulu. I'm going back to St. Maarten…now…as soon as I can." Her eyes shift to Jean-Paul. "Can you help me."

"Let's all go back. Now." Juliette's steady stare is suddenly on Jean-Paul as she speaks. "If you can make the arrangements, I'll pay for the flight. And a place to stay."

"Of course you will," Christopher says, shaking his head and smiling at her at the same time. Then turning to Sam, his own eyes suddenly moist, he continues, "I'm so happy for you...for all of us."

Sam knocks loudly as she calls "Andre," then depresses the lever and pushes the door open without waiting. Hearing the shower in the small apartment, she sprints the four steps to reach the bathroom, yanks the curtain back, and jumps into his soaking arms, squeezing him tightly as she is wracked with sobs.

"Sam" is the only word he can speak before she interrupts him. "No. Don't talk. Just hold me." Clothes and body totally drenched, a current of joy, elation, sublime bliss...courses through every fiber of her being.

Sam finishes loading her belongings into the large backpack, heads up the companionway to the deck of Zulu Warrior, and wonders if Alan will be at his favorite bar.

As she emerges into the lovely, soft, green-gold light just before sunset, the booming "Hello Luv" tells her she won't have to look. A couple of long strides and he steps onto the gangway, then the aft deck of Zulu, now tied stern-to to the government dock.

"That pack looks awful full. What the hell, Sam?"

"I'm staying here Alan."

"New boyfriend really persuasive, huh?"

She says nothing, stares straight into his eyes.

"Well, Luv...I'll never be able to replace that gorgeous little body and once-in-a-lifetime ass."

"Why did I know that's what you would miss."

His face breaks into a small, warm grin. "And your soul,

Sam. Most of all your beautiful soul. I've always been envious." She drops her pack and embraces him.

"Please stay in touch, Luv. Will you?"

"Yes. Definitely. I promise." She quickly picks up the pack, moves past him and onto the gangway. After a few steps she stops and turns. "I'll miss you, Alan. A lot. Thank you." Eyes moist, he only nods.

Andre has been inside the villa above the harbor of Phillipsburg only long enough to exchange embraces with Jean-Paul, Christopher and Juliette, when there is a knock on the door and he opens it to let Sam in. After a quick embrace, they turn, his arm across her shoulder, to see Juliette sitting at the large, round dining table, the dim light of dusk through the wall of windows backlighting her face. The others still stand.

"Come and take a seat. We're all waiting for your story." A warm smile covers the face of the gorgeous Brit.

Once everyone is in a chair at the table, with beers in front of them, Andre speaks. "I just remember being almost out of air, needed to come up, when I found the through-hull with my hand. I think something hit me, not sure, but I swallowed a lot of water, still 10 feet down, thought I was dead." He takes a swig from the Heineken, is silent for a few moments, then continues. "Don't know how long I was out, but I came to with a lot of pain in my chest and throat. They must have brought me up, pumped out the water and revived me. Huh…" A smile crosses his face. "Killed me then brought me back to life a few minutes later."

There is silence as the three others wait for him to continue.

"I was in and out, my mind was foggy, but I could tell by the motion we were moving. Don't know if they gave me anything. I was in a small cabin on a bunk. Really nasty guy, blond spiked hair, wild eyes, angry, kept calling me nigger...he was the only person I talked to. Wasn't a problem not to tell him much, act like I didn't know much."

"What did you tell him?" Juliette asks, a flat expression replacing the smile.

"That I was an independent security contractor. Had no idea who hired me...through an agency. I just get the mission. He thought I was trying to blow up his boat, didn't realize the device was just meant to slow them down."

"And he believed you?"

"Hell no. Said he was going to come back and kill me. But I left before he came back. I did hear a female voice in the cabin next to mine...heavy, multiple locks on the door. Could be the Brockton girl."

"How did you escape?" Christopher asks.

"Real dumb move by one of the crew."

"Did you see anything else that might help us?" Juliette has the look of a detective in the middle of an interrogation.

"In the couple of fast strides it took me to get across the deck and over the rail, I remember a dark, maybe black, smooth surface...it was still dark...on the deck. The first time I came up for air and was far enough away to look back, the hull was the same color. Probably trying to camouflage the boat. White gives off a lot of reflection. And they didn't spend a lot of time looking for me. Surprising. My guess is they're on a schedule. By the way, where's El Tigre?"

"In a couple of pieces, off the beach in Barbuda. PURITY ran over us, right across the rear third of the hulls, a couple of hours after you left. We're lucky as hell we were able to jump in time. Only real casualty other than your boat was Juliette's forehead," Christopher says, as she pulls back the dark hair to reveal a flesh-colored bandage. "What was left of her was turtled, ripped away hulls sticking up from the water. Sorry."

Christopher keeps the floor. "While you were away, after I told Jean-Paul what happened and what we're trying to do, he found out the yacht came back to St. Bart's. He took me to the bay where she anchored and the house at least some of those on board probably stayed in. A large Zodiac had been spotted tied to the dock that belongs to the house."

"Dark blue and gray? 30…35 ft." Andre asks?

"Yeah. Fits the description." Jean-Paul chimes in.

"What was in the house?" Andre asks.

"Nothing. Obvious it had been cleaned, meticulously…so whoever showed up wouldn't find anything." Christopher continues. "But we did find a small bag of trash they must have dropped by mistake, floating under the dock."

"And…?" Andre leans forward on his forearms, his steely eyes suddenly alive.

Christopher glances at Jean-Paul, who nods for him to continue. "We went through every scrap in the bag. One yellow HAZMAT glove, a broken vial…test tube…and a small piece of paper torn from a notepad with letters, maybe a word, and numbers…but only a few letters that the water didn't blur out." Christopher pauses. "A kidnapped daughter of a billionaire, a camouflaged yacht, broken test tube and a hazmat glove. The nasty guy on the boat – any idea where he's from?"

"British probably, maybe Aussie accent. Lower class, cockney don't they call it?" Andre asks, glancing at Juliette.

"Anything else about him that might help us?" Christopher and Andre are fully engaged…a two-man conversation.

"Something I keep thinking about. When he was threatening to kill me, said something like "one more dead nigger won't matter. I'm gonna kill more than you can count, in a week." Andre pauses, then continues. "I'm not sure if he meant he wanted to kill more than I can count in a week. Or he was going to kill them in a week."

Christopher's response is immediate. "Could your nasty friend's accent be South African."

"Yeah. I guess."

"You've got a lot of Brothers in South Africa. Way more than you can count." He continues before anyone else has a chance to speak. "If it all fits somehow, we're going to need some help. Some official help."

"I was going to suggest that anyway," Andre says. "Even if the Brockton girl and her daddy's money is all there is to it."

Juliette's response is quick. "They will screw it up. I guarantee you. We've got to find out more before we let them show up with an army and thought process that will get her killed for sure."

"Please don't take this personally," Andre eyes lock on Juliette as he speaks, "but I've got a writer, a gorgeous, brilliant philosophy student, a beautiful, smart, classy, wealthy lady…all with no special-ops skills that I know of. And a capable, highly skilled bar owner who probably wants to remain a bar owner rather than accept overwhelming odds he will die. Don't forget, the only reason we're having this conversation is because a dumb-ass in their gang kept me alive."

"You're too modest, selling yourself short." Sam joins in, looking at Andre. "You'd have found some way to get away."

"We're out-gunned. Way out-gunned." Andre looks first at Sam, then at the others.

"There may be a compromise." Christopher leans forward, rests his forearms on the table. "Assuming we can find out anything else that helps, somehow stay in contact with them...we might be able to alert the authorities and keep them on the sidelines, but close, until we need them."

"How do we do that?" Sam asks.

"Juliette has...shall we say...a contact and a bit of leverage with an Interpol agent." Christopher says, glancing quickly at the piercing stare of his current bedmate, then away. "He's in the islands. Has known the girl might be on PURITY somewhere around here, but nothing else as far as we know." Christopher pauses for a moment as four sets of eyes shift to Juliette. "If she throws him a bone, a little more information, and we play it right, it could work out."

"Must be some serious leverage." Andre says, a sly smile creeping across his face as he looks squarely at Juliette. "But I'm sure the boat has left the islands, is God knows where, headed to God knows where. Interpol, the FBI...have the resources to track and find her. We sure as hell don't."

"Yes we do." Juliette's expression is still flat, her tone matter of fact. "Where's the tube, the glove and the slip of paper?"

"In my bag." Jean-Paul speaks for the first time.

Chapter 27

Robert walks past his wife Jane, sitting on the couch with the TV tuned to a cooking show, dozing, which is most of the sleep she claims to get these troubled days. "Honey," he says in a loud enough voice to wake her. "Follow me. Please. She's alive." He turns and walks briskly toward their bedroom.

Since he received the most recent video, he has resigned himself to showing it to his wife, in the hope it will ease her tortured mind, if only a bit, and restore at least some confidence in his decisions. Only a few feet behind him, her voice is frantic. "How do you know? How do you know?"

Without saying a word he slips the video in, turns the TV on and to the correct input, and waits silently until their daughter's image fills the screen. Jane says nothing until the image and voice fades, then he hears the sobs. When he puts his arm around her and pulls her close, she doesn't resist.

Chapter 28

The unrelenting thrum and vibration of the huge diesels since they were revved to cruising speed are distractions, along with the painful breaths and aching neck that keep Brian from resting comfortably. He has tried reading his Bible, to doze off, to find a comfortable position, all without success. Worried about what his attacker might have learned, if he attached any other tracing device other than the one they found on the hull, if anyone else knows their whereabouts, his mind suddenly shifts to the beginning.

A lonely, isolated only child from a prominent, wealthy, but cold and distant family, he was in his late teens when his parents were killed in a private plane crash. Although much of his eventual wealth is in a trust he won't be able to fully access until he turns thirty, he is quite rich by most standards.

Long drawn to religion to spite his parent's atheism, he fell in with a group that welcomed and embraced him...included him as a member of what he sensed was as close to a loving, caring family as he might ever find. Their beliefs closely mirrored Evangelical Protestantism, but they were adamant that true believers of the Caucasian race were the only legitimate children of God. Over the years the sect turned more radically racist, and the more enthusiasm he showed for their views the more he became an acknowledged leader. Although not physically attractive, with a short, pudgy body and complexion problems, he was well-educated and well-spoken enough to stand out from many of the others.

A year ago, Ian spoke at one of their services, and emphasized the need for action to save the integrity of their race. Now yet fully radicalized, Brian was intrigued by his rough, loud, but dynamic personality. They met a couple of times in private, and a plan began to emerge.

Ian and his group were secular. Brian got the feeling their embrace of religion was pandering, but they nonetheless shared similar goals. While the total cost of their plan was out of Brian's league, he had enough for the down payment – leasing a yacht and the initial million- dollar deposit for Dr. Lefont.

Lefont was a brilliant French epidemiologist and infectious disease specialist who played a significant role in the early, landmark breakthroughs in HIV research. But before his work was complete or he received significant credit, charges of connection to a child pornography ring ruined his career and left him broke, bitter, and revengeful. Ian read an article about the sordid allegations against him, contacted him, and the rest is history.

Brian's central conflict never leaves him. The Bible and more contemporary religious publications have chronicled instances of the violence necessary to liberate believers and God's chosen people from the infidels. He is a true believer. But also a gentle soul, with a fear of being in the middle of any serious conflict.

How did I end up here? Is it really a noble quest...a holy crusade? Or am I just a gullible guy with a lot of money desperate for acceptance. And a total lack of guts to resist giving in to someone like Ian.

Chapter 29

Jean-Paul lifts the weathered and worn leather backpack from beside his seat, unzips the large compartment, and lays the glove, bottom half of the broken test tube, and the small slip of paper on the table. In unison, Juliette, Sam and Andre lean forward on their forearms to get a closer look. "Are we sure there is nothing dangerous on the surface of the glove or tube?" Juliette asks, looking first at Christopher, then Jean-Paul.

"No we're not," Christopher answers. "But Jean-Paul and I both touched them, examined them pretty closely, and we're not writhing in agony...yet."

The slip of paper makes the rounds and undergoes close scrutiny from each of the three who have not seen it. After allowing plenty of time and silence Christopher asks, "Let's hope there's an Atlas on the bookshelf in the living room? Or if not, is there a library on the island? We've got to hope the blurred letters are a place. We'd have to get the authorities and their technical enhancement capabilities to make any sense of the numbers."

Sam stands and walks into the living room as the others continue to contemplate the riddle on the slip of paper. "Atlas requested, Atlas produced," she says, placing the large, worn, hardbound book on the table. "But in French."

"No problem," Christopher chimes in, "our beautiful financier speaks more than enough of the language to make sense of an Atlas."

Christopher turns toward Andre. "Do you have any idea of

265

the range, speed of PURITY?"

"Size, design…I would guess 25 to 30 knots and at least a couple of thousand miles at that speed, depending on sea conditions."

Christopher replies. "Well, I'm guessing they're not headed to the US with Miss Brocton. If it does have anything to do with South Africa they should be going south if they can't make it directly. Has to be at least five thousand miles. They would have to refuel somewhere. At least once."

"Unless they abandon the boat and fly the rest of the way," Sam chimes in. "I think ten, twelve days at sea leaves them exposed for too long…at the mercy of whoever might find them, the yacht. If we accept some South African plot premise, we need to look for a harbor and an airport along the way."

"Ah…my lovely critical thinker," Andre pipes in. "The best bet, if time is their enemy, would be South America. Somewhere approaching half-way; south, then southeast."

Christopher pulls the piece of paper in front of him with his left hand, draws the atlas across the table and opens it with his right. Thumbing through it until he finds the page he wants, he glances back and forth from the paper with the blurred letters and numbers to the pages of the Atlas. Deep in thought, he is oblivious to Juliette's trip to the refrigerator for more beers.

"Recife, Brazil." Christopher looks up, then to each set of eyes. Silence around the table. He continues. "The three letters we can read are REC. If it's a place they're headed, on the way to South Africa, Recife would be the ideal place to stop for fuel, or to transfer to a plane. The route from there to Cape Town, or points north, should allow a trip by air or sea without refueling. It's south of here, then southeast."

Andre reaches for the Atlas and slip of paper, turns them, stands and bends his long body across the table to get a closer look, then looks back at Christopher. "Excellent work. Brazilian authorities can be bribed."

"Yeah...but it feels like I'm trying to make sense of clues for a made-up parlor game...not real murders, kidnapping, maybe genocide." Christopher again surveys the eyes around the table. "I mean...we've got three letters that could be part of the name of a person, a business, an acronym...a broken test tube, one glove...and the racist rant of what sounds like a berserk, crazy dude in one, one-sided conversation. I'd guess the odds of us having figured this out at about five percent. Against that, we're going to risk our lives and Caroline Brocton's, if she's still alive, with our gang of three special ops imposters led by one, and only one...true, qualified warrior." Again, he pauses. Silence around the table. "Oh...and we have no weapons, operational resources, or money."

"We have resources, depending on our plan," Juliette quickly replies with a flat, matter-of-fact tone to her voice and no change of expression.

"Look," Christopher says, staring squarely at Juliette, "We let the FBI know what we know, Juliette can do the same with Interpol, and we've done what we could to help. Let the folks who know how to deal with this stuff, who have the resources, handle it from here?"

"But there are a lot of ways for her to die if they realize the authorities know, are closing in...when she's no longer leverage. When she becomes more dead weight to drag along if they have to move fast." Sam scans each set of eyes as she speaks. "Isn't that the conflict in these kidnapping for big money cases? The family, the company, whoever is supposed to pay, doesn't want the authorities involved because they believe their best chance to get their folks back is to follow instructions, do it on the sly, and pray." She settles her eyes on Andre. "How many resources do you think the government would throw into a case like this based on our information? Coming from us?"

"Hard to say. FBI and Interpol for sure. If our wild assumptions about genocide in South Africa are believed, a hell-of-a-lot. But some serious vetting would have to occur, it would take time, and it wouldn't be pleasant for any of us."

"I'm pretty sure some of us already have liability for withholding information," Christopher adds.

"All the more reason to keep moving forward on our own. If there is more certainty to our information, or we can save her, they will forget about that." Juliette again confronts Christopher.

Andre looks at Jean-Paul. "What do you think?"

Silence as the two men lock eyes. "I think it's a crazy-as-hell longshot with bad odds. But if you're in...I'm in." More silence. "Can your man in Antigua help us?"

"Yeah." Andre looks down at his hands, clasped on the table, no emotion on his face. "But it's going to get expensive." He hesitates, looks back at Jean-Paul. "You sure you're in? This could get really crazy."

"Yeah."

Andre looks back at Christopher. "We have another highly capable warrior."

"Thinking about what might happen if we do this...quite frankly...scares the hell out of me." Sam, her eyes staring directly at Andre, commands the immediate, total attention of the others. Hesitating, then looking down, she slowly raises her head and scans each set of eyes staring back at her. "But we just may have the right combination of skills, bright minds…passion…and compassion. An intersection bringing together 'the right stuff'…if I may be so trite. That might give us a chance at this intersection of good and evil. It's a noble cause. And hopefully we are noble people up to the task. But we can't let that idea blind us to an honest appraisal of the challenges we may face. And the decisions we'll have to make." She looks squarely at Juliette. "If at any point a majority of us think we need to contact the authorities…we've got to make that move."

Later that same night, as Christopher and Juliette lie in bed, both awake, each lost in their own thoughts, he breaks the silence. "I need an answer to a question. Please be honest with me. I think you're terrific…in so many ways. And if there's anything I'm about to say that may offend you…well, I'm sure it's one of the main reasons I'm so attracted to you."

She says nothing, keeps staring at the ceiling.

"Why are you so stubborn about doing this on our own? Is it the wild-child heiress looking for an adventure or a firm belief in your strategic reasons? Informed, of course, by your incredibly quick and penetrating mind."

"I suppose a bit of both. But the "wild-child" doesn't take precedent. I really believe she'll die if they know the authorities are coming. Maybe not right away. But before this is all over." She pauses. They both still stare upward. "And there's the book. Or scoop. Before you get self-righteous and preach a sermon, hear me out. It's not in the top two or three reasons. But you could be a hell-of-an-investigative reporter. You just don't know it. And…"

Christopher waits. She doesn't continue. Doesn't move a muscle. A long period of silence. "And what?"

"Perhaps…just perhaps…I would like to use my extraordinary luck in the gene pool…my privilege…to do something worthwhile in the world."

Juliette climbs out of bed early the next morning, to find Christopher on the patio with a cup of coffee. Walking back to the small kitchen to grab a cup, there is a knock at the door. A jolt of alarm shoots through her as she steps into the bedroom for the short robe to cover her naked body.

"Yes, who is it," she says in a strong, steady voice, as she steps back to the door.

"Thatcher Wilson. We need to talk."

Jesus. "Give me a moment." Stepping again into the bedroom, she pulls on a top and shorts that aren't as revealing as the robe, heads back to the door, unlocks, unlatches it, and pulls it open.

"May I come in?"

"Yes."

Christopher is standing just inside the open doors to the patio, looking at Wilson as he appears in the doorway.

"Hello, Cabot. Imagine finding you here." A slight, knowing smile fills the Interpol agent's face. "Will save me time with both of you in one place. Have you learned anything else?"

"Not much." Juliette replies immediately.

"Well, we have. Karl Mueller, the trainer for the Austrian ski team, came to us. Peter Molterer gave him some early information, whether he was involved, or just heard it from contacts who had been around someone with loose lips. When Molterer was killed, Karl figured it was connected and worried he was next if they knew Molterer confided in him. He hid out for a while under the guise of mourning Nydegger's death, couldn't decide what to do. Said he couldn't sleep, had nightmares for a week. Then finally came to us for protection." Wilson trains his best stare first at Juliette, then Christopher. "I got the call in the middle of the night. The FBI, the Swiss and Austrian authorities had to be told. Mueller didn't give us much beyond what I knew – PURITY and the Leeward Islands. But he did say Molterer mentioned something about a terrorist plot. Maybe the girl for money was only a part of it. Do you know anything about that?"

"No." This time it's Christopher that replies quickly. "We found out PURITY was in Antigua, but by the time we got there she was gone. No trail, no disgruntled crew left behind. No directions in a bottle where to look for her."

"Yeah. We found out she was in Antigua. Must have been crawling with competing agents yesterday afternoon and last night. Haven't heard that anyone found anything else." Wilson pauses. No one speaks. "What's your next move? Are you going to keep trying to do what we are qualified to do and you're not?"

Again, Christopher speaks quickly. "No way. Now that you and the rest of the world's finest are hot on the trail, we don't want to get caught in the circular firing squad. Wish the Brockton girl had the same option."

"If she's still alive." Thatcher stares directly at Christopher.

"Yeah. Let's hope. You two may have private business to discuss," he says, a smirk on his face. "I'll get another cup of coffee and leave you alone."

Once he is back on the patio, the glass doors shut, Wilson

asks Juliette, "At this point you need to tell me everything you know. If you don't want serious trouble."

Juliette's expression is flat, but her eyes flash. "If I don't communicate by certain dates, or show up back in London, or send a certain message...our little video will be released to numerous media. Don't even think about threatening me. I have all the leverage. Don't forget it. Ever."

"So what do you do now?" Wilson's menacing tone has disappeared.

"Enjoy the beach, the windsurfing, and the French cuisine. And listen to the news to hopefully learn you don't screw this up."

As the agent turns to leave, he looks back at Juliette. "He knows, doesn't he?"

She hesitates, smiles. "Surely you don't expect me to answer that."

The Interpol agent slams the door shut on his way out.

Juliette steps out onto the patio. "Our sense of urgency just increased dramatically."

Christopher doesn't turn to look at her, to encourage any conversation between them. Hearing her footsteps back inside the villa, he returns to his thoughts. *Should I try to convince her again, now that they know? Now that they may be watching us as well as chasing them? Now that there's an army on the move to find PURITY. Two things I know. Juliette may be right about the chances of them getting her killed if she's still alive. And I'd love to beat Wilson at his own game.*

Sam knows within moments of her eyes opening that she won't be able to fall back asleep. Still dark outside, she doesn't look at the time, rolls onto her side and snuggles close to Andre's warm body, laying her arm and leg across him. Contrasting thoughts of security, love, foreboding and anxiety compete for a foothold in her mind. She wonders how long it might be…what might transpire…before they can lie together again and share a sublime embrace.

Chapter 30

Joseph is tempted for only a split second to take the severed finger joint from the small, covered container in the freezer of his office refrigerator and throw it on the desk in front of FBI agents McCrary and Waite. Opening his safe, he does remove the two tapes and notes he has decided to share, walks back to the desk, and drops then squarely in front of the two men, his steely glare never leaving the older McCray.

"Is this all?" McCrary asks. "We need everything. We'd be closer to getting her back if you gave us this when you got it."

"The hell you would. She'd be dead. There are no clues there. None. And yes, it's all I have. Now, are you going to be honest with me...tell me all you know other than she may be on a boat in the Caribbean? And you're hot on the trail." His stare still unwavering, he continues. "I'm guessing you don't have children, McCrary. Am I right?"

There is a hesitation. "No. I don't."

"Well, what else?"

"We've told you all we know."

"You sure as hell got the best of that trade." Joseph's voice is almost a growl...his anger spitting out through clenched teeth.

"Get the hell out of my office. I have nothing else for you." The two agents get up and turn to leave. Brockton's voice stops them at the door. "Don't fuck this up, goddamit. Don't fuck this up."

Chapter 31

For over twenty-four hours Brian has stayed in his cabin, sore from the attack, but also reluctant to confront Ian, who was enraged by his naïve decision that allowed the escape. Screwing up his courage, he walks into the steering and control room where Ian is talking to one of the crew members.

As Ian turns and sees him, his smile and tone break the ice. "So you're upright. Pain better or just toughing it out?"

"Little of both, I guess. Can we talk for a minute?"

"Sure." He glances at Michael, who immediately turns and walks out.

"We've got the money. We need to let the girl go. That was always the deal."

Ian's smile disappears, his face now a hard mask. "Well the deal has changed. We need her as leverage. If they find us, she's the only bargaining chip we have."

"Nobody knows anything about the rest of the operation. If they get her back alive, know her father paid up, they'll have no reason to continue to look that hard for us."

The large, blond man hesitates for a second. "Are you kidding me? I was hoping you got all the dumbass out of you when you let Mr. Commando get away. The original deal didn't include killing the skier. Or the hotel guy. We're murderers. Killed somebody really important. A national hero. They're all looking for us. Will keep looking. She's our ace in the hole…and only if we play it right."

"I didn't sign up for this, Ian. We agreed. When we got the money, we'd let the girl go."

"Even if they hadn't killed the skier, where in the hell would we let her go? On some deserted island? Wherever we let her off they can track us. At this point I don't think anyone has any idea where we are or where we're going."

"Are you sure? The guy knows where he was when he got ashore. He knows where we were."

"We're running a zig-zag course. East, then south, southwest, back east. We could be headed anywhere. And we don't look like PURITY from the air anymore. But if you're right and somebody can track us, even more reason to keep the girl in case we need her."

Feeling miserable, aware he's descending into one of his dark places, Brian walks quickly away, down the steps and out to the fantail of the yacht and sits on one of the molded lazarettes. *Knew it...or at least always had doubts. That he would release the girl as he promised. As I made him promise. Do I really believe it's an acceptable sacrifice if we're successful? Just one more life. But not one of them. Have I been wrong about the whole premise? Am I a monster? In the worst way? How did I let it go so far? Too late. Up to my neck. Only one way out. And I'm too much of a coward.*

Intersections

Book 3

Chapter 32

Jean-Paul's coconut telegraph has come through again. The captain of a private charter yacht on passage from the Canary's to St. Lucia, in the Windward Islands, reported what might be PURITY, well east of Martinique headed southeast. "He's a friend, got my notice to be on the lookout, said it was the right length, and through the glasses had a weird-looking dark finish."

Christopher, looking at the map, offers an opinion. "Based on the cruising speed from Andre, and if it's Recife, they're slow. May be changing course occasionally to throw anyone off who might see them. If they're going south, or east, instead of southeast…lots of possibilities to consider."

Once again sitting at the table in the villa where Juliette and Christopher are staying, the room that has become their command center, Andre speaks. "Charles has come through with flying colors. Everything we asked for will be at the airport by midnight."

"How does he have access…that kind of stuff should not be easy to get? And so quickly." Juliette interjects.

"Don't ask." Andre's expression is flat, dead serious, before breaking into a slight grin.

"Can I ask what we have?" Juliette replies.

"No more automatic weapons than this group of green horn desperados is qualified to operate. A few handguns, grenades, some smoke grenades, tanks, regulators, a few tracking devices." Andre hesitates, then looks slowly around the table. "And an affidavit for me to sign stating I'm crazy as batshit."

"Is there any system of contacts, any folks around Recife, that could be on the lookout? I mean...if our hunch is correct, if we've got the right place...from the maps it looks like there are harbors, inlets, places she could anchor, for miles around Recife." Christopher continues. "Assuming she'll come in the last 30 miles or so from offshore at night, blacked out...chances are really good no one will see her. Won't know where in the vicinity she is. Unlikely we'll find her by chance, without help. And I'm guessing if they do come ashore, they won't be in one place long."

"For the guy who's leery about this whole adventure, you're on top of it." Andre says as he leans back in his chair and folds his arms. "I had a brief talk with Charles, also Jean-Paul, about this. You're right. Could be a real problem. We're working on it. But it would help if we took a closer look at the map and identified the most likely spots for them to get off."

"Jesus...that's way under my budget. What the hell is it?" Juliette speaks to no one in particular as they all cross the tarmac, at midnight, wheeling bags and wearing backpacks...toward the ancient, nose-up silhouette of the DC3.

"It's the perfect aircraft," Andre replies. "Flies slow and low, has good range, lands on short runways. And won't remind anyone of anybody's government."

After climbing the steep steps, entering the sloping fuselage, stowing bags and finding seats, they listen to the deep rumble of the plane's engines come to life. There are no lights as they start moving, slowly, toward the end of the runway.

The five passengers, scattered among the twenty or so rows of seats, are silent during the taxi and as the plane pivots sharply to move into position for take-off. Sam, by a window, next to Andre, gazes into the blackness, her face void of emotion, her arm across her lover's, resting on his leg. Five rows farther back, Juliette snuggles close to Christopher, who also stares out the window. Jean-Paul, in a seat closer to the rear of the plane, eyes closed, dozes.

Christopher feels the old plane vibrate and shake as the deep roar rises in pitch and intensity, and they begin the long, lumbering roll toward takeoff. "Here we go." Juliette says, in a light, playful voice, squeezing his arm with excitement. He doesn't' respond, continues to look out the window, deep in his thoughts.

The exit from the runway is slow, labored, and the feeling of flying only a few feet off the ground takes him back years to another old plane, from the belly of a third-world country, in a very different climate. As they fight to gain altitude, the buffeting and bumps from the trade winds cause Juliette to snuggle tighter. Speaking almost the instant the thought enters his mind, he turns his head just enough from the window to allow her to hear, then whispers, "Will you ever settle down?"

A few silent moments pass before she replies. "And what do you mean by settle down?"

"Get married...you know...or at least stay with one guy. Have kids. Back off on the nonstop hedonism and adventures."

"You may have the wrong impression. Look, this is the biggest adventure of my life. Yes...the nature...the excitement of it appeals to me. That you have right. But as I keep repeating, I truly think what we're doing offers the best chance to save the girl's life. And if that's all we do, we've done a very, very good thing. I'm a more serious, caring person than you may think. I told you I like to do good. Make a difference. Help people."

"I don't doubt your seriousness. Your compassion. A lot of the reason I'm so attracted to you. But that doesn't mean you'll ever want to change your lifestyle. Settle down."

"I really believe in you, Christopher." She is looking up directly at his face, still turned slightly away from her toward the window. "I keep telling you...I think you can be a terrific reporter...write a great book. You're going to come out of this with some excellent options. And that's okay. There is no problem with a secondary, even ulterior, motive. Altruism is rarely pure."

"Hmmm." Deep in thought, that's the only sound he makes.

She continues. "Settling down may not mean the same thing to me as it does to you. What's your description – 'wild child'? Can't I occasionally be a wild child and also be a wife." Maybe even a Mom?"

"I suppose so." Christopher still does not face her, continues to look ahead as he speaks. "But if you're too wild...or wild too much...maybe your fetish could be helpful."

"Oh my. I'm shocked," she replies, as she lifts her head, stares into his face, and squeezes his arm. "Had no idea you can think like that."

"Not sure. Tried a couple of times. Attitude adjustment I guess."

"When this is over...we definitely need to talk."

"If we're both still here...and still able to talk when it's over," he replies.

"Christopher, I've got to teach you to stop being so negative. Have more confidence."

Without saying a word, he slowly turns his head and snuggles it against the top of hers.

Andre, having moved past the others to the rear of the plane as soon as they leveled off at altitude, is unstrapping the crate lashed down in the space where the rear rows of seats have been removed. Aware of Sam suddenly next to him, he says nothing, just looks up, then back down to the task at hand. The sharp screech of stressed wood and fasteners pried with a crowbar fills their ears moments before the top of the crate comes free. "Wow." Sam eyes lock on what's inside. "You guys don't mess around, do you?"

After a quick count, Andre looks up at the lovely face, shaded and highlighted by the dim cabin lights, only inches from his. "We need all the help we can get. And then some."

"Can you tell me, in military terms, what we have here?"

"Two M16A-3s, three Beretta 9MM handguns, four M67 grenades, two smoke grenades, scuba gear for two…tanks are in another crate…couple of knives, night vision scope and goggles, flak vests, first-aid kit equivalent of a field hospital, etc., etc."

"Charles?" Sam asks, looking only slightly down into her tall lover's eyes, who is still on one knee.

Nodding ever so slightly, he responds. "As long as I don't agree out loud I won't have to kill you." His face breaks into a wide grin, white teeth flashing.

"Are you going to show us how to use this stuff? Or just cut us loose?"

"That would be very risky. Good chance you'd kill or maim me by mistake. It will have to be classroom only. Sorry, we don't have the luxury of training time here."

How did I get myself into this? Am I over my head? Jesus...everything is moving so fast. Why do I have such strong feelings for this guy? This amazing human being? So fast? The amazing part, dumbass!

Sensing her silence and blank stare means doubt, Andre stands and pulls her into his arms. "Just do what I tell you. And nothing else." He pauses, pulls her closer, holds her tight. "I'm counting on being on another big cat with you, soon, on another tramp, making love as we haul ass off the wind."

Along the eight hundred plus mile first leg to Georgetown, Guyana, where they will refuel, the DC-3 makes several wide circles. Andre had calculated the possible positions of PURITY and thought it worth the extra hour of fuel they have on board to make the effort...even though he realizes sighting them in the vast stretches of ocean is a long shot. He was right. They don't. As they lose altitude on the approach to the runway at Georgetown, the quiet cabin of dozers and ruminators begins to stir to life.

Just before strapping into his seat for landing, Andre quickly moves along the seats that are occupied. "A reminder...we stay in our seats here. Curtains down. Just a quick refuel and we'll be on our way again."

The plane touches down in the pre-dawn darkness and continues moving, at a good pace, to a far corner of a taxiway. Andre pushes the curtain slightly open, peaks out, doesn't see what he is looking for, steps across the isle to look out another window, and sees the silhouette of the fuel truck moving on a parallel course, at a similar speed, toward where they will stop. Stationary for barely 30 minutes as they take on fuel, the engines, never completely shut down, rev again, they make a sharp turn, and taxi back to the end of the runway.

From a slight opening in the window curtain, Andre now looks toward the terminal and taxiways in the first, barely perceptible light of dawn, trying to discern any alarming movement or signs. He sees none. Ahead of him, Jean-Paul is also scanning their surroundings, as they move faster, toward rotation speed. Feeling the nose of the plane elevate and the wheels finally leave the runway, he sits back in his seat, satisfied and relieved.

With enough fuel on board, they have decided to parallel the coast and fly a slightly serpentine pattern between thirty and fifty miles from shore during the daylight hours. Again, on the chance they might sight PURITY. Having calculated the yacht should now be somewhere off the coast of South America, the old plane's passengers are all alert and peering outside as they head offshore. Everyone is seated by a window. No more cuddling, dozing, or reading, as the horizon continues to brighten.

Chapter 33

For the second morning in a row, the fleet of small, brightly colored fishing boats from the settlements surrounding Recife are approaching the designated, five-to-ten-mile offshore areas, where they will cast nets. And watch. Depending on the weather and sea state, it can be a perilous journey, and day. But with luck, highly profitable. Once they reach their assigned spots, similar boats that have been out overnight head back to shore.

Chapter 34

Christopher scans the water outside the starboard side of the plane as it moves steadily offshore...until his ruminations invade and capture his thoughts. Competing thoughts, but all part of the whole.

On a great adventure, with the most fascinating, alluring, bright, sexual woman he's ever met. Hands down the best, most sophisticated lover, who appears to derive sublime pleasure, whether giving or receiving. Who will introduce him to sexual adventures he's only dreamed about...or hasn't ever dreamed about...much less considered. Who seems to truly value his intellect, conflicted values and impulses, and deep, often troubled thoughts. His core. The gentle kindness. Who might actually believe in his ability to write about this adventure. And cause him to believe it. And...by God...who has lots of money. Unimportant to him in relation to her other qualities. Well, maybe not. Hell-of-a-bonus.

But as so often, he returns to the knife-edge difference between bliss and tragedy. She's admitted she might leave. And he suspects it could be in a heartbeat. An integral part of her personality and needs that may be inseparable from what so excites him. And they could all die on this great adventure. Or at least end up maimed. Or in jail for withholding information. If the Gods are with him, it all works out, and she stays...for how long? And can he continue to be himself, reveal more and more of his conflicts. Will that eventually chase her away? Does she have a time limit...for anyone?

The idea of the book takes over. Descriptions and organization have started to coalesce in his mind. But he readily accepts the difficulty...and luck...of finding a publisher. She hasn't boosted his confidence that much. He's sure he would have enough time to write it from prison if convicted of a crime associated with their adventure.

Starting to pray...he keeps it short. Doesn't ask for the pleasure, security and success he's been thinking about. Only health and safety. And helping what's right and good to prevail. Far too much chaos, suffering and pain in the world to be selfish.

Across the aisle, in her seat by the window, Juliette also looks out, but she too has lost her focus on the search for PURITY. Worry fills her thoughts, even fear. Is she going too far this time? Is her obsession for adventure, for maintaining a striking, commanding, exotic, avant-garde, sophisticated presence...in large part to hide her insecurities and guilt at being so privileged...will it get them killed? Can she follow through on her recent urges to open herself to Christopher? To share her secrets...finally drop her nonstop façade for someone she really cares for? Maybe in love with?

There's a chasm between my persona, my act, that attracts most men, intimidates many...and who I'd need to be to keep anyone engaged on a depth beyond the face and body, the sex, the always-on-the-move adventure. Is that person hidden inside me? If I ever have the guts to let her out. Have I been this me for so long it's too entrenched to dislodge? The wall may not be impenetrable...but it could be beyond my ability to remove it. If I can feel that other me...if I can imagine her...doesn't that mean she's there?

After a long day of watching...and seeing no sign of PURITY as the plane lumbers in the serpentine pattern twenty miles offshore, the pilot turns west and starts a slow descent.

Crossing the shoreline at low altitude, Christopher sees development, but also deserted stretches of isolated beaches. Their destination is a small runway at an old army base northwest of the Brazilian city of Recife.

Once on the ground, the real wait begins. They will remain on the plane until there is some sighting or information about PURITY'S location. There is enough food and water on board for a couple of days, and the hope is the bathroom and air conditioner will continue to work. Christopher crosses the aisle to join Andre and look at the black van moving slowly up to the side of the plane, where it will remain until needed.

Twenty-six hours have passed, a full night and day, and those inside the old plane are growing restless. There's only so much exercise you can get inside a small tube, and sleep has been fitful for all but Andre and Jean-Paul. Transferring the gear and weapons they will need from the crates into the van was accomplished swiftly under the darkness of night.

Chapter 35

Julio and his brother Juan have just pulled up the anchor holding their twenty-foot fishing canoe in place, cranked the small outboard, and started the ten-mile trip back to shore. Suddenly Juan grabs Julio by the shoulder and points out to sea. In the faint light of dusk, a dark shape is barely visible. Clearly some distance away, Julio kills the motor, and they watch intently through the binoculars they were given until they are sure the vessel, appearing to move slowly, is headed toward them, and the shore. Ten minutes later darkness has settled over them and the ship has disappeared. There are no lights. Now worried about their position, Julio again cranks the motor, and they move slowly south to be sure they are not in the path. Pulling the walkie-talkie from his jacket pocket, he relays his position and what they have seen.

Closer to shore, Gustavo, who has just arrived at the position he will maintain until dawn, moves his boat a half-mile to the south, on a line closer to Julio's position. Waiting to cast his net, he tries to pierce the darkness with his stare, only occasionally using the binoculars. Scanning the blackness again and again…he sees, hears nothing. There will be no moon. If the ship is moving slowly, with no lights and little sound, he knows he will have to act quickly if he is too close.

The night stretches on, the darkness now deep, and Gustavo only occasionally, half-heartedly, sets and retrieves his net. He is focused on the dark, and the large ship he hopes will appear. He will earn more from each night he keeps watch than he does in weeks. If he sights and reports the ship, there will be a large bonus.

At some point, with no awareness, his eyes close and he drifts into sleep. Jolted back awake, his boat rocking, he bolts upright, looks around, and sees the stern of a massive, dark vessel no more than a few hundred feet away. Moving very slowly, creating little wake for such a large boat, he wonders if he would have seen it if it were not so close. Gustavo waits until there is more distance between them, then slips the oars into the locks and starts to row. Not wanting the sound of the motor to give him away, he pulls hard on the oars and finds he can keep the stern in sight. Engaging his walkie-talkie, he reports his position and heading, that he is following and able to keep the ship in sight.

Andre picks up the sat phone as it buzzes him awake inside the plane. A pad, pen and map are on the seat next to the case, and as soon as he has jotted down the information and coordinates he needs, he is up and moving down the aisle. "Rise and shine. We've got some action. Be ready to leave on quick notice." He slips into the seat toward the rear next to Jean-Paul. Rapid movements and tension suddenly fill the inside of the fuselage.

Gustavo senses he is gaining on the ship. His oar handles rest on his lap, as he doesn't want to get too close. He estimates they are just over a mile offshore, approaching the jetty extremely slowly, barely moving.

On board PURITY, everyone except Caroline Brockton and Dr. LeFont are on the bridge, at the steering station, staring intently into the black night and lights on shore. Now in neutral, they have slowed from five knots to four, to three, as the momentum of the large vessel, with short bursts of power, will carry them close to the point outside the jetty where the Zodiac will be launched. Ian looks to Keith, manning the controls and helm, and receives an affirmative nod back.

"Okay, thirty minutes to go. Everyone needs to be in the Zodiac. Ready. In twenty."

Brian heads below, to get the girl and LeFont.

"Just south of Olinda Beach, outside the northernmost jetty," Andre says to Jean-Paul, as he holds the map open and points to the location. "My guess is they'll come ashore in the launch, to the beach. Shaped like a triangle, there are no structures between them and the road. Probably have a vehicle waiting."

"Makes sense." Jean-Paul replies, tracing a line with his finger. "No cover there. If that's where we try to take them, it will have to be total surprise. Fast. We'll need to be set and ready."

"We should hear from the boat guy again," Andre says. "Let's roll now, get as close as we can to where they'll come ashore. And hope we'll have enough time if we have to change the location."

Walking down the steep steps from the plane, single file, dressed head to toe in black, they enter through the back of the van. Settling onto bench seats on each side, each of them gathers the weapons and armored vests they have been assigned. Christopher tries to remember the instructions for operating the semi-automatic pistol. Andre and Jean-Paul sling the automatic long guns, with silencers, over their shoulders. A shudder floods Sam's body as she watches the others. She glances at Juliette, who appears confident, cool, and in command...while desperately fighting any visible signs of the jolt of fear squeezing her chest.

It takes about 15 minutes to arrive just north of Olinda Beach, and the van, with no lights, creeps to within a few hundred yards of the northernmost end of the beach and parking lot. The rear door opens and Andre steps out, stays very low for a man of his height, and moves quickly and silently along the foot and bike path that parallel the road, toward the open expanse of sand. Reaching the edge of the shark-tooth shaped beach, the night vision goggles allow him to clearly see it is no more than a hundred yards wide and exposed to the parking lot except for a stand of trees on the south end. He moves quickly across the sand until he can see the stand of trees are actually two large trees, with an open path to the parking lot, probably no more than 50 feet across, then a thick stand of trees another hundred feet south that continue down to the edge of the beach. Moving to the large trees, he takes note of the distance to the parking lot and a place the van might fit behind a small building at the end of the lot.

Crouched behind a large tree trunk, he scans the sea, the jetty highly visible in the greenish glow of the night vision goggles. Pulling out the scope, which allows him to see at a greater distance, he looks south. The shape of the dark, unlit yacht fills the lens. *Less than a mile off the jetty.*

Retracing his steps, he is quickly back at the rear of the van, knocks four times, and the door opens. "They're out there. We move, now, to the south end of the beach."

The driver, who came with the van, all courtesy of Charles's vast network, has the van moving, slowly, on Andre's command. Passing the parking lot, they turn left, and ease into the space behind the building. Andre sees an opening in the trees, motions forward from his kneeling position beside the driver, and the van eases into a small space just inside the stand of trees but still hidden from the beach.

Chapter 36

Ian, three members of his gang and crew, LeFont, Brian and Caroline Brockton climb into the Zodiac, joining the man at the helm, and wait for the lift to lower it over the side and into the sea. PURITY is slowly drifting, a single crew member at the helm, without power, a steadying drogue chute deployed, on a course that will take her toward the southern end of the jetty. Once the launch settles into the water, it starts toward shore, moving slowly enough that the engine noise blends into the sound of the surf and wind.

"Follow me, crouch low, try to stay behind the trees," Andre says. "When we are in position...remember...those of you with pistols...if I say "fire"...keep firing in the general direction across the beach. And high. Can't take a chance on hitting the girl. You probably won't, but the sound will confuse them, make them think we're more than we are. No one speaks, coughs, sneezes...no sound...once we're out of the van."

Andre leads them to a position behind a few of the larger trees, on the border of the sand, about a hundred feet from the water. As he turns, reaches back with his arm and signals for them to stop, he notices a black van pull into the parking lot midway across the beach. Looking back toward the sea through the scope he sees the green, illuminated image of the Zodiac move slowly inside the jetty. Turning, he points to the sea, then closes his fist. Hearts pound. Shivers flood spines. Jean-Paul removes the automatic rifle from across his body, checks the night vision sight one last time by sighting the Zodiac, and readies the gun.

Andre feels the familiar tension, but also the laser focus and steely, cool composure, as he watches the boat inch closer to shore. Through the rifle scope he recognizes the large man who steps across the bow onto the beach, an Uzi in his grasp, as the man who questioned him on PURITY. Three men quickly follow him, all with backpacks, two with automatic weapons, one carrying two large black cases, then a smallish figure, also with a backpack, who has difficulty climbing over the high, inflated bow, and what appears to be a slight, slender woman in a blindfold, followed by another man, who helps her climb out.

Starting up the beach single file, the men with rifles and cases scan the terrain, the small figure follows, stumbling along with his head down, and the man in back steers the figure with the blindfold by holding her arm with one hand while his other is on the small of her back. Making their way up the beach toward the parking lot, they come even with Andre, now peering intently through the scope at the figure with the blindfold and her escort. A split-second separation of only inches, as she stumbles, brings the instantaneous, smooth trigger pull, *phfft phfft* of the two silenced rounds, and an agonized, piercing scream from the escort as he crumples onto the sand.

Without conscience thought, Christopher is up and in a dead sprint, Andre yells "Fire"… and the still, silent night explodes with the startling fury of automatic weapons unleashed. Reaching the figure with the blindfold, standing, frozen in place, Christopher grabs her around the chest, pushes her forward until they both stumble and fall, then begins rolling with her like a log down the gentle slope toward the water, aware that rounds are kicking up sand around them.

Fire is coming back toward their position in the trees,

ripping off bark, tearing into the ground, as Andre and Jean-Paul lay down a wall of lead to shield Christopher. A piercing, unintelligible yell is heard above the roar of the firefight. Andre, eye still at the rifle scope, watches the men, through the green, smoky haze, backpedal from scattered positions, continuing to fire as they near the parking lot and van. Unable to sight the man with the cases, he resists the urge to take down a few of the others and turns his attention to the man writhing in agony on the sand, Christopher, and the person he is laying on top of as a protective shield.

As the incoming fire slows and he hears voices yelling at the van, Andre quickly makes his way to the fallen man, notices the growing dark stain of blood on the sand beneath his leg, and yells. "Christopher, we need to go. Now. Quickly. To the van." Lowering his mouth to inches above the man's ear, he says, "You have a clear choice. And you need to answer quickly. I can leave you here to bleed out, which will only take minutes, or I'll patch you up and you'll eventually be good as new, although your track career is probably over. But if I save your life...you've got to tell me everything. Understand. Everything!"

There is no hesitation, and the words come between gasps. "Okay. Okay." Just give me something. The pain's ungodly. I can't take it."

Andre quickly removes the tourniquet from his vest and tightens it above the man's knee, then in one motion stands and lifts him onto his shoulder as his blood curdling scream shatters the suddenly quiet night.

Christopher is now on his feet and has helped the girl to hers. Gently pulling off the blindfold, he looks at a lovely, pale, female face with a petrified stare. "I'm here to help you. Follow me. Quickly."

Andre reaches the trees and the others in a jog, with the man slung across his shoulder. "In the van, fast." Arriving first, he notices the engine is already running, knocks four times, and as the doors open, dumps his cargo onto the floor between the benches.

As the others scramble in, they see the open medical kit, Andre ripping off the man's shirt and injecting a needle into his arm. "Morphine...but not so much he can't talk. I'll give him a local in his leg. Jean-Paul, can you help me with the splint?" The van is moving before Christopher pulls the doors shut. Along the street, in back of the beach, lights are coming on and a few people are cautiously stepping outside. Smoke and the smell of cordite drift on the breeze.

When Andre finishes with the emergency medical assistance and the victim is stabilized and momentarily quiet, he looks for Sam and sees blood on one side of her face. Moving in front of her, he notices the small, superficial wound on her left cheek. "What happened to you?"

"Didn't pay enough attention to your instructions on recoil. First time I pulled the trigger it jumped back and hit me in the face."

"Sorry. Was hoping to avoid that much of a firefight. But then," he says, looking at Christopher, "superman here pulled on his cape and we had to cover him. Anyone else hurt?" he asks as he scans the other faces and sees no blood or bruises. Andre's face breaks into a broad grin as he looks at the girl huddled between Christopher and Juliette. "And you, I presume, are Caroline Brockton."

"Yes. I...I am. Thank you. Thank you so much." Tears begin to run down her cheeks, and then she is sobbing.

"Can we question him...get him to tell us where they are headed next so we can follow them?" Juliette asks. After waiting until the girl's sobs subside, Sam has moved just in front of her, bends down on one knee, gently places a hand on her shoulder, and wipes her tears and nose with a tissue. As Sam glances at Andre she senses a rare flash of steely, controlled anger through the clipped tone of his voice and hard eyes as he looks at Juliette.

"You've had your adventure. We have Miss Brockton. It's over. We're going to tell the authorities all we know. If he confirms what we've guessed, stopping a terrorist attack is a hell of a lot different than rescuing a hostage."

Michael arrives back at PURITY after driving the Zodiac at full speed from the beach. Once the fire fight erupted, engine noise was not an issue. Keith, the former Royal Naval officer who stayed on board, helps him raise the boat enough for them to board it again quickly, then returns to the bridge and helm. Turning PURITY onto a north by northwest course for Reykjavik, Iceland, he engages the autohelm, and brings the boat speed up to 10 knots. They will stay on board for another ten minutes, until PURITY is well off the jetty, then abandon her and take the Zodiac to a beach just north of Recife and a waiting car that will take them to the airport.

Inside the van on the long drive to Recife International Airport, south of the city, Ian has resisted the urge to scream his frustration at those who made it off the beach. Fighting to focus on what the attack and loss of the girl and Brian mean for their next moves, he is uncharacteristically silent...deep in thought. LeFont's question suddenly jolts him and unleashes the rage. "The car will be ready for me? Correct?"

"Fuck you, Doc. You ain't going nowhere. Everything has changed."

"You idiot." LeFont replies through clenched teeth, a mocking sneer on his face. "Don't you think I planned for this. That you were never going to keep your part of the agreement? Your plan…every drop of the pathogen in every vial…will do nothing, infect no one…without one more procedure."

Ian fights to squeeze out a few words amid the exploding chaos of his emotions and thoughts. And resist his overwhelming urge to kill LeFont on the spot. "Keep talking, Doc."

"As soon as I arrive at an address on this continent, you will receive a call on your sat phone. You will hear an address of a post office in South Africa, and the number of a post office box at that post office." Lefont pauses to gage Ian's reaction. Red face, contorted grimace…trembling lip. Silence. "Inside the box will be a box. It will contain a device and instruction for the final, simple task your men must perform for the pathogen to remain active once in the water." Again he pauses. "If I don't arrive at the house you will never know the address of the post office or box number. Also, if I don't arrive at the house within the next two days, a letter will be sent to Interpol and the major daily newspapers in Cape Town and Johannesburg that will detail every aspect of this operation, including names."

"What if I just fuckin' kill you right now? God, I'd love that." Ian's restraint has totally disappeared, he is on his feet in the moving van, his face a tortured mask of rage, towering over LeFont, his finger pointing only inches from the tiny man's face.

Without any hesitation LeFont stares back into the violent eyes. "That would be unfortunate for me…but also for you. You will have nothing for all your planning and efforts, will never get a chance to spend the money and will spend the rest of your life in jail. Unless the state or one of your hated blacks kills you."

"I'll just torture you until you tell me the address and number."

"Goddam. Are you so slow you don't think I thought about that. I can't tell you because I don't know."

"You gotta know the last step. The procedure."

"Of course, but I don't have the box number, the device, can't get one in less than a week, you can't get one anywhere. And by then the letter will be at its destinations. And, of course, if you haven't wired it as you were supposed to after I finished my work, the last two million must be in my account." LeFont's face explodes in pain as the large hand slaps him hard enough to slam his head against the metal wall of the van.

Chapter 37

Inside the DC3, their captive has been laid out across a row of seats toward the back, is resting as comfortably as possible after Andre and Jean-Paul have done all they could to stabilize him and ease the pain. Andre picks up the sat phone and takes it to where Caroline Brockton is sitting, across the aisle from Sam. "Tell me your parents phone number. You should call and let them know you're OK. But don't tell them anything else at this point…and tell them not to let anyone else know you called or that they know you're alive and well. Tell them you'll call again soon and let them know where they can send a plane for you. You'll be on your way home soon."

As the girl looks up into his eyes and tells him the number, he smiles down at her. "We'll give you some privacy." Andre points and the others move toward the rear of the plane and their captive.

"Ready?" Andre says, standing over the man with pain etched on his face as he lays across the seats, his left leg braced by two splints, the large white bandage showing the slow seep of blood. He nods. "We'll start at the end of this story since we need to know what happens next. If you answer the questions, quickly, we can have you in a hospital, quickly. Your choice." Again, the man nods.

"Where are they going from here?"

There is no hesitation, but the voice is weak. "Cape Town, South Africa. At least until tonight."

"Why South Africa? Is there terrorism involved."

"They have a pathogen. Deadly virus. It's waterborne. They want to poison the black population."

"Who's they?"

"Leader is Ian Carlson. Five others, including me, on the boat. Twenty more throughout South Africa. White Supremacists, racists. Radical. He's crazy."

"When do they leave for Cape Town. How?"

"As soon as everyone's off the yacht and meets at the airport. Chartered jet."

"The main, international airport?"

"Yes."

"Do they have documentation?"

"Yes...but don't need it. You can buy anything, pay off anybody, in this country."

"How does the pathogen work? How did you get it?"

Raising his head from the pillow on the armrest, he glances at his leg. "I'm bleeding bad again. Please get me to a hospital."

"You'll live. Unless you stop answering questions."

Laying his head back on the pillow, he starts again. "We paid a world-renowned scientist, an infectious disease specialist, French guy named LeFont...paid him a lot of money to make a waterborne pathogen, a virus that kills quickly. No antidote. Can't pronounce it. Vibrio Vulnicus...something like that. It's a version of the flesh-eating virus that gets in the press. LeFont said if it gets in the water source, the system, hundreds of thousands will die."

"Jesus." Andre continues to stare down at his captive. "Do you have info on the plane. Manufacturer, size?"

"No. Ian arranged it. Just know it's a private jet that can hold everyone and fly nonstop."

"What's your name?"

"Brian."

"Last name?"

"Richards."

"What happens, Brian, when they land in Cape Town? If they still do?"

"Twenty other guys will meet them, spread out to population centers, townships around the country, and put the pathogen into the water systems."

"I need a list of the systems they'll attack."

"Ian never told me. Said nobody knew but him. Until they all meet."

"You must have some idea?"

"I'm being honest. I'd guess some around Cape Town...heavy black populations...but I swear I don't know."

Andre bends across the seat and looks out the window, then straightens back up in the aisle. "There's a car waiting out there to take you to the hospital. We'll get you in the car. But remember what you said - you can pay anybody off, buy anything here. You want to change any of your story? Anything you didn't tell me? I'd hate to send some guy into your hospital room who doesn't care about your health. Or your life."

"No. Nothing else. I told you what I know," Brian answers, through the clenched teeth of serious pain.

Andre looks toward the others. "OK, let's get him to the car. Be gentle."

After placing Brian on the back seat of the car that Jean-Paul arranged, on short notice, again through Charles' local contacts, the three men join Sam and Juliette back on the plane. Juliette looks at Andre and asks, in a slightly annoyed tone, "Why didn't you ask him more details? Where in Cape Town? When will they arrive? Where will they meet the others?"

The elegant, tall black man is silent for a moment, staring directly back at Juliette. "The authorities will get all the details. You're going to call your Interpol contact, right now, and tell him everything we know."

"We can't give up now." Juliette's voice is now a plea. "You heard him. There are hundreds of thousands of lives at stake."

"I told you. It's over. At least for us. If you want to save all those people...you better call right now. There may not be much time."

"Christopher?" Juliette's voice hardens. "You've got to help me. Help all those people."

"Call the guy, goddamit!" Christopher's anger and frustration are palpable in his voice and expression. "Andre's right. Do you want this on your conscience? On your head? We're way out of our league. We can't waste a minute. Jesus. Are you that self-centered?"

Andre thrusts the sat phone in front of Juliette, who is still staring at Christopher...who stares back with equal fury. Rising from her seat, she walks to an empty section of the plane with the phone.

A deathly quiet…a cloud of tension…fills the cabin of the chartered Gulfstream GIV, parked on the perimeter of the airport. After setting the Zodiac on a slow course to the open ocean from the beach, Keith and Mick walked ashore and have just entered the cabin. Within moments the engines begin to rev for the taxi to an active runway.

At the same time, Dr. Gerard LeFont sits in the terminal's gate area, under an assumed name, with a forged passport, waiting to board a flight to Buenos Aires. His head is resting on his chest, cap pulled low on his forehead, as if he's sleeping.

Juliette sits next to Christopher after she finishes her call. "I'll be leaving to go to the international airport in Recife. I'm going to try one last time to talk you into coming with me."

"What?" Damn." Frustration, rather than anger, fills his voice. "You just won't quit. Let me guess where. Cape Town? Probably flying private, too. No expense too much for you to keep the adventure going."

She waits a moment, for his expression to soften. "Yes. I talked to Wilson, told him where to find Brian, but that I wouldn't tell him all I know unless he meets me in Cape Town. He's sending a plane. Remember, he doesn't have a choice."

"Why? Why can't you let them handle it? Tell him now. It's over for us."

"I want to keep my leverage as long as I can. And you need to be there too." She watches a flat look spread across his face. "The book, Christopher. It's a hell of a story. I'm confident you can write it. But you need to see the last chapter."

Offering no reply, Christopher slumps in his seat and looks out the window of the old plane. She is not deterred. "Look, I know you and I likely can't do anything else to stop them. But I want to see this out." She snuggles her head against his shoulder as he continues staring out the window without moving a muscle to acknowledge her. "How long do you think it would take you to write the book." She waits. No reply. Then finally, "Six months, five months, nine months, a year. Hell, I don't know. I've never tried to write a book."

"I'll rent a quiet villa somewhere...on the coast or in the mountains...the perfect place for you to write. No interruptions. Except for me trying the quiet, domestic life thing. God...I ought to know in six months."

"You've always got an angle, don't you? Always strong, determined enough to get your own way." Christopher's head still hasn't moved as he continues to stare out the window. "Guess you'd have chartered a jet, gone by yourself if your Interpol guy hadn't been blackmailed into sending a plane."

"Why can't you understand that such a major part of this is my faith in you. That you can...and need...to tell this story. And I don't want to leave you."

Chapter 38

Once the Gulfstar reaches their cruising altitude of 36,000 feet and is thirty minutes out of Recife, Ian walks into the cockpit. "Do we have enough fuel to land at Port Elizabeth instead of Cape Town?"

"I'll calculate it, but I'm sure we do." The man in the left seat of the two-man crew answers quickly.

"Please confirm that as soon as you can," Ian responds.

"Only take me a minute," the pilot says, as he opens a pad and checks a few gauges on the console.

Ian, his tall frame hunched over under the low ceiling, stares at nothing, his mind racing.

"Yes, we can make it."

"Okay, don't change course until we're closer, but that's where we're going."

Back in the cabin, Ian uses the sat phone to call Christian, the leader of the group that will distribute LeFont's ghastly handiwork to water systems in designated townships and densely populated black areas of South Africa. The revised plan is to have the van waiting in Port Elizabeth to meet them, then arrive in Cape Town by road. He informs Christian.

Chapter 39

The flight back to Antigua in the DC3 will be slow, but not as slow as the flight down. They are no longer looking for a black yacht in the vast expanse of Ocean. After the long hugs, heartfelt, emotional goodbyes, and arrangements to talk at key times, the mood during the first couple of hours is subdued. But then Andre emerges from the back with a bottle of champagne, cold beers, and the four passengers quickly become joyous. Once everyone has a glass, he raises his. "To Miss Brockton. We are so glad you are safe. And with us."

Caroline looks up at the broad, beaming smile of the tall, handsome black man, and tears again fill her eyes. Sam hands her a tissue as she struggles to calm herself to speak. "Thank you. God, I'll never be able to thank you enough. You're all saints. You risked your lives."

"Ah…no big deal. Just another day…another adventure," Andre says, the dynamic smile still in place as he looks around at the others.

Laughter and shouts of joy fill the cabin after Jean-Paul raises his glass and his deep baritone booms. "Here's to saved damsels and great adventures."

Chapter 40

Their course altered for Port Elizabeth, the Gulfstar has crossed the South African coastline, and Ian is still in a foul mood. Sensing disaster, he is plotting a grisly death for Lefont when the sat phone rings. He immediately recognizes the familiar, scratchy voice and heavy French accent. An address in Cape Town and a box number are stated slowly, clearly. Then silence. Ian jots the message quickly. "Lefont...Lefont. I'll hunt you down like a dog if you're fucking with me. I swear to God."

Silence. Then, "Do you have the information?"

"Yes, goddamit! What's the final process?" Ian asks as he hears the line go dead.

His rage at Lefont and thoughts of failure momentarily softened by the phone call, Ian feels his energy level spike. Mind racing, he dials Christian's number.

"We also need a car, not another van...a fast car...at the airport in Port Elizabeth. I've got to get back to Cape Town ahead of the van." After listening to Christian's questions and information on where the plane should taxi, he replies. "I'll explain everything when I get there. There's a letter in a box at a post office in Cape Town that I need before we can move forward. I'll pick it up, then meet everyone else, and we'll split up just as we planned. Nothing changes once we're together in Cape Town...other than where we'll meet. I'll figure out where and let you know."

Chapter 41

Thatcher Wilson fastens his seat belt as the Interpol jet banks for the final approach and landing in Cape Town. Deep in thought, he wonders if the F.B.I. or US Intelligence has arrived in force ahead of him. Waiting as long as he could to contact them after the call from Juliette, he knows they have more assets in and around Cape Town than he does. His agents barely beat them to the hospital in Recife, even though they had a few hours head start. Luckily, they got to interrogate Brian Richards first. He didn't give up any information about where they would gather once they landed, so no one will know any more than he does until he talks with Juliette again. He'll play dumb, maintain radio silence until he knows more, and his other agents arrive at the hangar. Once on the ground, they will taxi to a hangar with a secure room…where he will meet Juliette, the other agents, and local authorities. Thatcher checks again for other airports and distances to Cape Town, as he feels it likely the group's plans have changed since they know Richards might have talked if he survived and was interrogated.

Chapter 42

After hours of silence, with Christopher still deep in thought and Juliette making soft, purring sounds of sleep while curled up on the seat, her head on his shoulder, the pilot announces they are approaching the coast of Africa and will begin their descent. Stroking her cheek and gently shaking her shoulder, Christopher sees her eyes open, then look at him with a warm smile. "We're getting close. Before the chaos and intensity start, I have a few questions."

Shaking her head as if to clear it, she responds "Sure."

"One more time. Are you serious about the villa and settling down with me? At least for a while?"

There is no hesitation. "Yes."

"Why me? Why now? Evidence says I should be leery."

"You're different. Far different than any other man I've known. You're...classy. And not afraid to admit your vulnerabilities...your faults...your fears. Other men...they're so compulsive about proving their manhood, toughness. Inner strength. What a joke. So dishonest. So easy to see through."

She continues after he says nothing, and they stare into each other's eyes. "Look, I know I'm crazy. Wild. Untamed in some ways. Need more honesty? But I think...and I hope...a lot of it is my protective act. An act I'd like to get rid of. Or at least some of it. Maybe it won't work. But I want to try." She waits. He says nothing. "Please believe me, Christopher. I really believe in you." Bending forward, he kisses her lightly on her forehead. "And another reason. You're quite a good lover...and you've got terrific potential."

The unmarked Interpol jet taxis, all lights now off, to a hangar at the end of a row of hangars. Thatcher arranged for his flight to have no record of take-off, flight path, or landing, as he did Juliette's. He knows the plane and terrorists he is trying to find has likely done the same. No problem to buy silence with enough cash.

Once inside the hangar he and the agent travelling with him walk quickly to the back and through a door being held open by a large man in tactical gear. There are ten or so men in the room; a few he recognizes as Interpol agents stationed in South Africa, others he assumes are local authorities. "Any sign of their plane?"

"No. Nothing." One of his agents responds.

"No surprise." Thatcher continues. "Hopefully we'll learn more from Miss de Montfort." He turns to the men he doesn't' know, and before shaking hands and introductions, asks, "Who knows how many water plants there are and their locations…in predominantly black townships around Cape Town and areas of the city? And other cities?"

Before there is an answer his sat phone rings and he sees it is David McCrary with the F.B.I. Reluctantly, he answers. "Yes. Where are you?" After he finds out McCrary is hours away but has men at the airport, Thatcher says, "I've just arrived. I'll get back to you soon with a location."

After landing, the plane carrying Juliette and Christopher follows directions from Thatcher, parks on the other side of the hangar, and they disembark quickly. Once inside they see a large man holding a door open toward the back, they enter, and find the room filled with serious looking men they don't know, with the exception of Thatcher. He speaks first.

"Juliette, could I have a word with you alone?"

"He knows as much as I do," she responds, nodding to Christopher. "He's smart as hell…you want his perspective."

Christopher feels his pride soar, his shoulders and chest shift and puff a bit as they move to the far corner of the room. "These are Interpol agents and local authorities, agents…and I'm sure the F.B.I., CIA will be here shortly. Is there anything particularly sensitive that you don't want anyone to hear?"

"No." She responds immediately, her voice flat and powerful. Thatcher stares at her for a moment, then turns and they follow him back to where the others are standing.

"What are the basics of the plot? What do we need to know to stop it? How much time do we have? Start with the important stuff." Thatcher's eyes never leave Juliette.

"They have a number of vials with a deadly, waterborne virus they're going to put in the water supply of numerous townships…those with large black populations. And areas of the city. Or cities. Technical name is Vibrio Vulnificus…leads to necrotizing fasciitis. Eats soft tissue. Often referred to as the flesh-eating virus." Juliette waits before continuing, looking into the eyes of the men to judge their reactions. "Tens of thousands…perhaps hundreds…could die."

Juliette and Christopher answer as many questions as they can over the next thirty minutes but spend more time on what they don't know than what they do. Thatcher reluctantly accepts the fact they will learn little more than they did from the interrogation of Brian Richards. And once more how the camera in Juliette's room created leverage he can't combat. But he still asks one question for the third time.

"I'm not going to accept the fact you don't know where your friends took the Brockton girl. She's out of danger.

Where the hell is she?"

Christopher answers for Juliette this time...quickly. "Think. They didn't tell us because they knew we were going to meet you. They're smart. They're not going to make a mistake at this point. We'll know, you'll know...as soon as she's on her way home." Pausing, he stares directly at Thatcher. "Look, these are good people. The best. They risked their lives and spent their money to save someone they had never heard of. Do you really think they're going to withhold information that could save hundreds of thousands of lives? You know what they know. You know what we know." Again, he pauses. The veins on his neck and steel in his eyes betray his anger and frustration. "Surely you learned where the townships are, the water supplies, from Brian?"

"Only a few that he guessed. Said Ian selected them...he didn't have much to do with that part of the operation. This guy Ian, the leader, who came up with the plan, is a real beauty. Domestic violence, racism, member of known hate groups."

"Do you have men on the ground at the systems he suggested? Other airports?" There is no response from Thatcher as his eyes remain hard on Christopher, who continues. "There can't be many airports around Cape Town where a private jet can land totally under the radar."

"Don't fuck with me. Don't tell me how to do my job." Thatcher's eyes narrow, his face hardens. "I can cause you a lot of trouble if I want to."

Juliette suddenly speaks in a sharp, cutting voice, looking squarely at the agent. "You don't want to. Because you still need our help. I'm sure I've seen the scientist...the guy who made the vials, the virus. And a couple of the men. Likely Ian. I can identify them."

Thatcher stares into Juliette's eyes...unflinching...then shoots a glance at Christopher. "I have a room for you at the Hotel Verde. It's close. We'll drive you. Don't leave your room until I call. I'm sure you can afford room service." Turning, he steps quickly to the door, signaling the other men to follow him.

Once they are alone, Christopher turns to Juliette. "How the hell can you identify them? You never saw them."

"Well..." She looks warmly into his eyes, lifts an eyelid slightly, a barely perceptible grin on her face. "Sam told me she saw a creepy little old man a couple of times on St. Bart's. With some other men that could be our kidnappers." Her grin widens. "Should I be punished for lying?"

Chapter 43

The Mercedes sedan speeds along the two-lane rural roads toward Cape Town. In the back seat, Brian is oblivious to the scenery or their location as he runs through the finale of the operation. *Thirty townships or districts where the water supply is controlled by a corrupt government or private company. Mostly old, antiquated systems involving above-ground storage and simple piping. Thirty individuals paid off to lead the guys to the best place to dump the vials with the virus and look the other way.* Images of the agonized expressions, horrible suffering, and deaths of hundreds of thousands of blacks fill his mind, and a smirk crosses his face before his thoughts shift to the post office and LeFont's letter. *If there's a problem I'll hunt him down. Pay whatever I have to. I'll pour a vial down his throat, or find a way to make him die harder than having his flesh eaten.*

"How much longer to Cape Town? To the address I gave you?" Brian asks his driver. A member of Brian's group, the man answers, "Two and a half, maybe three hours."

Chapter 44

Tears flow freely down Sam's cheeks and well up in the eyes of Andre and Jean-Paul as they watch Caroline Brockton run in a dead sprint and collapse into the arms of her father. The DC3 has just landed at V.C. Bird International Airport in Antigua, taxied to the edge of a runway where a gleaming private jet is parked, engines running, Joseph Brockton waiting at the bottom of the plane's stairs. Their embrace lasts…and lasts…until they pull back to look at each other. Then another tight hug, before both wipe their eyes with his handkerchief and walk, hand-in-hand, to where the others stand beside the old plane.

"I can never thank you enough. But I'll try. I don't want to insult you because I have a hint of what you're made of. But money? Anything?" Joseph Brockton, looking every bit the master of the universe in appearance and statue, is emotional, his voice cracking.

"No. Certainly not." Andre replies. "Our pleasure. We're so glad it all turned out. Some long odds." He continues. "Any idea how much time we have before the authorities arrive?"

Joseph answers quickly. "I did all I could to throw them off my trail. You should have time to get out of here."

Chapter 45

The Mercedes pulls up to the address Ian has, in front of a large, ancient, ornate post office building. Knit cap pulled low over his forehead, wrap-around sunglasses in place, leather satchel over his shoulder, he scans the sidewalk and steps, exits the car, and looks around again before walking purposely, but not too fast, toward the entrance. Once inside he quickly locates the boxes, the box number he wants, opens it with the key, and is relieved to see a small, padded package inside. Withdrawing the package, he closes the box and retraces his steps. The Mercedes has moved farther down the block. Again scanning the sidewalk and street for any signs of trouble, he moves the hundred yards until he arrives at the car, opens the door, and climbs in a split second before the car lurches forward. Once seated, Ian frantically tears at the package, ripping it open to reveal a small, square, white box with a single piece of scotch tape holding it shut. He rips the box open rather than the tape, and a silver, flip cigarette lighter and folded piece of lined paper tumble to the floor next to his feet.

"Jesus fucking Christ," he shouts as he flips the lid open…to reveal the wick and roller mechanism of a standard lighter. Reaching for the folded piece of paper, he quickly unfolds it, then reads the carefully hand-printed message.

> The pathogen in each vial must be heated
> in order to activate it before it goes into
> the water supply. Hold a lighter flame 1" under

each vial for 20 seconds, then introduce it
into the supply within 1 minute.

Ian slumps back against the seat of the Mercedes, trying to quiet his fury, calm his gut-wrenching anger, with rational thought. Activating the sat phone, he dials Christian's number, and waits for the answer. "Get each man to bring a cigarette lighter...hell, a flip-top lighter, to Murray's house. Every single man, goddamit. The whole operation depends on it."

An hours' drive away, Ian knows some of the men are already at the place they will meet to stage the final phase of the operation. Murray lives on a ten-acre farm, with the small main house, garage and barn out of view of the road down a long, dirt driveway framed with large, silver oaks. "We can't afford to be stopped, but we need to get there fast", Ian says to his driver, as he gazes out the window, deep in thought.

Walking into the barn, Ian sees the men scattered about, some talking in small groups, a few sitting on hay bales. "Who doesn't have a lighter? Have you tested them? How many do we need?" His voice booms, rings with frustration. Eight to ten hands go up. "Tony, John, go to two or three different stores and buy at least twenty flip lighters like this," he says as he holds up the lighter from the package. "Don't buy enough at one store to raise suspicion. We need extras. And haul ass."

"We lost Brian. We don't know if he's alive...or if he talked. Better assume he did. If there's any good news...I didn't tell him the location of the systems. Only a few we aren't going after."

Christopher comes awake to the gentle touch of fingers and a wet tongue playing down his body. Momentarily confused after his first hard sleep in days, he quickly recognizes the inside of the hotel room and Juliette's head of dark hair on his chest. Surrendering his mind and body to a respite from days and nights of grating tension, for the next hour he revels in the uninhibited variety and mind-blowing expertise of his lover's sexual skills. And then does his best to reciprocate.

The warm afterglow of yet another sublime erotic episode with Juliette settles over Christopher, as she now snuggles against him, her head on his chest. "Aren't you glad we're here? That you came with me?" Her eyes sparkle as he gazes into them.

"I'm glad as hell I'm with you. But we don't have to be in South Africa chasing a gang of blood-thirsty racist terrorists to do that."

"Do you believe in God?"

Caught off guard, he fights to shift gears. "I've tried. Really hard. All my life. I want to. How about you?"

"I like the way you put it. I've tried. Can I use that as my answer?"

"It's the old, ever-present conflict. All life, from the simplest organism, is so incredibly complex, so perfectly designed...it's inconceivable it happened by chance. But there is so much pain, suffering, tragedy in the world...and so often experienced by the most innocent, the most vulnerable. It also seems inconceivable that a benevolent supreme being could be behind it.

Ian has the four vials zipped into the pocket of his jacket

as he exits the jeep and heads toward the small building beside the water tower. His heart pounds with the excitement and realization that he is very close to fulfilling his twisted dream. Scanning the darkness with the night vision scope, he sees nothing suspicious, moves swiftly, crouched low. The door is open, access to the metal climbing bars right there, no guard or keeper in sight. *Exactly as planned.* The failure...or success...of the other men crosses his mind before he begins to move up, hand over hand, silently but quickly. All but two of the water systems he chose are relatively small, and rural. Only two large systems where more people will die, but the chance of failure is greater. As the only man who will contaminate more than one system, Ian will next head to one of the larger systems, closer to the city. After he is confident at least thousands will die from this success.

Chapter 46

Shadow, the large, black, ocean catamaran, sister ship to El Tigre, flies downwind over the waves at close to twenty knots, her bow pointed into the spectacular mural of blues, reds, golds and greys after the sun has dropped below the horizon. Andre steps onto the soft, thick elastic of the trampoline and heads for Sam, who is lying, naked, screaming in joy at the scintillating, sublime ride. Lowering his body gently onto hers, they both giggle and kiss as the bow rises and plunges with the steady rhythm of following seas and spray sprinkles their bodies.

"How long can we do this, love?" Her voice rises in pitch with the adrenaline rush. "God, can you make it never end? Come on, you can do anything."

"Couple of more hours. We'll stop in St. Bart's for the night."

"In that case, guess I better shift my attention from this gorgeous sunset...to your gorgeous...no, stunningly gorgeous...body."

Chapter 47

Flipping the lighter open and activating the flint, Ian holds the flame under the vial, counts, then dumps the contents into the water below the open valve. Any desire to linger and reflect is overcome by his urgency to get to the next system. As he quickly climbs down the rungs from the tower, images of the excruciating deaths of thousands...tens of thousands...hundreds of thousands...of hated black men, women and children...again flood his thoughts. *How many depends on the success of the others.*

Back in the jeep, adrenaline still pumping, the images continue. Of international headlines, congratulations for the organization, the envy of white nationalists around the world. *Largest attack in history...and I engineered it.* He knows there will be many successful, accomplished people...those who cherish and revere the historical tradition and personal advantage of unobstructed white power and rule...who will silently applaud the results, if not the method. Eyes narrowing, jaw set, Ian pushes the accelerator and surges down the two-lane road.

Zeke, high on amphetamines and cocaine, is driving much faster than the speed limit Ian insisted they observe. As he nears the water tower, he reaches inside his jacket to touch the handle of the semi-automatic pistol with silencer tucked into the waistband of his pants. Braking hard, he almost drives past the gravel drive leading to the system he has been assigned. Out of the car, his muddled mind tries to remember the sign from the night watchman that he will need to return.

His hand pats the pocket with the vials. Seated just outside the gate, the man doesn't move as Zeke approaches. Dozing, he suddenly awakens, sees Zeke coming toward him, and puts his hands on his upper thighs to help him stand.

With lightning speed, without conscience thought, the gun is drawn, two shots are fired, and the man drops in a heap. Heart pumping wildly, trying desperately to clear his muddled thoughts, Zeke quickly takes the keys from the man's belt and opens the heavy lock on the gate.

Chapter 48

Inside a gated neighborhood on the outskirts of Buenos Aires, on a quiet street, a stylish but modest house sits nestled between large trees. Inside, empty soda cans, wine bottles, stacks of magazines and books cover most of the tables...a few scattered on the furniture. The back yard is surrounded by a ten- foot-high stone wall and has a small pool. On a large, double size chaise lounge there are two stunning young women. A raven-haired, dark-skinned, voluptuous beauty, and a fair-skinned blond with the tall, slender frame and patrician features of a model. Both are naked. Between them is a small, frail looking, extremely thin older man, with white, pasty skin. Dr. Gerard LeFont is also naked.

Each of their hands holds a glass of red wine as he continues his story. "They wanted me to test it on a human but I refused. Killed a cat and a couple of dogs with supermarket poison." Pausing, an odd, scratchy laugh escapes his lips. "What goddam morons. I filled the vials...all of them...with cloudy water. Nothing but water that I'd drink. Dumb bastards."

Epilogue

Stepping through the door of the bakery into the cold, crisp air of the early fall, alpine morning, Juliette de Monfort starts her walk past the quaint shops and red, geranium-laden window boxes of the classic Swiss Chalets in the lovely mountain village of Grindlewald, Switzerland. As has become her habit, she stops for a moment to gaze up at the towering magnificence of the Eiger.

Strolling past the chocolatier, she notes the need for an afternoon visit. Shopkeepers sweep and wash the sidewalks, and as she approaches, smile and wish her a good morning. A night-owl for the most part, she has always loved the mornings when she rises early. At the end of the small commercial part of the village, she turns up a steep gravel driveway that rises between large, ancient trees.

Juliette opens the heavy wooden doors of the chalet, walks up the stairs into the bright morning light of the open, main floor, and toward the kitchen.

"Let me know when you want another cup of coffee. Croissants and quiche are on the counter when you are ready for a break."

Never looking up from the keyboard, Christopher replies, "I'm ready. Another coffee would be wonderful." Hearing footsteps, he looks up to see her round the corner, a steaming cup in each hand, the ankle-length, fur-lined, shearling coat unbuttoned and open enough to reveal the long, lithe, luscious, naked body underneath.

Tearing his eyes away and back to the screen, he fights to

keep his voice flat, all business. "You know I need to concentrate." After placing a cup on the desk, the sound of her steps tells him she is walking away. Realizing quickly any chance of regaining his concentration...of typing another meaningful sentence...has vanished...he marks his place, pushes save and gazes out the large window in front of his desk on the spectacular alpine vista as a smile creeps across his face.

www.ingramcontent.com/pod-product-compliance
Lightning Source LLC
Chambersburg PA
CBHW030927260626
47169CB00002B/393